PRAISE FOR DEN

"*Love, Unscripted* has it all—the funniest meet-cute ever, unique characters, and a charming beach town setting. If you love sweet romance with a lot of heart, this one has 'Hallmark movie' written all over it. Highly recommended!"

—COLLEEN COBLE, *PUBLISHERS WEEKLY* AND *USA TODAY* BESTSELLING AUTHOR

"Hunter (*Bookshop by the Sea*) opens this heartwarming romance with Queens, N.Y., western writer Sadie Goodwin learning that her publisher wants her to switch genres to romance . . . Hunter's charismatic and complex characters effortlessly propel the story. Readers won't want to put this down."

—*PUBLISHERS WEEKLY* FOR *A NOVEL PROPOSAL*

"A heartwarming tale written by an undisputed queen of the genre, *A Novel Proposal* is a love letter to readers, to writers and, above all, to romance. As Sadie and Sam were forced out of their comfort zones, I sank deeper and deeper into my reading happy place. This cozy, clever, captivating love story is the perfect beach read and an absolute must for fans of happily ever afters. Denise Hunter charmed my socks right off with this one!"

—BETHANY TURNER, AUTHOR OF *PLOT TWIST* AND *THE DO-OVER*

"A tragic accident gives a divorced couple a second chance at love in the warmhearted third installment of Hunter's Riverbend Romance series (after *Mulberry Hollow*) . . . Readers looking for an uplifting Christian romance will appreciate how Laurel and Gavin's faith helps dispel their deep-rooted fears so they can find a way to love again. Inspirational fans will find this hard to resist."

—*PUBLISHERS WEEKLY* FOR *HARVEST MOON*

"Denise Hunter has a way of bringing depth and an aching beauty into her stories, and *Harvest Moon* is no different. *Harvest Moon* is a beautiful tale of second chances, self-sacrifice, and renewed romance that addresses hard topics such as child death and dissolved marriages. In a beautiful turn of events, Hunter brings unexpected healing out of a devastating situation, subtly reminding the reader that God can create beauty out of the most painful of circumstances and love from the most broken stories."

—PEPPER BASHAM, AUTHOR OF *THE HEART OF THE MOUNTAINS* AND *AUTHENTICALLY, IZZY*

"A poignant romance that's perfect for fans of emotional love stories that capture your heart from the very first page. With her signature style, Denise Hunter whisks readers into a world where broken hearts are mended, lives are changed, and love really does conquer all!"

—COURTNEY WALSH, *NEW YORK TIMES* BESTSELLING AUTHOR, FOR *MULBERRY HOLLOW*

"Hunter delivers a touching story of how family dynamics and personal priorities shift when love takes precedence. Hunter's fans will love this."

—*PUBLISHERS WEEKLY* FOR *RIVERBEND GAP*

"Denise Hunter has never failed to pen a novel that whispers messages of hope and brings a smile to my face. *Bookshop by the Sea* is no different! With a warmhearted community, a small beachside town, a second-chance romance worth rooting for, and cozy bookshop vibes, this is a story you'll want to snuggle into like a warm blanket."

—MELISSA FERGUSON, AUTHOR OF *MEET ME IN THE MARGINS*

"Sophie and Aiden had me hooked from page one, and I was holding my breath until the very end. Denise nails second-chance romance in *Bookshop by the Sea*. I adored this story! Five giant stars!"

—JENNY HALE, *USA TODAY* BESTSELLING AUTHOR

"*Carolina Breeze* is filled with surprises, enchantment, and a wonderful depth of romance. Denise Hunter gets better with every novel she writes, and that trend has hit a high point with this wonderful story."

—HANNAH ALEXANDER, AUTHOR OF *THE WEDDING KISS*

"*Autumn Skies* is the perfect roundup to the Bluebell Inn series. The tension and attraction between Grace and Wyatt is done so well, and the mystery kept me wondering what was going to happen next. Prepare to be swept away to the beautiful Blue Ridge Mountains in a flurry of turning pages."

—NANCY NAIGLE, *USA TODAY* BESTSELLING
AUTHOR OF *CHRISTMAS ANGELS*

"A breeze of brilliance! Denise Hunter's *Carolina Breeze* will blow you away with a masterful merge of mystery, chemistry, and memories restored in this lakeside love story of faith, family, and fortune."

—JULIE LESSMAN, AWARD-WINNING AUTHOR

"*Summer by the Tides* is a perfect blend of romance and women's fiction."

—SHERRYL WOODS, #1 *NEW YORK TIMES*
BESTSELLING AUTHOR

"Denise Hunter once again proves she's the queen of romantic drama. *Summer by the Tides* is both a perfect beach romance and a dramatic story of second chances. If you like Robyn Carr, you'll love Denise Hunter."

—COLLEEN COBLE, *PUBLISHERS WEEKLY* AND
USA TODAY BESTSELLING AUTHOR

"I have never read a romance by Denise Hunter that didn't sweep me away into a happily ever after. Treat yourself!"

—ROBIN LEE HATCHER, BESTSELLING AUTHOR OF
CROSS MY HEART, FOR *ON MAGNOLIA LANE*

"*Sweetbriar Cottage* is a story to fall in love with. True-to-life characters, high stakes, and powerful chemistry blend to tell an emotional story of reconciliation."

—BRENDA NOVAK, *NEW YORK TIMES* BESTSELLING AUTHOR

"*Falling Like Snowflakes* is charming and fun with a twist of mystery and intrigue. A story that's sure to endure as a classic reader favorite."

—RACHEL HAUCK, *NEW YORK TIMES* BESTSELLING
AUTHOR OF *THE FIFTH AVENUE STORY SOCIETY*

BEFORE WE WERE US

Also by Denise Hunter

RIVERBEND ROMANCES

Riverbend Gap

Mulberry Hollow

Harvest Moon

Wildflower Falls

BLUEBELL INN ROMANCES

Lake Season

Carolina Breeze

Autumn Skies

BLUE RIDGE ROMANCES

Blue Ridge Sunrise

Honeysuckle Dreams

On Magnolia Lane

SUMMER HARBOR NOVELS

Falling Like Snowflakes

The Goodbye Bride

Just a Kiss

CHAPEL SPRINGS ROMANCES

Barefoot Summer

A December Bride (novella)

Dancing with Fireflies

The Wishing Season

Married 'til Monday

BIG SKY ROMANCES

A Cowboy's Touch

The Accidental Bride

The Trouble with Cowboys

NANTUCKET LOVE STORIES

Surrender Bay

The Convenient Groom

Seaside Letters

Driftwood Lane

STAND-ALONE NOVELS

Sweetwater Gap

Sweetbriar Cottage

Summer by the Tides

Bookshop by the Sea

A Novel Proposal

Love, Unscripted

NOVELLAS INCLUDED IN

This Time Around, Smitten,

Secretly Smitten, and

Smitten Book Club

BEFORE WE WERE US

DENISE HUNTER

THOMAS NELSON
Since 1798

Published in Nashville, Tennessee, by Thomas Nelson. Thomas Nelson is a registered trademark of HarperCollins Christian Publishing, Inc.

Thomas Nelson titles may be purchased in bulk for educational, business, fundraising, or sales promotional use. For information, please email SpecialMarkets@ThomasNelson.com.

Publisher's Note: This novel is a work of fiction. Names, characters, places, and incidents are either products of the author's imagination or used fictitiously. All characters are fictional, and any similarity to people living or dead is purely coincidental.

Any internet addresses (websites, blogs, etc.) in this book are offered as a resource. They are not intended in any way to be or imply an endorsement by Thomas Nelson, nor does Thomas Nelson vouch for the content of these sites for the life of this book.

Library of Congress Cataloging-in-Publication Data

Names: Hunter, Denise, 1968- author.
Title: Before we were us / Denise Hunter.
Description: Nashville, Tennessee: Thomas Nelson, 2024. | Summary: "Before We Were Us is a cozy, autumnal, opposites-attract Hallmark movie mixed with 50 First Dates. Denise Hunter weaves a charming romance between a woman who can't remember her own love story and the man who couldn't forget her even if he wanted to. The perfect escape into a happily-ever-after"—Provided by publisher.
Identifiers: LCCN 2024016189 (print) | LCCN 2024016190 (ebook) |
    ISBN 9780840716682 (paperback) | ISBN 9781400349586 (hardcover)
    ISBN 9780840716699 (epub) | ISBN 9780840716705 (ebook)
Subjects: LCGFT: Romance fiction. | Christian fiction. | Novels.
Classification: LCC PS3608.U5925 B44 2024 (print) | LCC PS3608.U5925 (ebook) |
    DDC 813/.6—dc23/eng/20240412
LC record available at https://lccn.loc.gov/2024016189
LC ebook record available at https://lccn.loc.gov/2024016190

Printed in the United States of America

24 25 26 27 28 LBC 5 4 3 2 1

CHAPTER 1

JONAH LANDRY ELECTED to stay busy on the day his entire future hung in the balance. That's why the axe was poised over his head when the death rattle of his sister's Jeep Gladiator reached his ears.

Finally.

He swung the axe down, slicing into an upright log, and left it there. Then he grabbed his Henley shirt and headed up the slope of the resort's wooded property. A carpet of pine needles padded his eager steps and a nattering squirrel cheered him on. He drew in a deep breath of crisp autumn air heavy with the smoky scent of last night's bonfire.

His long strides made quick work of the distance. He pulled his shirt into place just as Meg stepped from her truck.

Her shoulder-length auburn waves glinted in the sunlight, and her pale skin was flushed from the trip to Portsmouth in her air-conditioning-free vehicle. "You know we have a log splitter, right? Or were you just hoping Lauren would catch a glimpse of your six-pack and start drooling?"

"It's called *nervous energy*. Where is it?"

She gave him a blank stare. "Where is what?"

His heart might have stopped beating. It definitely seized in his chest for a long, panicked moment.

"Just kidding," the little brat singsonged, smiling as if his whole future wasn't on the line here.

He was just about to throttle her when she shoved a small cream-colored box at him. He grabbed it and withdrew a rich blue velvety box.

"You're welcome. I had to park three blocks away and wait fifteen minutes while they——"

"Thank you." The lid gave a quiet squawk as he opened it—and there it was, tucked into a soft blue nest. His irritation lifted like autumn fog off the lake.

Lauren had changed a lot in the six months since she'd come to work at Pinehaven Resort, but she still had a penchant for sparkly things. And the brilliant oval diamond dazzled.

Tonight he would take her out to eat at The Landing. Then they would go for a ride on the lake in the same boat where he'd professed his love for her a month ago. The memory of that moment sent a rush of heat through him. When she'd stared up at him, her heart in those beautiful eyes, he'd wondered if he'd died and gone to heaven. What had he ever done to deserve this beautiful, resilient woman?

The sound of Meg's laughter pulled him from the sweet memory.

He scowled at the teasing sparkle in her eyes. "What?"

"You are such a goner." She was still laughing.

He snapped the case closed, unable to work up any real irritation on today of all days. "Shut up."

A few weeks ago he'd seen the ring in a display window in Portsmouth but knew a proposal was premature. Oh, he'd wanted to marry her. He'd known right away she was the one for him. Well, once he'd stopped hating her. But he hadn't been sure Lauren was quite there yet.

Until two weeks ago when they'd sat in the gazebo at Bayview Park. Swaths of pink streaked the sky, a glowing stage for the sun's final act of the day.

Her head rested on his shoulder and her hand lay on his chest. "I think I could stay here forever."

It wasn't often she was so open, so unguarded. He was careful not to overreact, though he couldn't prevent the way his heart two-stepped in response. "In Pinehaven?"

She snuggled closer, burying her face in his chest, uncharacteristically shy. "In your arms."

Jonah had called Garrett Jewelers the next day and purchased the ring.

"What are you wearing?"

His sister's question snagged his attention. "I don't know. Khakis and a button-down, I guess."

Meg rolled her eyes, seeming more sixteen than twenty-one. "Wear the navy khakis with your camel oxfords and matching belt and the blue button-down—she likes the way it matches your eyes."

"She does?"

"Don't wear a blazer—she'll be suspicious. You never wear a blazer."

"You're a little bossy." Sometimes he forgot his sister was all grown up. Hard to believe this was the same freckle-faced little girl he used to help with algebra and chemistry.

"You made a reservation, right? The Landing fills up on Saturday nights."

Give me a break. He spared her a look.

"What time should I bring the boat to the marina?"

"As soon as we leave for supper." What would Lauren think when she saw their boat just steps from The Landing? Would she realize what was about to happen? How would that make her feel? Would she be excited? Nervous?

"You know what you're gonna say, right?"

"I believe 'Will you marry me?' is traditional."

3

Meg sighed. "You'd better come up with more than that. This should be the most romantic moment of her life."

A knot of worry tightened in the pit of his stomach. "No pressure there."

"Just tell her how you feel. Is that so hard?"

He'd given this plenty of thought already. He had a few ideas swimming in his mind. But he didn't want to memorize some speech. Didn't want this to be scripted. It should come from the heart, in the moment. Hopefully his heart wouldn't go blank.

And when he was finished she'd give him that wide smile, green eyes lit and happy and perhaps glazed with a sheen of tears . . . and she'd say yes.

His thoughts slipped gears. The ground dropped from beneath him. She would say yes, wouldn't she?

They hadn't dated very long, but *he* was sure. That didn't necessarily mean she was though. Maybe she needed more time. She hadn't been raised in a warm home with a solid example of love and marriage. His hands shook as he pocketed the jewelry box, which missed the pocket entirely. He fumbled with it before it plunked to the ground.

Meg chuckled as she retrieved it. "Look at you. You're a mess. Relax, it's gonna be fine. She doesn't suspect a thing."

Hardly his biggest concern at this point. Was he rushing things? Why hadn't he put more thought into this? What if his proposal scared her off for good? "Like, doesn't expect it because tonight seems like an ordinary day, or doesn't expect it because it's months too soon for a lifetime commitment and she's not even sure I'm the man she wants to make it with?"

Meg tilted her head, a smile curving her lips. "Aw, you're cute when you're insecure. I'm so telling Lauren about this once she has that ring on her finger—and she will have that ring on her finger." Meg patted his arm, wrinkled her nose at the sweaty dampness, and withdrew her hand. "She's gonna say yes, Bro. Would I set you up for failure?"

"There was that time in middle school . . ."

"Please. You could've done so much better than Maddy Benton."

His sister had had uncanny insight even as a gangly teenager. And though she loved messing with him, she always had his best interests at heart. She and Lauren had grown close over the summer. If Lauren wasn't ready for this, Meg would know.

"Stop worrying. Tonight's gonna be perfect." She moved to the bed of the truck. "But you can work off that nervous energy by helping me unload all this stuff."

Jonah checked his watch, then grabbed a bag. Three hours and counting.

FROM her spot on the bay, Lauren Wentworth's pet project was just a patch of weathered red peeking through the dense forest. The trees were just starting to turn, a sprinkle of gold and orange against the deep green pines. She had no doubt the New Hampshire fall would delight her.

She drew the oars through the water, pushing the boat toward the pier, where her dog, Graham, sat waiting. His yellow coat gleamed in the sunlight.

"Look, honey," Beth Cabot said from the back of the boat. "It's a loon."

George lifted his old-school camera and snapped a photo. "He's a little late heading to the Atlantic, isn't he, Lauren?"

"The young ones sometimes linger longer than their parents." She'd learned a lot about loons since her arrival in March. She'd learned a lot about many things.

She rowed closer to Graham and the boat dock belonging to Pinehaven Resort. The resort traffic had slowed since last week—Labor Day weekend. High season was officially over, and their guests would now consist mostly of older couples. Some of whom couldn't get out on the water without assistance. Leaf peepers would soon flood the state, but peak season was still weeks away.

Lauren could finally turn her attention to the big barn on the property adjacent to the resort. The "buffer" property, Tom Landry had called it. Lauren had found the old relic by accident one day, back when she considered her position at the resort a mere stepping stone to her dream job back in Boston.

My, how things had changed. She gave the oars one final pull and the boat drew alongside the pier.

Graham stood, backend wagging, ears perked, brown eyes sparkling.

"Miss me, buddy?" Lauren grabbed the dock post and pulled them in, tied the rope around the cleat with some precision. She offered a hand to the couple, who were in their upper seventies but still spry.

"Thank you, dear." Back on land, Beth petted Graham, who soaked up the attention. "We so wanted to take a lap around the lake this year, but our shoulders just aren't what they used to be."

"I'm always happy to get out on the water. Let me know if you want another ride before you leave."

A minute later as Lauren waved them off, she spotted Jonah heading down the sloped ground toward her. Her heart clutched at the sight of him. Even in an old T-shirt and jeans, he did it for her. His work around the property kept him fit and muscular, and the summer sun had darkened his skin to a deep bronze. The ball cap, worn low, called attention to his handsome facial features: light blue eyes, a slightly crooked nose, and lips that were perfection.

Those lips tipped as he approached. "You took the Cabots out on the lake?"

"Great day for a boat ride."

He brushed her mouth in a quick kiss that made her anticipate their upcoming evening. Their gazes held for a beat. Yeah, a night with Jonah was just what the doctor ordered. Their summer schedules had been hectic, and working for a family meant there was a lot of family time. She wasn't complaining. She loved each one of the Landrys. But time alone with Jonah?

As if reading her mind, he pulled her close and kissed her again, his lips taking their sweet time with hers.

"Mmmm," she murmured long seconds later. "Nice."

"Just nice?"

"Just perfect."

He gave her that sleepy-eyed look she'd come to love. "Ready to be wined and dined?"

"I can hardly wait. But a shower's definitely in order, and I think I'll lose the ponytail and resort polo."

"But you're so cute in resort wear." He kissed her nose.

Impatient for his attention, Graham nudged between them.

Jonah ruffled his fur. "Hey, bud. Yes, I see you. It's been all of thirty minutes. Meg just got back with the supplies. Did the Browns finally check out?"

"Just in time. Fran's cleaning it now. Should be done by three. I was just gonna head back to the barn and see how the hayloft looks with all the stuff gone." While she'd been working yesterday, he and Meg cleared out the space, which had been filled with decades of junk.

"If anything, it seems even bigger. Let's go." He grabbed her hand and they set off, Graham on their heels, across the property toward the path that led through the woods.

Birds chirped from the spiny branches of a hemlock tree, and the wind whispered through the leafy canopy. They'd spent their recent spare time clearing brush and weeds from around the barn's exterior, exposing the stone base. It would take a lot more work to transform the old building into the venue she saw in her imagination, but Lauren was eager to see her vision materialize.

She was excited for the future. It might look far different now at twenty-six than she'd once imagined, but it was somehow better and clearer than those wispy dreams that had carried her through college. The reminder that she might be running from her past pressed like a boulder on her chest.

But she pushed away the unsettling thought as their conversation turned to business matters. They made their way through the thick woods, their footfalls silenced by damp pine needles. Soon the path opened to the clearing, and the sun shone on the structure, highlighting the recently exposed side walls and rock base. Lauren couldn't help but smile.

"You gaze at this eyesore like it's the Holy Grail."

She jabbed him with an elbow. "She's not an eyesore. She's a diamond in the rough and she's gonna be beautiful. You just wait—every bride in the county will want to say her vows here."

He squeezed her hand. "I don't doubt it for a minute."

He slid open the creaky barn door, and as they passed through the doorway, the air immediately cooled. Lauren's nostrils filled with the musty scent of earth and time long past. Sunbeams flooded through filmy windows, and slivers of light cut through cracks in the vertical boards, dust motes dancing in their beams.

Now that the space was clear of debris, she could envision the final product even more clearly. They would maintain the barn's rustic integrity but add embellishments: twinkle lights, a chandelier, and a grand stone fireplace at the west end of the barn that would seem as if it had grown here.

"You have that look on your face again." His smile was full of affection. "Just a peek at the hayloft—we have reservations. And you have all winter to whip this place into shape." He grabbed the aluminum ladder that leaned against the wall adjacent to the loft. "Ladies first."

And up she went as he steadied the ladder. A moment later she caught her first glimpse of the open loft. It wasn't her first time up here, but the junk had hidden the square window in the center of the back wall of the loft. It now shed a soft glow over the space. Some rags and a bottle of Windex sat on its ledge, but judging by the film of dirt on the panes, they hadn't been used yet.

She stepped onto the platform that didn't even squeak at her weight. "Oh, this is perfect. We'll be able to fit at least six extra tables up here. We'll need a railing built to code. And another chandelier to cozy it up. But the view is great, isn't it? They'll be able to see all the action from up here, and the photographer will have a wonderful vantage point."

Jonah cleared the ladder, then stepped up behind her and wrapped his arms around her waist. "I love your passion for this place. Have I mentioned that?" He pressed a kiss to the crook of her neck.

Smiling, she tilted her head to give him greater access. "You just love my passion, period."

"You're not wrong."

She closed her eyes and sank into the moment—something new to her. She still had to remind herself to stop and savor the moments. Not to be in such a rush to do more, climb higher, get ahead. Oh, she still wanted to do all those things.

But the tranquil moments were also nice. Very nice.

His lips had worked their way up her neck and jaw, and then he was turning her in his arms, his eyes hooded with want.

"You have that look on your face again," she said.

And then his lips were on hers. She never tired of his kisses. He somehow hit the mark between commanding and reverent with expert precision. His touch and taste were familiar by now, equally soothing and stirring—and she craved both with an addict's obsession.

His hands roved over her back as hers worked into his short brown hair, displacing his cap. She barely heard it thunk to the ground. Her hands followed the line of his shoulders and down to his arms. She loved his arms. Adored how secure she felt within their confines. Her heart was so full. She didn't know love could feel this way. But now that she knew, she was greedy for more.

From below, Graham's impatient bark brought her back to planet Earth.

Jonah decelerated the kiss, reluctance in the slow steps of his withdrawal. In the way he set his forehead against hers, as if not quite ready to let go of her. Their breaths came heavily, mingling together. "Reservations."

She took delight in the ragged edge of his voice. "I know." And now that her brain was starting to function again, she remembered she'd planned to wash her hair, blow-dry and curl it, the whole deal. Not to mention her nails. They were in terrible shape.

"I can't wait to have you all to myself tonight," he said.

"Me too—also the black-and-blue filet, if I'm honest."

He chuckled, pressed a kiss to her forehead before he drew away. "That's my girl."

He glanced back at the window. "I'm gonna clean that window before I head home to shower. Ran out of time yesterday."

"All right. I'll meet you in the lot a little before seven?"

"No way. I'm coming to your door like a proper gentleman."

"Have it your way," she said, secretly delighted. She gave him a peck on the lips and tossed him a smile before she stepped onto the ladder and began her descent. Her gaze took in the spaciousness of the barn from above. She would almost hate filling those cracks where the sunlight sneaked through. It would be such a beautiful place for a wedding. Perhaps someday, in the not-too-distant future, she and Jonah would—

Her weight-bearing foot slipped. She grasped the sides. Too late.

Gravity took her. Panic stole her breath. A startled cry ripped from her throat.

And then there was nothing.

CHAPTER 2

JONAH PACED THE length of the hospital hallway, the past thirty minutes replaying in his head like a horror film. He couldn't erase the terrible thud of Lauren's body hitting the floor. The clatter of the ladder's fall reverberated in his head. The sight of her unmoving body on the ground below him flashed in his mind on repeat. She'd looked as if she were—

Stop it. Stop. It. She's gonna be fine. She has to be.

His mind returned to his panicked 911 call. To the long, helpless minutes of waiting, when all he could do was call her name. Hold her hand. Let the steady pulse in her neck give him hope.

Graham whined mournfully, tail tucked, licking her other hand.

What had seemed like an hour later but was probably only minutes, the EMTs stabilized Lauren's neck with a brace. They put her on a board and carried her through the woods to the parking lot, where they loaded her into the ambulance. Jonah insisted on riding along, and since he'd gone to school with one of the EMTs, he'd gotten his way.

Upon arrival at the hospital, they'd swept her through the ER and into a room for a CT scan. He wasn't allowed in.

At the end of the hall, Jonah pivoted, said his hundredth silent prayer, then glared at the closed door. How long could this take? It seemed like hours since the door had swung shut behind the gurney.

His phone vibrated in his pocket, and he checked the screen. Meg. He hit the Accept button. "Hey. I don't know anything yet. They took her straight in for a CT."

"Is she awake?"

"Not when she went in." He ran his hand over his face. How could this be happening? Less than an hour ago she was smiling up at him with those big green eyes. Kissing him with those soft lips.

"She's gonna be fine."

"You don't know that." His throat was thick with emotion.

"She has to be."

That picture of her, sprawled lifeless, pale blonde hair fanned out on the floor, flickered in his thoughts again. He blinked against the sting in his eyes. "She fell from so high, Meg. Her head hit that old wood floor and——" He stopped talking before he lost it altogether. Swallowed against the knot in his throat.

"She's a strong woman. She's gonna wake up and she's gonna be fine. You'll see."

"I should've gone down first. I should've held the ladder." He squeezed his eyes shut. "Why didn't I hold the ladder?"

"Honey, it's not your fault. It was just an accident."

The words ricocheted off his heart. Why had he stayed behind to clean that stupid window?

"Take a breath, and for all that's holy, don't blame yourself. It was a freak accident, and we'll all be sitting around next week relieved and grateful that she's fine."

Please, God. "Hope you're right."

"I am. You'll see." A beat of silence followed. "I got hold of Mom and Dad. They'll be there as soon as they can. Poor Graham is confused. He keeps going to the door and whining. I think I'll take him for a walk. But don't worry about anything; everything's under control here. Just take care of our girl."

"Thanks, Meg." His empty stomach churned. Sweat had broken out on the back of his neck. "I'm gonna go now. I'll let you know as soon as I find out anything."

"All right. I'm praying hard."

JONAH paced. He took off his hat, ran his fingers through his hair, and put it back on. Glared at the closed door. Took off the hat again and slammed it to the floor. Paced more laps. Picked it back up again.

Finally the door opened. He rushed over as two orderlies wheeled her out on the gurney. She was still strapped to the board, still in a neck brace.

Her eyes were open!

"Lauren." Jonah fell in step with them. "Honey, I'm right here."

Head braced, her eyes tracked until they settled on him. She blinked them, and then they fluttered closed.

"She has a whopping headache," the older orderly said. "The bright lights aren't helping. Once we get her to the room, they'll get her something for the pain."

"Is she okay?"

"She's a little confused. We'll know more once the doctor examines her and we get the results of the CT."

"Everything's gonna be okay, Lauren."

If she heard him, she gave no indication. But the frown line across her brow indicated she was still conscious. That was good, right? Conscious was good.

The orderlies wheeled her into a room and transferred her on the backboard onto the bed. "A nurse will be in shortly."

Jonah moved to her side, took her hand. "You gave me a scare. How are you feeling? Do you need anything?"

She tried to open her eyes, squinted against the lights. Then she pulled her hand from his and put it over her eyes.

13

"I'll turn them off." He moved away, swiped at the switch, and the fluorescents extinguished. The room was still plenty bright with the light flooding in from the hallway. He returned bedside. "Better?" When she lowered her hand he took it again, needing to feel her skin, warm and alive beneath his.

"What happened?" she croaked. "Why am I in the hospital?"

"You don't remember? We were in the barn, checking out the hay-loft. You fell off the ladder. I'm sorry. I should've been holding it for you. You fell from pretty high up. An ambulance came and brought you to the hospital."

She pulled her hand from his. Blinked up at him. "What barn?"

Before he could register the question, Carson McConnell swept into the room, wearing teal scrubs, a white lab coat, and a stethoscope slung around his neck. He was a friend from church and a pediatrics intern at the hospital. His brows pinched when he spotted Lauren. "Hey. One of the nurses told me you took a fall. What rotten luck."

Lauren's eyes swung his direction. "Hi." Her hand trembled as she tried to smooth her hair.

Carson greeted Jonah and they shook hands. Then Carson approached the bed. "How are you feeling? Nasty headache, I'll bet."

The tips of her ears pinkened as she met Carson's eyes, reminding Jonah of the crush she'd had on the man when she first arrived in town. "It's pounding. I'm—I'm a little foggy."

"No doubt. I'm just coming off my shift, but I'll see if I can get you bumped up in line."

Jonah moved closer to Lauren, took her hand in both of his. "We'd appreciate that. She just had a CT scan. She could use something for her headache."

"I'll see what I can do. Can I call anyone for you? Your dad and mom?" He glanced at Lauren. "Your family?"

BEFORE WE WERE US

The guy was already attractive. Did he have to be thoughtful too? Never mind that Lauren didn't have any family to speak of. He'd call her best friend Sydney later. "Thanks, but it's taken care of."

Carson gave Lauren his anchorman smile. "All right then. I can see you're in good hands. Just wanted to stop by and check on you. I'll see if I can get someone in here quickly."

"Thank you." Lauren's lips lifted. "Very kind of you."

"Least I can do for a friend. Let me know if I can do anything else," Carson said to Jonah on his way out.

"I will. Thanks."

Lauren watched him go, then closed her eyes.

"Hopefully they'll be in soon to check you over." Jonah recalled the way she'd smiled at Carson. Something seemed off. She didn't seem her usual self. She wasn't particularly demonstrative, but she'd hardly glanced at Jonah since she'd awakened, and her hand was lying as limp as a dead fish in his.

Her chest rose and fell slowly. Her finely arched brows were drawn together over eyes that moved behind closed lids. Her tangled lashes fanned out above pale cheeks.

Her eyes flashed open and her gaze darted wildly around the room before jerking to him. Her chest rose and fell with quick breaths.

"Hey . . ." He squeezed her hand. "It's gonna be okay. I'm here. I'm not going anywhere."

Confusion flickered in the depths of her eyes. "What happened? Where am I?"

15

Chapter 3

LAUREN COULDN'T THINK. Her head was full of cotton, and her pulse thrummed in her temples. Something was around her neck; she couldn't move her head. She didn't remember coming here. Didn't remember any of this!

What's happening to me?

"Hey, it's okay." Jonah squeezed her hand. "We're at Pinehaven Hospital. You took a fall—that's why you have a neck brace, just a precaution. You've had a CT scan and we're waiting for the doctor."

"I hit my head?" She removed her hand from his and raised it to the back of her head. Winced at the tender lump. Her stomach roiled. She lowered her hand and closed her eyes against the pain. She didn't want to see Jonah. Where was his mom? She'd rather have Tammy at her bedside. Would rather have anyone here, even Carson, though she must be a fright.

Good grief, how vain could she be? And why wouldn't someone come in and give her something for this awful headache?

"That's it, close your eyes, rest a bit."

At least Jonah was being nice for a change. Sad that she had to get whacked upside the head to wring a smidgen of kindness from him. She opened her eyes. He looked different. He'd cut off all that long dark hair and shaved his scraggly beard. When had he done that?

"Who's at the resort?" she asked.

"Don't worry, Meg's taking care of everything. Mom and Dad will be here soon. Graham's worried about you."

Gram. Did he have a grandmother she hadn't met? And why would the woman be worried about Lauren? "Who?"

"Graham."

Gra-ham. Still didn't ring a bell. "No idea who you're talking about." All this thinking was making her head throb. Why couldn't he just leave her alone?

"Lauren . . . You don't remember your dog?"

"I don't *have* a dog."

His lips slackened. His brow furrowed and he took her hand again.

Her hand.

She homed in on her fingers. The calluses weren't concerning, though she didn't remember them. She was a hard worker and was employed as a manager at a rustic resort.

It was her nails. She always, *always*, kept her nails manicured and painted. Currently they were bare of the polish she'd last used—Ballet Pink, if memory served—and her cuticles were an abomination.

What was going on? Why weren't her nails painted? Why did Jonah think she had a dog, and why in heaven's name did he keep touching her? Her breath felt stuffed in her lungs. They, too, were filled with cotton and unable to draw in a breath.

She ripped her hand from his. "Stop touching me. Stop talking to me. Why are you even here?"

He leaned forward, gaze sharpening on her. "Lauren . . . What's going on? It's *me*, Jonah."

"I know who you are! I'm not stupid." Why was he being so weird? She needed Sydney. She'd be trying to make her laugh, not confusing her. She'd help Lauren make sense of all this. She would go out there and demand someone get in here. She wanted to talk to Sydney, never mind that her friend was back home in Boston.

17

Lauren felt for her pocket, but she wasn't wearing her jeans. She was in a hospital gown. "Where's my phone? Get me my phone."

"It's probably still in your pants." Jonah turned and opened a cubby, grabbed her jeans, and fished through her pockets. "It's not here." He lifted her shirt, her shoes. "It must've fallen out in the barn."

She couldn't catch her breath. "I want to talk to Sydney!" Lauren couldn't seem to draw in oxygen. She needed air. The neck brace was choking her. She clawed at it.

Jonah grabbed her hands. "Honey, don't do that. It's okay. You're okay. I've got you."

"Get this off. Get it off! I can't breathe."

"I need help in here!" he hollered. "You have to stay still. Please, sweetheart. You're gonna hurt yourself."

"Leave me alone!"

A terrible foreboding filled her. Anxiety swarmed like a dozen angry bees in her head.

A commotion sounded as a nurse entered, Carson on her heels.

"Something's wrong," Jonah told the nurse. "My girlfriend can't breathe."

"Not . . . girlfriend," she squeezed out. Breathe. She needed to breathe. A horrible sense of doom washed over her, nearly swallowing her whole. Her pulse raced, pounded in her chest, in her head. She was gonna die.

God, help me.

Carson edged past Jonah. "Does she have panic attacks?"

"No, never."

Carson got in her face. "Hey, Lauren? Lauren, look at me, look at me. Let go of the C-collar, okay? I'm gonna take it off. Your CT showed no neck or spinal injuries. That's good news, huh? Off we go." The rip of Velcro sounded, and he slipped the thing off her neck. "There, is that better? What's going on?"

The constriction didn't go away. "I feel . . . anxious. Can't breathe."

"Does your chest or anything else hurt?"

She couldn't think. Couldn't breathe.

"Lauren, does anything hurt?"

"Just—just my head."

"Something's wrong with her," Jonah said. "You have to help her."

"Her brain appeared normal on the CT. Lauren, I know you're scared, but I think you're having a panic attack. I want you to focus on breathing slowly and deeply. Watch me."

Lauren's gaze clung to Carson's. She pushed away the panic and shifted her breathing to match his.

"One breath at a time. That's it. You're doing great."

She took three more deep, slow breaths. Okay. She could breathe. Maybe she wasn't dying after all.

JONAH'S hands knotted into fists. He felt so helpless. He'd never seen that wild look in her eyes before. Never seen the complete and utter panic on her face. Lauren was cool and calm. Not flustered and fearful.

"Lauren, try counting back from one hundred." Carson's voice was soft and measured. "Can you do that for me?"

"One—one hundred." Her voice quavered. "Ninety-nine . . . ninety-eight . . ."

"There you go. Keep it going."

She was breathing normally. Her features relaxed a bit. That wild look in her eyes faded.

Relief swamped Jonah, making his legs go weak and wobbly. She wasn't having a heart attack. And she didn't have brain damage. But if that was true, why didn't she remember Graham or the barn? Why was she acting like they weren't a couple? The questions hovered like annoying mosquitoes. It was as if she didn't remember him—or at least, remember *them*. But that couldn't be true, could it? The possibility punched the air from his lungs.

"You're feeling better, right?" Carson asked a few minutes later.

Lauren nodded.

"Hang in there. You got this." Carson edged away while the nurse stepped in and took her vitals.

He joined Jonah at the edge of the room. "I'm reasonably sure that was a panic attack, but they'll likely run some tests just to make sure. What brought this on exactly?"

Jonah shook his head. "We were just talking. She said she didn't have a dog, and she didn't remember the barn, the one she's making into an event venue—the place where she fell! And she said she's not my girlfriend—you heard that."

"Listen, she's obviously confused. I know it's disconcerting, but what matters is that we keep her calm. She's got a concussion at the very least. She needs rest." Carson glanced at Lauren who, for some odd reason, was glaring at Jonah.

"Why's she so mad at me? I swear I didn't do anything to make her angry. I'm telling you, she's not herself."

"No, I get that. Try not to take it personally. A bump on the head can cause all kinds of symptoms, including irritability. They almost always go away with time. The normal CT is a very good sign. But we don't want her having another panic attack. The less stimulation, the better." His face softened as he set a hand on Jonah's shoulder. "You might want to give her a little space."

"Okay. I'll sit over there and be quiet. I don't want her to be alone."

"Stop talking about me," Lauren snapped at Jonah.

The nurse had removed the backboard and inclined her bed a bit. She seemed so small. So helpless.

"It might be better if you step into the hall," Carson said. "Just for a little bit. Give her some breathing room."

Jonah's heart gave a sudden crack. Because Carson was right. He wasn't doing Lauren any favors. His presence, for whatever reason, only seemed to annoy her. And despite the terrible fear leaking into his veins, he had to put her health first. "Okay, you're right."

"The doctor will be in in a few minutes. I'll stay until then if you want."

"Yeah, yeah. All right." Whatever was best for Lauren.

CHAPTER 4

LAUREN HEARD CARSON shift on the bedside chair, but she kept her eyes closed. He'd said she needed to rest and she was trying to do just that. But she kept reliving that terrible panic and praying it wouldn't come back. Between that and the fuzzy thinking, she couldn't calm herself.

Fortunately, it wasn't long before someone slipped into the room— the doctor, judging by his scrubs and lab coat. He was bald with warm brown skin and a kind smile.

"Hello, young lady. I am Dr. Kadambi."

"Lauren Wentworth."

"Congratulations. You have already passed my first test." His gaze flickered to Carson. "You are friends with Miss Wentworth? It is good if someone who knows the patient is present for the questions."

"Ah, in that case, I think it would be better to bring Jonah back in. That okay, Lauren?"

She pressed her lips together. "I guess."

"Tell me how you are feeling," the doctor said as Carson left the room.

"My head's a little better." The nurse had put something in the IV. "I'm a little nauseated."

"We can get you something for that. Any weakness, tingling, or numbing anywhere?"

"Um . . . no."

"The light is off, so I assume your eyes are sensitive?"

"Yes."

"This probably will not be pleasant, but I need to check your pupils." He leaned in and shone the light in her eyes. "Good. Now follow the light with your eyes only. Good, good."

She heard Jonah slip into the room, but she was still seeing spots from the light.

"Come in, Jonah. I am Dr. Kadambi and I will be asking Lauren some questions. We may need a bit of help."

"Okay." Jonah came as far as the chair and perched on the edge of it.

"Lauren, can you tell me where we are?"

"At the hospital. Pinehaven Hospital."

"What happened to bring you in today?"

"I . . . I fell."

"I told you that," Jonah said. "I had to tell her that twice. She didn't remember falling."

Dr. Kadambi raised his brows at her.

She thought hard. Back to the last thing she remembered. She wanted to prove Jonah wrong. But she couldn't recall the accident. "I—I don't really remember falling."

"That is not unusual with a concussion. You might never remember the moments before the accident. What is the last thing you remember?"

"Um . . ." She thought back. "We were on the pier. I just came back from a boat ride."

"That's right." Jonah voice was laced with excitement. "That was this afternoon."

"We—we argued."

23

"Who argued?" Dr. Kadambi asked.

Her eyes flickered to the corner. "Jonah and me."

"That's not true. That didn't happen."

She nailed him with a look. "Yes, it did. I remember very clearly."

"What did we argue about then?" He searched her face. Where was all this warmth and concern coming from all of a sudden?

"I didn't wear a life jacket. You got all bent out of shape."

His lips parted. Otherwise his features froze. Then he glanced at the doctor, who in turn glanced at her.

"What?" she said. "It's true. I know I'm a little fuzzy, but the memory's very clear." Why was Jonah disputing this?

"Is that what happened, Jonah?"

He blinked. "Yes." He stared at her again, those blue eyes holding secrets she was suddenly sure she didn't want to hear. He cleared his throat, his focus like a laser beam on her. "The argument on the pier did happen. But it didn't happen today."

The doctor returned his attention to Lauren, and his gaze sharpened on her. "Can you tell me the date?"

Seriously? She huffed. What kind of trick was Jonah playing on her? She glared at him.

"Humor me, Lauren," the doctor said.

"It's Sunday, April twenty-eighth." She rattled off the year for good measure.

A beat of silence passed. The clock ticked away the seconds. Something shifted in the room as the doctor made eye contact with Jonah.

"*What?* I know it's Sunday, but it could be the twenty-ninth, I guess. I'm a little foggy, remember? Cut me some slack." She sometimes lost track up here—something she'd never done in the city. But why had Jonah insisted they hadn't argued that very day? She was still peeved about it. He could be such a pain, a real stickler for the rules. She was a perfectly good swimmer, for heaven's sake.

24

The doctor touched her arm. "Lauren . . . You seem to have lost a bit of time, which can happen with a concussion. We'll need a few more tests, and I'd like to keep you overnight as a precaution."

Her thoughts got hung up on his first sentence. "How much time?" Her gaze toggled between the doctor and Jonah. Had she lost a few days? Was that why Jonah said they hadn't argued that day? That made sense, didn't it? When thinking was like slogging through mud, it was hard to tell.

"Lauren . . ." Dr. Kadambi said. "It is not April. Today's date is September seventh."

JONAH sat frozen to the chair. Lauren thought it was the end of *April*. That would've been only about a month and a half after her arrival. If Lauren didn't remember the past four months, she hadn't just forgotten about the barn and Graham.

She'd forgotten about *them*.

"I'm not his girlfriend."

She didn't remember all the weeks they'd spent working their way from antagonism to love. She didn't remember their first date or her steady slide into his heart. She didn't remember when he'd professed his love or when she'd finally vocalized her own feelings.

No wonder she was behaving so strangely. She was still neck-deep in animosity. Dread seeped into his bloodstream.

"That—that can't be true." Lauren's eyes, full of confusion, darted from the doctor to him. "It's *April*."

Dr. Kadambi pulled his cell phone from his pocket and held it up for Lauren. "This is my home screen. Can you read the date?"

She blinked. Gaped at the screen for a full five seconds. Then she lifted a hand to her face. "I don't understand. How can this be possible?"

"Jonah, this memory Lauren had of the argument on the pier. When did that occur?"

He tried to slow his spinning thoughts. "Um, I couldn't tell you the exact date, but it would've been toward the end of April, like she said."

Her gaze fastened on his. Disbelief warred with fear in her familiar green eyes. And he hated that he'd helped put them there.

The doctor laid a hand on Lauren's, his voice softening. "I know this must be unsettling, Lauren. But you seem to have what is called temporally graded retrograde amnesia. It is a form of memory loss that can sometimes occur after a traumatic brain injury."

Her fingers tightened on the sheet. *"Traumatic brain injury?"*

Jonah popped to his feet and approached the bed. "I thought her CT was normal."

"A concussion is a traumatic brain injury, and the brain is a very complex organ. An injury that damages the region where memory is stored can cause this type of amnesia."

He had to ask the question that was surging up from the deep, sludgy well inside him. "Will she—will she get her memory back?"

"I cannot say for certain, but often memory is restored within days or weeks."

"Weeks?" Her breath rushed out. She blinked back tears. "This can't be happening."

"It's gonna be okay." Jonah started to grab her hand. Grabbed the railing instead. She wouldn't welcome his touch. Once again he was just the pesky son of her boss, the man she had to deal with on a daily basis.

Only now that man was madly in love with her.

JONAH approached the ER waiting room where his mom and dad waited in hard plastic chairs. They jumped to their feet at his approach, his dad, gray hair windblown, towering over his mom.

26

His mom's dark hair was caught up in a youthful ponytail. But worry lines marred her forehead and empathy filled her brown eyes. "How is she?"

He found himself swallowed up in his mother's embrace. His dad's beefy hand settled on his shoulder. Gave a firm squeeze.

"Physically she seems okay. The CT scan was normal and they're running more tests."

"That's good news," Dad said.

She hadn't wanted him there for the tests. It was written all over her face. Since Mom had texted that they'd arrived, he used that as an excuse to slip away. Plus, he really did need some time to absorb all this.

April.

Mom's intelligent eyes homed in on him. "What aren't you telling us?"

He opened his mouth to relay what had happened. He could hardly believe this was happening. It felt so surreal. Maybe saying it out loud would help. "She's lost some of her memory. When the doctor asked her the date, she thought it was April. But she understands now it's not. She's reeling a bit."

Mom gasped. "April? That's a lot of time to lose." Her eyes flashed with a succession of emotions, putting it all together. Then they filled with compassion. "Oh, honey. She doesn't remember . . . ?"

"No."

"She'll get it back though, right?" Dad asked. "The memories will come back."

Jonah swallowed around the boulder in his throat. "The doctor seemed optimistic they'd return in days or weeks. But he couldn't say for sure. Hopefully they'll know more after the tests."

Mom squeezed his arm. "They'll come back. They just have to. We'll be praying hard."

"We'll do everything we can to help with her recovery," Dad said. "Whatever she needs."

"I have no idea what that'll entail."

"Doesn't matter," Mom said. "She's family and we'll be here for her. Now, you should go be with her. She must be scared and confused, poor thing."

Jonah squeezed his neck as another piece of his heart cracked off. "She, uh, doesn't really want me in the room, Mom."

Her eyes watered. "Oh, honey."

"You remember how things were between us in April. She had some kind of panic attack earlier. It was awful. I don't want to put her through that again. But you should go back. A friendly face would probably be comforting just now, and I don't want her to be alone."

THE plastic chair was hard. Jonah shifted regularly. Got up and paced. People came and went. The TV screen mounted to the wall played *Wheel of Fortune* and *Jeopardy!* He had no idea how much time had passed when his parents returned to the waiting room, but his mom's face was tight with worry, her ever-present smile nowhere to be seen. His dad lumbered behind her.

Apparently Lauren's memory hadn't magically returned. Jonah met them near the check-in desk. "How's she doing?"

"Holding her own," Mom said. "But losing all that time . . . It feels like we've gone back to square one in our relationship. They were just starting some tests, and I didn't feel she wanted us there." She wrapped an arm around his waist. "I can't even imagine how this feels to you."

"They're keeping her overnight," Dad said. "They'll be moving her upstairs soon."

"Thanks for going back there, being with her."

"Of course, sweetheart."

He longed to be with her himself. It was killing him to stay out here. But the memory of that panic attack, or whatever it was, was fresh in his mind. He could still see the raw fear in her eyes as she struggled to draw breath. He never wanted to see that again. Never wanted her to feel like that again.

"I'm gonna stay here."

"All night?" Mom asked.

"Yeah." He couldn't leave her. And if her memory came back, she'd want him. "Would you guys check the barn for her phone? She wanted to call Sydney earlier. It must've fallen out of her pocket. I'd call her myself, but I don't have her number in my phone."

"I'll do that soon as we get home," Dad said. "And we'll bring your truck and leave it for you."

"I'll gather a few things she'll be wanting, toothbrush and whatnot."

"Thanks, Mom. I'm sure she'd appreciate that."

They left a few minutes later and Jonah resumed pacing. He hadn't realized how much he'd been hoping they'd come out and report that Lauren's memory had returned. That she was asking for him. If he deflated any more, he'd be a limp, airless balloon lumped on the floor.

He got water from the vending machine and stared sightlessly at the TV screen until his parents returned with a bag for Lauren and a backpack for him.

Dad handed him the keys to his truck and they talked for a few minutes. Offered to stay. Jonah insisted they go home and get some rest. They wanted to be updated of any changes no matter the time of night, and Jonah promised he'd call. Then they left.

He asked the desk attendant to take Lauren's things back to her. Then he resumed his long-distance vigil, only remembering belatedly that he hadn't used Lauren's phone to call Sydney. But she'd no doubt do that herself. He hoped Sydney would come because Lauren needed someone she could trust. But then he remembered the woman was flying to Florida this week for her brother's wedding. What terrible timing.

Sometime later he opened the backpack and found a small blanket, toiletries, water bottles, protein bars, and homemade cookies. The sight of food reminded him he hadn't eaten supper. Then he remembered the reservations at The Landing. He glanced at the utilitarian wall clock. Ten twenty-six.

Had the night gone as anticipated, right now he would've been engaged to the love of his life.

CHAPTER 5

ALL THE WORDS the doctor had said this morning swirled around Lauren's head like debris in a hurricane. The woman came in just after six, awakening Lauren from a dead sleep. She hadn't had time to orient herself, much less have coffee, before the talking started. The only thing she knew for sure was that she'd be discharged soon.

She inclined her bed, sat up, and turned until her feet hung over the side. Were those her socks? Her nails still looked like someone else's. The headache was better at least. But her thoughts were still fuzzy. If she'd been awake and coherent, she would've asked the doctor how long that would last.

She glanced out the window that faced the parking lot and the woods beyond. It was almost six thirty and the sun was barely up. The trees held autumnal tinges of yellow and orange.

September, not April. Even with visual proof, it seemed impossible.

She recalled Tom and Tammy's visit last night. Odd to have her employers in the room while she swam in a hospital gown and felt mentally vulnerable. They were good people. Tammy was a warm, motherly woman. Tom had a gruff exterior, but she suspected he was as soft as fresh fudge on the inside.

Did she already know that for a fact but had only forgotten it? The thought flittered away.

She spied the bag of things she assumed Tammy had gathered for her. Lauren wanted to get out of this gown and start feeling like herself again. She wanted to return to her cabin where strangers weren't telling her what to do and when to do it. It was her childhood all over again.

Why could she remember her miserable childhood and not what had happened two days ago?

She came to her feet and hesitated until she was certain the room wouldn't spin. Then she grabbed the bag off the corner chair and rooted through it. Toothbrush, toothpaste, a change of clothes, her hairbrush. She wanted to weep at all the familiar things. She wanted to hug the entire bag.

And that was before she found her phone in the side pocket. She needed a lifeline. She needed her best friend. Sydney would be up torturing herself in the gym at this early hour. Lauren found her number and tapped the Call button.

The woman answered on the third ring with a breathless, "Hey, what's up?" The whir of a treadmill and the rhythmic thumping of footsteps carried across the distance.

Lauren sank into the chair. "I am so glad to hear your voice. You have no idea."

"What's wrong?" Beeps sounded and the background noises silenced. "What happened?"

"I fell yesterday and hit my head. I'm in the hospital."

"Lauren! Are you all right?"

"My head hurts and I can't remember stuff, like entire months, and my thoughts are all disconnected and fuzzy."

"Oh no. What did the doctors say? Wait, did you say you can't remember *months?*"

"I have a concussion. But yes, I have no memory of the last—" April to September would be . . . She couldn't even do basic math! "My last memory is in late April. I have no idea what's happened since, and I'm not sure I even want to know.

"Jonah was here when I woke up in the ER—you know, the Landrys' son. And he was being all nice and weird. I think he said I was his girlfriend at one point? But I was having some kind of panic attack at the time, so maybe I misheard. Please tell me I'm just confused." She closed her eyes tightly. Her pulse throbbed in her head.

"Oh, you poor thing. Will you get them back?"

"I don't know. They don't know. Maybe in weeks or months. Or maybe not at all."

"Oh, Lauren, that's just awful. I'm so sorry. You're gonna have to be careful. You're supposed to limit stimulation—I got a concussion playing soccer in high school. No internet, no TV. You're supposed to be resting. You really don't remember anything that happened the past four months? Nothing?"

"I seriously feel like it's springtime right now, but the leaves are already starting to turn. I missed the entire summer."

"Well, you didn't miss it, really. It did happen . . . You just don't remember it."

Something about her tone sent a tremor of fear through Lauren's system. "My brain might not be working right, but I'm pretty sure you haven't answered my question about Jonah."

A pause ensued. Then, "You know what? I'm coming up there. My flight isn't until tomorrow morning. I can be back in plenty of time."

"Flight . . . ?" *September.* Something teased the tattered fringes of her brain.

The wedding. Last Lauren had checked, Syd's brother's wedding was still months away. Now it was this weekend. "No, don't do that. You'd no sooner get here than you'd have to turn around and head back. I'm fine. I'll just be resting in my cabin. The Landrys will make sure I have what I need."

"I'm your best friend. You need me."

"Please don't. You should be getting ready for your trip. Your brother's big day. If you want to help me, just tell me the truth. I'm going back to the cabin in a bit, and I need to know what I'll be facing."

"Right. Um, have you looked at your phone, at your photos and texts and stuff?"

She hadn't even thought of that. "My brain's like a tangled skein of yarn right now, Syd. I'm dating him, aren't I? He somehow charmed me like he does everyone else and I'm dating him."

"Um . . . yes? Sort of?"

She flopped back in the chair, careful with her head. "Oh. My. Gosh. I'm so humiliated."

"Humiliated?"

"I don't even like him! I made that very clear to him and to you."

"Honey, it's not as bad as you think. In fact, you guys seem great together, though I don't entirely like that—"

"How do you know we're great together?"

"That's right. You don't remember. This is so weird. I came up in early August for a weekend and got to know him a bit."

"He worked his charm on you too."

"He worked it on you first, my friend."

Lauren groaned. "This is not happening. Were we serious? We can't have been serious, right? Not in only four months."

"Um, well . . ."

The pause continued so long that Lauren pressed her hand to her thudding heart. *"Syd?"*

"The last couple months you guys have gotten pretty serious. The last time we spoke you even mentioned not returning to Boston at all."

Lauren gaped. That couldn't be true.

"You were in pretty deep, Lauren."

It was just talk. There was no way she would've given up her dream job. She moved her hand to her throbbing temple.

"Listen, you shouldn't be worrying about all this right now. You need to focus on your recovery. Resting is job number one."

"Oh, sure, I'm so great at that."

"They might have to tie you down. I'm coming up there, just for today."

"No, you aren't. You're packing for your trip and . . . doing whatever sisters of the groom should be doing." Her brain was a sieve. "I'll be furious if you drive up here today, and the emotion drain would be terrible for my concussion."

"You don't play fair."

"Finish your zillionth mile on the treadmill and start packing—you probably haven't even started."

"Guilty as charged. Okay, but promise me you'll rest. And stay off your phone—unless you need to talk, in which case you should call me, day or night."

After promising, Lauren ended the call and stared at the phone for a full minute. Some of the answers she sought were housed in this thing. The photos, the texts. But the thought of taxing her already overloaded brain had her dropping the device into the bag.

The mystery of how Jonah Landry had wormed his way into her heart would have to wait.

CHAPTER 6

March 18

IT WAS GETTING more real by the moment.

Lauren surveyed the passing landscape as she exited the highway and hit a country road leading to New Hampshire's lake region. Boston seemed a continent away. Good-bye skyscrapers, peopled greens, lively pubs, and stunning architecture. Hello barren trees, rolling hills, and low stone walls that seemingly served no purpose.

It was only nine months. She could survive nine months in the wilderness, couldn't she, when her dream job awaited? And so soon after attaining her hospitality management degree.

She could handle nine months as temporary manager of Pinehaven Resort. Oh, at first she'd been thrilled by the opportunity. Sitting in CEO Olivia Stafford's upscale office, Lauren had been eager to do whatever was necessary for the coveted position at Glitter. Work with complete autonomy under the umbrella of Boston's most prestigious corporate event planner? Yes, please.

"With Ella Franklin retiring at the end of year," Olivia had said, "we'll have an opening for an event planner. We think you'd be a good fit."

Lauren kept a neutral expression when she wanted to jump to her feet and scream at the top of her lungs. A lifetime of self-regulation kept her seated. "It would be an honor to work for Glitter."

"But first I'd like you to have some real-world experience. Management experience, I mean. I'm sure you've learned a lot serving for Elite."

"I have." For seven years Lauren had taken college classes while working full-time for a catering company, which was how she'd entered Glitter's orbit. They often hired Elite to cater their events.

Lauren leaned forward in her chair, hoping Olivia was about to offer her a paid internship at Glitter that would allow her to attain the aforementioned experience and also make rent.

"I have an old friend who's seeking a temporary manager for the small resort she and her husband own. He had a heart attack recently and needs a reprieve from the daily operations."

Okay, not Glitter, but still . . . a resort sounded nice. Wealthy clientele, spacious suites, a spa, perhaps a restaurant that required French fluency. Lauren beamed. "That sounds right up my alley."

"It would be a good experience for you. Running Pinehaven Resort would be very different from the position here at Glitter, but I consider that to be a good thing. You're already intimately acquainted with the service end of things. This would give you the chance to oversee something. And if all goes as well as I expect it to, the event planner position would be yours come January."

Lauren was warming to the whole idea. She'd graduated a month ago, and she was eager to exit the catering industry and start the life she'd been working toward since she was sixteen. "Count me in. How should I apply for the position?"

Olivia had already spoken with Tammy Landry, and the job was Lauren's if she wanted it, on Olivia's strong recommendation. A Zoom meeting would be scheduled, but it sounded like a formality. The job would require a move as the property was in New Hampshire. The pay was on the low side, but they would be providing her accommodations. Her lease was about up and she could simply store her furnishings for the rest of the year.

Full of optimism, though lacking in details, Lauren took Tammy Landry's contact information. She rushed home to her studio apartment in Lynn and went straight to her laptop. As the resort's home page opened, her jaw dropped—and not in a good way. The header showed a group of eight tiny cabins along a lake shoreline. The main lodge boasted a stone fireplace. The activities offered were boating, swimming, fishing, basketball, and canoeing.

Heart dropping to the floor, she clicked on Cedar Cabin—each was named for a type of tree. The interior was very . . . rustic. Small bedrooms, wood floors, wood furniture, a kitchenette, and a bathroom that looked as if a person could shower, use the toilet, and brush one's teeth simultaneously.

So no lavender-scented spa, snooty concierge, or five-star restaurant (or even a vending machine, apparently). Just a group of country cabins on a lake in Podunk, New Hampshire.

She slumped in her chair, measuring her breaths, and allowed herself a moment to process. Okay. So the place wasn't quite what she'd expected. Her secondhand Jimmy Choos and Givenchy bag were definitely headed for storage.

For a while.

But it was only nine months. She'd shared a childhood bedroom with three spoiled kids, lived under the roof of an autocratic foster father, and survived the jealousy of a foster mother for longer than that. She could survive nine months at Pinehaven Resort.

The memory evaporated when she passed a sign that read "Pinehaven—Prettiest lake town in New Hampshire." As she crested a hill she caught sight of Loon Lake, the afternoon sun gleaming off its frozen surface. She tried to imagine how the lake would look in the summer, teeming with pontoons, fishing boats, and kayaks, but failed.

She slowed to navigate the potholes as she entered town and scanned for a place to stop and freshen up before she reported to the resort. Most of the shops lining Main Street seemed locked up tight. Ah, there ahead, an Open flag waved from beneath a red canopy. The sign on the window read Birdie's Deli. Perfect.

She was too nervous to eat, but a Diet Coke and a change of clothes would hit the spot. She may have Olivia's recommendation, and the Zoom with Tom and Tammy had gone well, but she knew the value of a good first impression.

She parallel parked, then removed the clothes she'd hung in the back seat of her Camry and carried them into the deli. The delicious aroma of baked bread made her stomach rumble. Maybe just a slice of that bread to tide her over.

Since there was a line she headed for the restroom and changed. The navy cashmere sweater she'd purchased from her favorite Goodwill in North End seemed brand-new and flattered her blonde hair. Though jeans might be the uniform of choice for her job, she'd chosen a pair of quality khakis (Bargain Basement) for today, as well as her prized Prada suede ankle boots (Renew) in camel with a matching belt.

Her makeup was fine, but she fluffed her hair. Stepping back, she surveyed the overall effect. She appeared competent and put together if a little nervous. *Relax. You've got this.* Now that her initial disappointment had faded, she was eager to step in and run this resort through the high season and beyond.

Tom and Tammy hoped she could help bolster their flagging business, which had suffered since a new upscale resort opened across the lake last year. It was time to put her education and ingenuity to work. And the woman in the mirror seemed like she could handle the task.

She ordered her fountain soda and a slice of freshly baked bread, and a few minutes later she headed out to her car. The day was warming up, and with the sun shining it felt like at least fifty degrees. She had just enough time to review her notes from the Zoom call as she enjoyed her bread. She looked both ways, then crossed the street, navigating a pothole the size of Australia. At her car door she juggled the drink, sack, and hangers of clothing as she rooted through her pocketbook for her key fob. There it was.

A wave of cold water hit her. She gasped.

A guy called out of his blue pickup truck, "Sorry!" She caught a glimpse of his twinkling eyes in his rearview mirror.

Then she glanced down. Her pants and boots were drenched with muddy water.

FIFTEEN minutes later, Lauren followed the GPS to the resort, anxiety building because now she was running late. She'd had to change into wrinkled clothes from her suitcase since even the outfit she'd driven up in had been soiled by the jerk in the pickup truck. Her Pradas were probably ruined.

Following the verbal directions, she turned onto an unpaved road. This hadn't been the recommended route, but since she was running late she'd chosen the quickest one. Judging by the mud, Pinehaven must've recently survived a monsoon. So much for her clean car.

A few minutes later she questioned her decision. The road was getting worse by the minute. She topped a low hill, then started the descent, homing in on the standing water at the bottom. God only knew how deep it was. She should probably turn around, though it would make her even later. She slowed, pulled to the side of the road, and put the car in Park.

Once she rerouted the GPS, she shifted into Drive and pressed the gas pedal. The tires spun.

"No, no, no!"

She tried again, going easy, but still got no traction. She'd driven in enough snow to know to quit while she was ahead. Maybe she could put a floor mat under the wheel. She stepped from the car to assess the situation, and her low heels sank into the mud. Her front left tire was already several inches deep in the oozing sludge.

A car mat wouldn't fix this problem.

TWENTY minutes later she'd managed to walk back to the main road. Not a single car had passed, and her shoes were covered in mud. She'd been unable to reach Tammy because there was no cell service.

It would be at least a thirty-minute walk back into town where she could reach Tammy and ask for a ride—or she could take her chances with a stranger. As if her thoughts had summoned it, a gray SUV slowed as it passed and pulled off to the side of the road up ahead. Flashers came on. The Jeep Grand Cherokee sported a New Hampshire plate and a Red Sox bumper sticker.

A man exited the driver's side and headed her way. Handsome and wearing teal scrubs over his trim, athletic build, he could've stepped straight off the cover of *GQ*. But despite his appeal, her past had eradicated any naivety she might've had as a young girl.

As if sensing her guardedness, he stopped a couple car lengths away. "You okay? Need some help?"

She glanced at her mud-splattered pants and boots. "What would give you that idea?"

One side of his mouth tipped up. "Another innocent victim of mud season?"

"It swallowed my car."

"If it makes you feel any better, you're not the first. Can I make a call for you?"

Feeling a bit safer since he hadn't tried to cajole her into his vehicle, she closed the distance between him as she held up her phone. "No cell service." As she neared she spied a hospital ID clipped to his scrubs that identified him as Carson McConnell, pediatric intern.

He checked his own device. "Yeah, me neither."

He was even more attractive up close. His dark blond hair was clipped short at the sides and a little longer on top. His hazel eyes were deep set and he had a sharp, clean-shaven jawline. "I'm happy to give you a ride if you'd feel comfortable with that." He nudged his badge. "I'd say you could call the hospital and verify my identity but . . ."

She examined his photo ID. "Your badge kinda does that for you, and I'm late for an appointment, so I'll gladly take you up on your offer."

A few seconds later, he assisted her into the vehicle.

"Sorry about the mud."

"That's what the mats are for." He closed the door and headed around.

The inside of his SUV was clean and smelled of coffee and leather.

She glanced over as he got in. Ambitious, smart, handsome, and let's not forget, knight in shining armor. She sneaked a peek at his left hand. No ring. She could certainly do worse.

But no. Pinehaven was just a stepping stone, and she would not be distracted by a pretty face. Even one that pretty. Career first, then home ownership (complete with her very own dog), then husband and kids. She was firm on the order.

He buckled in. "Where you headed?"

"Pinehaven Resort? My little mishap has made me late for my debut. I'm their new temporary manager from Boston."

He started the truck and pulled onto the road. "Ah, the Landrys' place. Good people. You'll like working for them. We attend church together."

"I guess this *is* a small town."

"They hired someone from Boston, huh?"

She caught a note of humor. "That surprises you?"

"Folks around here have a thing about people from Massachusetts."

"I've heard, but I'm a good driver so maybe I don't count."

"You should get along just fine then. I'm from Boston myself."

"Oh, really? What brought you to New Hampshire?"

"An internship at the local hospital. I'm hoping for a residency at Mass General so I can once again reside in the same state as my girl-friend, Carina. She's currently getting her master's degree from Boston College."

A hopeful bubble burst. Probably for the best. "That's great."

He rolled through town, no doubt following the route she should've taken. "First time here?"

"Yeah. It's beautiful. Quiet."

"You won't recognize the place in a couple months. Come Memorial Day weekend, it's a tourist mecca."

"I guess that keeps you busy at the hospital."

"You wouldn't believe the messes people get themselves into while they're traveling."

She glanced down at her clothes. "Oh, I don't know. I think I can."

They chatted as they drove, and he recommended a place that would tow her vehicle from the mud. Lauren jotted *Sullivan's Towing* in the Notes on her phone.

Ten minutes later they pulled into a gravel drive. A sign out front read "Pinehaven Resort: A rustic retreat." The drive wound back through a pine forest. Despite the serene surroundings her nerves jangled. She was late and disheveled. So much for first impressions.

He followed a truck into a gravel parking lot and pulled alongside it. "There's Jonah now. He's the owners' son."

Lauren glanced over, recognized the blue truck and the driver inside, and gritted her teeth.

CHAPTER 7

Present day

JONAH SPLASHED WATER on his face and met his gaze in the mirror. They'd relocated Lauren to a regular room late last night, and he'd moved to the waiting room on the same floor. He'd gotten only a modicum of sleep on that chair, and his clothes were now disheveled. A shadow of scruff covered his jawline, his eyelids were swollen, and that cowlick at his forehead refused to be tamed.

But hope sprang up inside, relentless and buoying. Maybe with a full night's rest Lauren's memory had returned. Maybe he'd enter her room and her face would light up at the sight of him. Those green eyes would sparkle and turn to crescent moons the way they did when she laughed. He'd hold her tight and joke that someday they'd tell their kids about the time she'd forgotten him.

Common sense whispered in his ear, *If her memory returned, they would've come for you.* But maybe the staff had turned over and they didn't realize he was here. Maybe she hadn't found her phone in the bag his parents left.

Giving up on his hair, he left the restroom and proceeded past the desk and down the hall to her room. He hadn't visited her last night, hadn't wanted to upset her again, but they'd given him her room number. His footsteps quickened as the numbers ascended. He was eager to see her after the misery of yesterday.

There it was, Room 213.

The door was open, so he went right in. She sat on the edge of the bed, dressed in street clothes, the bag sitting at her side as if she was eager to leave. At his entry her gaze swung to him and she straightened. A guarded expression came over her face.

The hope inside him popped at her expression. He didn't even have to ask. She still thought he was her enemy. *What if her memory never comes back?* His stomach turned to lead.

He forced his lips into a smile. "Morning. How are you feeling today?"

She did a quick head-to-toe scan of him. "A little better. They're discharging me."

"That's great. I can take you home."

She opened her mouth, then closed it again.

"Was the doctor in this morning?"

"Yeah, she's the one who's discharging me."

"What did she say about your concussion?"

She put her hand to her throat, something she did when she was uncomfortable. "I'm, uh, not really sure. I wasn't quite awake yet. And I'm not thinking very clearly."

A middle-aged nurse bustled into the room with a wheelchair. "All right, young lady. We're busting you outta here." She glanced at Jonah. "Are you the ride?"

"Yeah."

"Perfect." She handed Lauren a packet. "The instructions are in here, basically a summary of what Dr. Wallis told you this morning, I'm sure."

Lauren started to say something, then put a hand to her temple.

"Up you go!"

Lauren stood slowly and pivoted to sit in the wheelchair. Once seated she cradled her bag and the packet to her middle as the nurse adjusted the footrests.

"All right, you got everything?"

"Um, I think so?"

Jonah swept his gaze over the room just to be sure. Peeked in the bathroom. Then, finding nothing, he followed them to the elevator. He had questions about her recovery, and no doubt Lauren did too. She probably wasn't thinking clearly enough to ask. The packet probably explained everything, but what if it didn't?

"Will she need someone to stay with her today?" he asked once they were inside the elevator.

"Definitely. Her tests looked good and we don't expect any problems, but you can't be too careful with a head injury."

"What should we be watching for?"

"If her symptoms worsen—vomiting, increased confusion, trouble waking, nonresponsive—you should bring her back to the ER."

"Otherwise, what are her limitations?"

"For the next couple days she should rest. She doesn't need to lay in a dark room, but no physical activity or anything that requires mental concentration. She should avoid stimulation in general: TV, the computer, reading, and texting."

"And after that?"

"She can gradually increase these activities and continue them as long as her symptoms don't worsen. What is it you do for a living, hon?"

"I manage Pinehaven Resort."

"Oh, I've been by there. Lovely property. Well, you can probably resume your work after a few days as long as the work doesn't make your symptoms worse. If it does, ease off. Let's see, what else? For the headache, no anti-inflammatories for twenty-four hours, just acetaminophen. After that you can switch to ibuprofen."

The elevator doors whooshed open and they exited. Jonah left them at the entrance while he went for his truck. The cab was chilly, so he turned up the heat and pulled around. By the time he got to the passenger door, the nurse had already assisted Lauren inside.

"Thank you for your help," he told her.

"Of course. Take care now."

He shut Lauren's door and turned to the nurse. "Wait."

"What is it, hon?"

He glanced back. Lauren leaned back against the headrest, eyes closed. He lowered his voice. "I wanted to ask about her memory, but I don't want her to feel pressured to remember."

"You're her boyfriend?"

"Yes." He grimaced. "Or at least, I was. I don't know what I am now."

She set her hand on his arm. "Bless your heart. Well, no one can say for sure if she'll get her memories back. Some people do and some don't. It might help to be around familiar things and people though. Be patient. The most important thing is that she takes it easy the next few days. After that . . . you'll just have to wait and see."

LAUREN shifted in the truck's cab, her headache throbbing in her temples. Jonah had slept in the waiting room last night. No one had to tell her that. It was apparent by his rumpled clothing and unkempt hair. He appeared so different now than he had when she'd arrived at Pinehaven. He'd looked like a lumberjack with his longish wavy hair and scruffy beard. She'd always preferred professional men—tidy haircuts and a clean-shaven jawline.

Had he changed those things for her?

She tried to reconcile the Jonah who'd slumped in a waiting room chair all night with the one who'd been a thorn in her flesh. It didn't compute.

The driver's-side door opened and Jonah got in and buckled up. "I bet you'll be glad to be home."

Home. She barely felt acquainted with the place. "Yeah." It was a nice enough cabin. Clean and kind of cozy even if the décor was a little primitive for her taste. The stone fireplace was nice on chilly evenings and the firewood abundant and free. The mattress was more comfortable than she'd expected, though she was glad she'd brought her own bedding. She still wasn't used to the night sounds: unknown animals yipped and howled and hooted. It was not the white noise of cars and sirens she was accustomed to.

Jonah cut a glance her way. "Did you speak with Sydney?"

"Yes. She wanted to come, but she's flying to Tampa today for her brother's wedding."

"I wondered about that. If you want, I'll ask Meg to stay with you the next day or so."

At least he hadn't expected to take the job himself. "Thanks." She wasn't sure what to say to Jonah. Didn't know how to behave around him. There was plenty of ground between bitter rival and doting girlfriend, but all of it seemed as mushy and treacherous as quicksand. But she was pretty sure the guy she'd known in April wouldn't have spent all night slumped in a hospital chair for her sake.

She had another wispy thought, but it fluttered away. That was happening a lot.

"Listen, Lauren. I realize this must be confusing and awkward for you. You must be wondering about . . . things. Maybe you have questions. There were quite a few changes over the summer."

He was still direct. That much hadn't changed. But her head throbbed and was still filled with fog. "Sydney explained how things were. But I really don't feel like thinking about that right now."

A long beat of silence passed. "All right. Fair enough. I don't want to stress you out. And it may end up being a moot point anyway."

She strained to connect the dots. "Because I might get my memory back?"

"Right. But as you said, you don't need to worry about that today. For now let's just focus on getting you better."

She could get on board with that idea. Because if getting her memory back meant she and Jonah were a couple, she wasn't certain she wanted it back at all.

CHAPTER 8

LAUREN WOULD'VE HIDDEN in her cabin all day, but she was bored out of her mind. Meg had stayed with her through the night and left after making her scrambled eggs. She'd been so attentive and affectionate. Clearly their relationship had progressed over the summer. Too bad Lauren couldn't remember it. Thankfully Meg had tiptoed around Lauren's memory issue. She just wanted to pretend it was still April and nothing had changed.

Her gaze fell on a framed photo sitting on her nightstand. A close-up of Jonah and her. Without peering too closely she grabbed the picture, laid it face down inside the drawer, and closed it.

When she stood her dog scrambled to his feet, tail wagging. Meg had brought him over yesterday when Lauren had come from the hospital. Apparently Graham had been upset by her fall and subsequent absence. It had been kind of Meg to take care of him.

Lauren ruffled the mutt's fur. He was a medium-sized dog with a terrier look to his friendly face. "You're a cute little thing, I'll give you that. Sure wish I could remember you." But he remembered her, that much was obvious. He hadn't left her side since she'd returned except when Meg took him out to do his business. "Are you feeling as cooped up as I am, buddy? Let's get out of here."

Her heart thudded as she left the comfort of her cabin, which was at the far end of the property. She could walk a ways and still stay out of sight of the lodge. Tom and Tammy had been by yesterday, bearing food and insisting she take all the time she needed to recover.

And Jonah came by this morning, shifting awkwardly on her doorstep, asking how she was feeling. After a couple minutes of stilted conversation, she used her headache to escape. He had an apartment just outside of town and was taking classes at the local college. At least he had been in April. He'd been planning to take classes throughout the summer to expedite his business degree.

Two days out from her concussion, it still seemed surreal that summer was already gone. But the leaves fluttering overhead and the slight nip in the air told her it was true. Someone—*her?*—had already decorated the property for autumn: bales of hay adorned with pumpkins and squash; potted mums in shades of maroon, yellow, and orange; and autumn wreaths hung on the cabin doors.

She followed the pine needle path toward the water, Graham trotting beside her. As much as she missed the city, she also liked being lakeside. And now, with the sun shining off its glossy surface, it looked much different than she remembered it. It seemed like only a few days ago that ice-out had occurred.

Tammy had told her about the significance of the day. Ice-out was declared each spring when the lake thawed enough for the shuttle boat to run from Pinehaven to the port in Bailey Harbor. A small plane from Air Tours flew over several times a day until the pilot declared the ice-out official. This year it had been April twenty-first.

Now it seemed as if the ice had never been there at all. The pier shimmied beneath her feet as she walked to the end and sat, letting her feet dangle over the water. Graham sat beside her, tongue lolling from his mouth. Her head throbbed from the walk and she couldn't remember what she'd been thinking about ten seconds ago.

It doesn't matter. Just relax. Rest your mind.

But resting wasn't really her forte. She still had a job to do. On a positive note, she now had less than four months before her job at Glitter began. The thought buoyed her spirits.

She let her gaze drift over the cove at the end of the property. She followed the shoreline to the private homes on the other side of the cove, then to the distant shores toward town and the marina and back around to where the lodge sat. She squinted at the resort's community pier where the boats were moored and beyond it to the shoreline.

Her breath caught at the sight of the pavilion. She'd presented the idea to Tom and Tammy only a week ago—or so it seemed. Now the gathering spot sat proudly at the water's edge as if it had appeared by magic. A large stone fireplace dominated the space, which was filled with picnic tables. It was just as she'd envisioned it.

Her eyes stung with tears. And she couldn't even make out the reason for them.

JONAH hunched over his economics textbook. He'd been home to sleep and shower, but he needed to study for tomorrow's exam.

The office was just off the big lobby, which boasted a fireplace and was a popular gathering spot for their guests. Before Lauren it had just been a lobby. Now it featured cozy furniture, a large-screen TV, board games, two vending machines, and a Keurig. Each morning they offered complimentary donuts and pastries. During rainy days guests gathered in front of the fireplace or at the game tables, chatting and laughing. Over the past few months they'd hosted watch parties for baseball—and now football—games.

The lodge closed at ten most evenings since his parents' living space—his childhood home—took up the entire second floor.

The office was less impressive: two desks, both wooden and age-scarred with nicks and scratches. One was his mom's and the one he currently sat at was Meg's. It was cluttered with papers, separated into piles only she understood. He'd pushed back the screen of her desktop computer to make room for his book and notes.

He focused on the pictures lining the wood-paneled walls. Photos going back to when his mom's parents started the place in the fifties. They'd bought the property for a bargain, intending to make it their homestead. But when a hurricane left the county with massive quantities of fallen timber, they'd decided to mill the logs and build cabins. The resort opened for business in 1954.

He loved sharing the history of the place with their guests. It would be an honor to carry on their legacy through another generation.

Jonah's gaze shifted to the picture window that overlooked the lake. What was Lauren doing? Was she taking it easy like she was supposed to?

He'd been texting with Meg for the past twenty-four hours, checking on Lauren. Her condition was unchanged. In other words, her memory had not yet returned. But he'd figured that out for himself an hour ago.

That black cloud of fear enveloped him again, the one that threatened to smother him every time he realized anew that Lauren didn't remember falling in love with him. That her memory might never return.

God, please. You have to bring her back to me. I can't lose her. He swallowed hard against the knot in his throat.

A sound came from out in the lobby, and minutes later Meg entered the office and stopped at the sight of him. "Hey. What are you doing here?"

"Studying."

Her face softened. Because Jonah studied at his apartment or at the campus library. Never here on property where there were so many distractions. He was doing so now only because he had to be close to Lauren.

"It's only been two days."

"I know." He was trying to be patient, but that wasn't his strong suit. And it was especially hard when his whole future with Lauren was on the line.

"You should go see her."

"I did." He'd made it as far as her doorstep. She hadn't invited him in or given him any indication he was welcome. Heat washed over him. "She doesn't want me around, Meg." It hurt to say that. Like an actual physical ache in the vicinity of his heart.

Meg perched on the desk. "I'm sorry. I can only imagine how hard that must be."

He kept telling himself her memory would return and they'd look back on this with gratitude. But what if that didn't happen? What if she finished the year and returned to Boston? A terrible thought occurred.

"Is there anything I can do for you?"

"Just . . . be there for her, I guess. Since I can't."

"Of course I will. I love her too. She's not the same, even with me, you know."

"Meg . . . Lauren doesn't remember turning down that position with Glitter a couple weeks ago. She thinks she's gonna finish out the year here and start that job. Unless Sydney told her what's happened—she called her from the hospital."

"Lauren and I talked quite a bit yesterday. I think she would've said something if she knew. She would've been upset about losing the opportunity."

"You know, she may not have told Sydney at all. She only told me a couple weeks ago and she never mentioned telling her. We had been pretty busy with the resort full and Labor Day weekend upon us." He tried to remember the Lauren he'd met in the spring. She'd been so driven, so determined to excel here so she could get that job back in Boston. "She'll be devastated that the opportunity's gone now."

But she seemed so fragile. He pictured her standing in her cabin doorway, blinking against the morning light, eyes searching for a safe landing spot. The memory of that panic attack was still fresh. "It probably wouldn't be good for her to find out just yet. She's still pretty shaky."

"Her take-home papers did say to avoid stimulation." Meg huffed a laugh and waved at the air. "Shoot, she'll probably get her memory back soon and it'll be a moot point anyway. No sense upsetting the apple cart."

"Right. She has a brain injury—it's a big deal. We don't want to make it worse. I'll let Mom and Dad know, just to make sure we're on the same page."

CHAPTER 9

DAY THREE WAS Lauren's breaking point. She'd napped and rested until she was about to turn into a zombie. Jonah had stopped over both mornings. Once with a load of firewood, once with a box of maple donuts from the Sugar Shack. He said they were her favorite—and when she'd bitten into one after he left, she believed him. She probably should've invited him to stay and enjoy them with her, but she couldn't bring herself to do it. She felt so awkward around him—caught in some weird dimension between enemies and lovers.

Now she was sitting on her deck, staring at the water through the trees. The surface glistened in the late-morning sunlight. If she didn't do something productive soon, she'd go mad.

The sound of laughter carried through the woods. The middle-aged couple who had checked in yesterday walked from Willow Cabin toward the community pier. She stood and followed. Graham scrambled ahead of her, tail flagging the air. She would just check on the couple. See if they needed anything.

She followed them down the dock where they were donning life vests. "Good morning. Beautiful day for a boat ride."

"We were thinking the same," the woman said. "Oh, who's this handsome guy?"

"Meet Graham—our resident mascot." Lauren extended her hand. "And I'm Lauren, the property manager."

They exchanged greetings while the couple gave Graham some attention. They were from Florida and had come north hoping for some early fall foliage. It was their first time at Pinehaven.

"We love it so far," Donald said. "Even if the leaves haven't fully turned yet. It's a beautiful area."

"I'm so glad to hear you're enjoying it. If I can do anything to make your stay more comfortable, just let me know."

"That's so kind," Kathy said. "We did use the last of the firewood. It got quite chilly last night."

"No worries." Donald assisted his wife into the boat. "I can take care of that when we get back."

Lauren beamed. "No need. That's what I'm here for."

The couple settled on the bench seats. "Well, thank you. It was nice meeting you. Off we go!" The two of them worked their paddles with a little trouble and a lot of laughter.

Lauren waved them off, watching for a moment, Graham at her side. Then she traipsed up the property toward the woodpile. It felt good to have something to do again. Her headache was just a faint throb in her temples as she walked up the incline toward the lodge.

She'd kept to herself since she returned from the hospital. It felt strange being around people who seemed more acquainted with her than she was with them. Made her feel exposed somehow. How much of herself had she shared? Anything they might've disclosed about themselves was lost somewhere in the complicated maze of her brain.

The wheelbarrow sat beside the log pile, so she began loading up. She was ready to start easing back into her job. The release papers said she could do so after a few days as long as her symptoms didn't increase. It wouldn't technically be three full days for another five hours or so—but close enough.

She loaded a few more logs, then stepped around to grab the handles.

"Lauren." Jonah appeared around the backside of the lodge, barreling her direction. "Hey, you shouldn't be doing that. Let me help."

"I'm fine. It's just a few logs."

"Go back to your cabin." He took the handles.

She tightened her grip. "The Garretts asked me to deliver them."

"I've got this. You should go lie down."

"You can't tell me what to do."

He wrestled the handles from her. "Actually, I can."

She bristled. Yes, Jonah was technically her boss. It was one of the sticking points between them as the authority figures in her life had been nothing but thorns in her side.

"I know you must be bored, but you're supposed to be resting."

"If I rest any more, I'll be comatose."

"You heard what the nurse said about——"

"She said three days, and that's what it's been!"

"Not yet it hasn't. Stop being so stubborn. Go sit on your deck and——"

"And what? Stare at the trees? I can't text, read, or watch TV. I'm bored out of my skull!" She shelved her fists on her hips, but to her mortification tears pressed behind her eyelids.

His gaze roved over her face for a long, searching moment. Then he set the wheelbarrow down. "I know this is hard."

"You don't know anything."

A muscle flickered in his jaw. "I know you like to be productive. I know your brain usually processes things so quickly you can make a plan and carry it out before most people have their first cup of coffee. I know you're dealing with brain fog and memory issues that have you confused and frustrated. You're thinking if you just get back to work, everything will return to normal."

She pressed her lips together and stiffened her spine when she wanted to sink in on herself. But she'd never admit that he'd hit a bull's-eye.

"But if you're not careful, you could actually do more damage. Be patient with yourself. If you need something to do, let's start with a chore less taxing than toting loads of firewood."

"It's just one load."

"Meg printed off the stickers for the brochures yesterday."

"What stickers?"

He blinked. "Right. It was your idea to update the brochures with stickers instead of purchasing new ones."

"Oh." Her brain seemed to have lost every little detail—and all the big ones too. "Stickers."

"It was a good idea and it needs to be done."

"Fine. I'll do the stickers." She glanced down at the logs. "Knock yourself out."

CHAPTER 10

April 15

JONAH PEERED THROUGH the lobby window, watching Lauren run the snowblower down the walkway surrounding the lodge. She was bundled up in a long, puffy coat with a fur hood that left the smallest circle of her face exposed. How could she even maneuver the blower with those thick, pink gloves?

It had snowed three inches last night, but already the morning sun was warming up the earth. If she just waited till afternoon, the snow would melt on its own. But who was he to give advice?

He hadn't exactly hit it off with their new employee. It wasn't because she was from Massachusetts as Mom had first assumed. It was true that many New Hampshirites held a certain animosity toward people from across their southern border. Yet Jonah knew plenty of decent Bay Staters—many of the resort's regulars, in fact. But if he felt the Massachusetts RMV could be more particular about handing out driver's licenses . . . well, he wouldn't be the first to hold that opinion.

No, his problem with Lauren began months before she'd even arrived. November was a slow month for the resort. A few snowmobilers or skiers per week. The extra downtime had allowed Jonah to load up on courses during the semester—for the degree he'd never even wanted.

Dad's heart attack had shocked them all. Tom Landry was a bear of a man, standing six-two, with strapping shoulders and a lumbering gait.

He was a man of few words, but he wasn't afraid of hard work and he could fix anything as long as it didn't involve a computer. To Jonah he'd always been strong and invincible.

Dad had been repairing a refrigerator in mid-November when the heart attack struck. A week later he was home from the hospital, a stent in place.

Mom pulled Jonah and Meg into their upstairs living room and lowered her voice. "Your father needs a break from this place. I know we'd talked about both of us retiring at the end of next year, but I guess God has different plans."

"That's fine, Mom. Meg and I have got this."

"Absolutely," his sister agreed. "I'll take over your part of the office work. I'll have plenty of time to do the books for us and Bartley's." Meg also did the accounting for a local insurance company.

"And I'll take over management. Consider it done." Jonah had been planning to do so in just over a year anyway, right after graduating.

Mom set her hand on his arm. "That's not what your dad and I want, honey. You need to finish your classes."

"I can do that later—"

"If you take them one or two at a time . . . it'll take forever. We want you to finish up."

Jonah pressed down the frustration this topic always brought to the surface. After Meg—who'd always planned to help run the resort—had discovered a love of accounting midway through her business degree, she'd shifted course. And this had made his parents worry that perhaps Jonah wasn't considering all the options for his future. They'd insisted that he, too, get a college degree before committing to managing the family resort.

But with just over a year left, he felt as strongly about it as he always had. Just because he was a good student didn't mean he had to aspire to something more intellectual. He loved this place. Loved the steady coming and going of familiar people. Loved taking care of a place that was a beloved annual tradition for dozens of families. Loved feeling connected with the family history. It was like opening his home to people who loved it just as much as he did.

He cleared his throat. "I will finish my degree, Mom. But I'm needed here now. I want to do this."

Mom's brown eyes softened. She'd aged ten years in the week since Dad's heart attack. "I know you do. But your dad and I thought it would be good to get some fresh blood in here for a while. Just till you graduate. A temporary manager who might bring new ideas. And come the end of next year, if you still want to run the resort—it's yours."

"That hasn't changed, and it's not going to." Mom had it stuck in her head that he should be a schoolteacher like his biological mother and grandmother. Sure, maybe he'd entertained the idea as a kid. But he was twenty-eight now—a man who knew what he wanted. For the hundredth time he wondered if she secretly hoped Meg would change her mind. Did Mom want to pass the resort to her biological child? After all, he wasn't technically related to Mom—or her parents—by blood.

"We've already decided. We're hiring a temporary manager as soon as possible. We can probably muddle through for a few months on our own. But we'll need someone full-time for high season next year. Once he or she is trained, your dad and I'll do some traveling. Heaven knows it's the only way I'll keep him from returning to work. This health crisis has reminded us we won't last forever, and your dad and I want to see something of the world. We were gonna do that the year after next any-way. We're just getting an early start."

In the following weeks Jonah tried to talk them out of the new hire several times, but they were set on it. He had, however, talked them into letting him train and oversee the new hire. That gave him some measure of control and made sense since they'd be traveling a lot. He applied himself to his classes, and the next thing he knew, they'd hired someone fresh out of college. As if a few courses could teach someone more about this place than a lifetime here had taught him.

He'd 100 percent rather be running the place than taking a full load of classes during the high season. But this was what his parents wanted, and he respected them too much to do anything but honor their decision.

Then four weeks ago, the woman he'd splashed with mud stepped out of Carson's SUV. Judging by her rigid spine and the flat line of her lips, she recognized him instantly. And in that fleeting second, he'd felt sorry for the incident and opened his mouth to apologize again.

Then he realized why she was here on his property. She was the new manager, coming to settle in for the next nine months. She must've changed clothes—no hint of mud splatters. She reminded him of his ex-girlfriend Monica with her designer pocketbook, heeled boots, and manicured nails. And her name—Lauren Wentworth—sounded like old money. He gave the princess a week.

He never had issued that second apology.

But a month later she was still here. His parents were now on the road, heading to the Florida Keys, and Jonah was staying on property for a few weeks to oversee their new hire.

Lauren had made a few small missteps, the worst of which was double-booking a cabin for a week in June—but his mom had caught the mistake quickly. Jonah would give Lauren credit for a surprisingly good work ethic. She was up and about at sunrise, always busy doing something, and didn't seem to mind being on call 24/7. Of course, she hadn't lived through high season yet.

"She's not so bad, you know," Meg said.

Jonah let the curtain flutter closed. "Didn't say she was."

"It was the smirk on your face. You could at least tell her the snow's gonna melt."

"Where's the fun in that? Don't you have some numbers to crunch?"

Meg crossed her arms, giving a smirk of her own. "You just don't like that she's doing a great job."

"I wouldn't go that far. And she's barely a month in. Also, it's not high season yet."

Meg shook her head in a patronizing way. "You poor thing. You don't even realize." With that she took off for the office.

Jonah frowned. "Realize what?" When she didn't answer he followed and found her settling into her chair behind the old computer screen. "Realize *what*?"

She started clacking on the keyboard. "Don't tell me you haven't noticed how beautiful she is."

The image of her sage-green eyes flashed in his brain. "What's that got to do with anything? I can barely tolerate her."

"And why do you suppose that is, brother dear? She's doing the job she was hired for and allowing you to get your classes over with. You should be grateful and yet you can't seem to be around her without bristling."

"She's the bristly one."

"Oh, really? The rest of us get along with her just fine."

"You've seen how she is when I try to give her instructions. She's practically belligerent." Okay, she might not say anything out loud. But that stubborn look on her face said it all.

Meg deigned to glance his way, holding his gaze a long second. "Since you seem to be the last to know, I'll do you a favor and enlighten you: The sparks between you two could ignite an inferno."

Jonah flinched. "That is ridiculous. Those are not *sparks*. We rub each other the wrong way, that's all. We can hardly be in the same room."

"Explain your dislike for her then, if it makes so much sense." That he resented Lauren for taking the job he wanted seemed pretty entitled if he couldn't explain his fear about being an outsider in his own family.

And he didn't want to go there with Meg. How could she possibly understand? Besides, if he told her he suspected their mom wanted her to run the resort instead of him, it would only make her feel guilty for choosing accounting.

He fumbled for words. "She's a city girl. She doesn't belong here." But he knew even as he said it that it was poor reasoning. Sure, she'd been a bit overdressed that first day. But since then she'd shown up to work in appropriate attire—if maybe a bit on the fussy side.

Meg was regarding him with something like pity. "Not everyone from the city is like Monica."

Because yes. She did remind him of Monica—from the designer bags to the big-city dreams. His ex-girlfriend had broken his heart when she left him and this "Podunk town" for the greener pastures of New York City.

It wasn't fair to take his hurt feelings out on Lauren. But somehow, when she tipped up that stubborn chin or pressed her lips in mutiny, all common sense went right out the window.

"I'll admit Lauren's a bit of a city slicker," Meg said, "but that's hardly a fatal flaw. She works hard and she's doing a good job, isn't she? Maybe you could ease up a bit—be a little less impossible."

"Me? She's the impossible one."

"See my former comment about sparks."

Good grief. Jonah rolled his eyes as he turned on his heel and left the room. "You read too many romance novels." His little sister had obviously never been anywhere near the vicinity of love. It didn't start with mutual dislike. It began with attraction.

Like when a guy caught the eye of a beautiful brunette at the Daily Brew and they shared a private smile. Or when he held the door for her half an hour later and she asked for directions to the post office and he thought his heart might explode from his chest.

That was attraction.

65

Jonah had escorted Monica to the post office, which was formerly a train depot. Monica had just been hired as an esthetician at the spa in the new Harborview Resort. She was from a tiny town in Maine he'd never heard of and had taken this job straight out of beauty school. Back in Maine she had two brothers, five sisters, and amicably divorced parents.

The conversation was fluid with plenty of give-and-take. He liked that she was direct, and that wicked smile she turned on him made him feel like a king. They reached the post office way too soon. He was still trying to figure out how to get her number when she pulled her phone from her pocket and said, "What's your number, Jonah Landry?"

A moment later his phone vibrated with a text.

"See ya later." She flashed a smile and entered the post office, those beautiful brown waves bouncing around her shoulders.

As soon as they parted ways, he checked his phone. *Call me*, her text said. And he did just that the next day—right after he looked up *esthetician*.

He mentally fast-forwarded through the months of courtship, full of ups and downs—mostly ups—until they reached the end of the road: a job offer from some spa in Manhattan.

Maybe he should've seen it coming a million miles away. She'd mentioned her determination to escape that small town where she'd grown up. Her search for bigger and better things than the lone town diner where she'd waitressed through high school and where her mother still worked. He'd thought of her as a small-town kind of person from a middle-class family, much like him.

He'd missed all the clues, and the cost of his ignorance had been a broken heart. The memory of that first meeting fizzled like a spent firework.

Now as Jonah headed off to find a quiet spot to read his assigned chapters, he caught a glimpse of Lauren through the window and scowled. No, he knew what attraction looked like, felt like—and it wasn't this.

Chapter 11

Present day

LAUREN WASN'T IN a social mood, but she'd simply had to get away from the resort. She watched an ember from the bonfire drift upward until it burned out against the black canvas of the night sky. She dug her toes into the sand as she scanned the row of residential homes lining the unfamiliar north shore of Loon Lake. Some of their windows were lit from within, but many of the homes must've been closed up on Labor Day weekend.

Another reminder that she'd missed the entire summer.

Her gaze drifted across the yard to Carson's house—or rather his aunt's, where he was apparently living while he completed his internship. The sound of laughter carried from the shoreline where Meg and some of the others from her friend group dared to wade into the cool water, clothes and all.

It was Lauren's first outing since the accident. It had been a week ago now and her headache had finally subsided. The fog had cleared, or most of it anyway. Her focus wasn't great when it came to numbers or figuring out complicated schedules. But she was back to work.

Meg had said something about the fall inventory, which apparently consisted of accounting for every fork and spatula in each cabin. Lauren would attempt that task next week.

She checked the time. Sydney's brother was married by now. Her friend would head back to the city tomorrow. She'd checked on Lauren every day this week, but Lauren hadn't wanted to usurp her time with her family.

Carson headed her way across the sand, barefoot and smiling. The golden glow of a fire had never danced on such a handsome face. Tonight he wore a white button-down and a pair of khaki shorts on his lean frame. The sight of him made her pulse race. That Carina was one lucky girl.

"Can I get you a drink?" he asked as he neared.

"No thanks." She held up her Diet Coke, then took a sip.

He sank onto the other end of the log. "How have you been feeling? Meg said you've returned to work."

"Nothing too strenuous, and I'm feeling much better, thanks."

"That's good. Just take it easy. You don't want to rush it."

"Believe me, they're not about to let that happen." Jonah was like Big Brother, popping up every time she tried to so much as pluck a weed.

She watched the others at the shoreline: Meg, Tori and Lori—fraternal twins—and Sam, a guy who appeared to be a few years younger than the rest of them. They all attended church together, apparently. Lauren and Jonah had been included in the outings throughout the summer. But she remembered none of it, of course. She'd only agreed to come tonight because Jonah had other plans.

"How's the memory coming along?" Carson asked as if reading her mind. "Anything coming back to you yet?"

She shrugged. "Not a thing." She hadn't exactly done anything to encourage the resurfacing of those memories. Hadn't looked at the photos on her phone or read the old texts.

"Well, give it a little time. The brain's an amazing organ. Just because you can't access them at the moment doesn't mean they aren't still in there."

The thought was meant to comfort but instead felt like an impending threat. Like they could appear any moment and ruin her future.

"I could put you in touch with a cognitive therapist if you'd like. Sometimes that helps."

"I'll let you know. Thank you. It's very sweet of you to offer." She decided to change the subject. "I was hoping to meet Carina tonight—or maybe I already have." She snorted. "I can't tell you how weird it feels not to remember my life."

"I can only imagine. No, you actually never met Carina—and I guess you're not likely to now. We broke up in June."

The information barreled through her mind like a train, destination unknown. She took in his wan expression and felt a prick of empathy. "I'm so sorry."

He shrugged. "It happens."

"How long were you together? Sorry if you already told me this."

"It's okay. We dated almost three years."

"You took this internship because you didn't want to be too far away." She remembered that from their first conversation when he'd rescued her on the side of the road.

He gave a wry grin. "Joke's on me, I guess. But no, she met some guy at school and that was that."

"That's the worst." Or she supposed it must've been. She'd never been in love before. Well, not that she remembered.

"It hasn't been fun. But it's been a few months now. And my work keeps me busy."

She studied his face. "Does that help?"

He met her gaze, then broke out into laughter. "No."

She smiled at his honesty. Wished she could think of something helpful to say. She'd had plenty of disappointments in her life, but romantic heartbreak was foreign to her. And truthfully, selfishly, she was a little glad to find Carson suddenly available. But she could hardly admit that.

Meg wandered over just then and rescued her from having to think of an appropriate response.

❦

LAUREN counted the mugs in the Hickory Cabin and wrote the number on the checklist. Eight. Two were missing. She moved on to the dinner plates. This kind of work, simple though it was, now took her full concentration. This was her fifth day doing inventory and she was only now on the last cabin. Of course she'd had other tasks requiring her attention—preferred tasks. She dreaded returning to this counting and math and spreadsheets. Jonah had offered to help, but he'd no doubt insist on working side by side, and that would make the chore even harder.

Because avoiding Jonah had become job *numero uno*.

He made her uncomfortable with his steady gazes and concerned looks. He was so different from the Jonah she remembered. It wigged her out and she didn't know how to respond.

A text message vibrated her phone. Seeing it was from Sydney, she finished accounting for the plates and took a short break. Her friend had practically begged to come see her after her brother's wedding last weekend, but Lauren put her off. As nice as it might be to have her friend nearby, Sydney was hoping to be promoted to manager at the restaurant where she worked. And taking off abruptly right after a week's vacation wouldn't help her cause.

How's it going? her friend had asked.

Fine, I guess. Doing inventory on the kitchen supplies at the moment. So thanks for saving me from that.

What are friends for? Still foggy?

Math has never been my friend.

How's everything else?

She hadn't really opened up to Sydney about everything. Hadn't opened up to anyone. Maybe it was time to unload.

Everything feels so weird. Jonah keeps coming around, staring at me with these hope-filled eyes. I feel so much pressure to remember. Like everyone's just looking at me wondering, Do you remember anything yet? *No, I don't! And you know what? I don't even think I want to.*

Oh, honey. I'm sorry. That's gotta be tough.

The Lauren everyone expects me to be—I don't even know who she is. She fell for someone I don't even like. I can't help but hope she's gone for good. I feel like a stranger in my own life.

Maybe you should come home, Lauren. Escape the pressure. Maybe you'll feel more like yourself.

Tempting.

You can stay with me till your job starts in January. I'm sure your new boss will understand.

But Lauren had committed through the end of the year. She couldn't risk losing the job at Glitter. She had to finish well here. She wasn't a quitter. And maybe Olivia would understand if she explained about the brain injury, but she didn't want to give the woman cause to worry about her mental health—she'd asked Tammy not to mention it to her friend. It didn't sound as if they kept in close contact anyway.

That's sweet of you, but I only have a few more months here. The family has been so nice to me, I'd hate to desert them. There are good things too. They've made a lot of the changes I've suggested. Meg says they're very happy with the increase in revenue, and she's been a good friend through this.

I had no doubt you'd do a great job. But just know my door is open if you change your mind about coming home or about me coming there.

Thanks. It helps knowing that.

She thought about this morning when Jonah had asked if she wanted to see the barn she'd apparently begun renovating. "You were really excited about turning it into a venue," he'd said. "We got it cleaned out and tore away all the scrub brush from the exterior. I thought you might like to see it."

He was obviously eager to spend time alone together. And maybe he hoped her seeing it would spark a memory. She wasn't interested in either. She told him she wanted to finish inventory today. The disappointment that spread across his face made her heart squeeze a little.

She stared down at the cursor in the text box. Then she began writing. *Did I talk to you about Jonah? What did I see in him?* Before she could second-guess herself, she sent the message. Then wished she hadn't asked. Because she didn't want to have feelings for Jonah.

Once you got to know him you thought he was sweet. You said he made you laugh.

That just didn't compute with what she remembered of him. *It doesn't seem possible.*

I was a firsthand witness. I've never seen you like that before.

Like what?

So happy. Unguarded. You don't drop your guard for just anyone. I was skeptical at first, but after seeing you together those few days, I could tell it was the real thing.

It doesn't feel anywhere close to real.

Trust me, it was. I was jealous! ☺ *Here I am on every dating site in existence, going out on multiple dates a week, and I can't even find a guy worthy of a second date. And you happen upon some prince in backwoods New Hampshire.*

But where was it all going? We were presumably in love, but my life is in Boston and his is here.

You were mulling all that over the last time we spoke in mid-August. I don't think you and Jonah had talked it through yet. But you thought he might expect you to change your plans, and you admitted that you were actually considering it.

This is such a mess.

Hey, it's gonna work out. Hang in there.

Thanks for chatting. I should get back to the spreadsheets.

Don't overdo it!

Yes, Mommy.

CHAPTER 12

THE FOLLOWING MONDAY morning Jonah found Lauren sweeping off her deck. He probably should've been home studying—his grades had gone to crap the past two weeks. But it was her day off and he hoped to spend time with her.

He caught sight of her through the pine forest, face freshly washed, hair still mussed from sleep. She nudged Graham playfully with the broom. The dog snapped at the bristles, then jumped to attention, tail wagging.

Lauren brushed at his feet. "Take that, puppers."

Graham barked.

"Mr. Broom's gonna getcha!" She let him grab the bristles, then tugged it away again, laughing.

The dog bowed on his front legs, back end in the air, and barked.

Jonah's heart twisted painfully. She didn't remember the dog any more than she remembered being in love with Jonah. Yet she was obviously letting Graham in. She'd taken him back under her wing. She was playing with him, affectionate with him.

I'm jealous of a dog.

It was an all-new low. But seeing her guard down made him miss her so much. Whenever Jonah was near her, Lauren was present—but she wasn't. The Lauren he'd fallen in love with was somewhere in there.

But she wouldn't drop her guard with him, and he didn't know how to convince her to let him back in.

Before, he'd gradually won her over by spending time with her on the job. It had taken months for her to open up about her mom's abandonment, her difficult childhood. But she wouldn't even give him the time of day now. And she'd probably be horrified to realize all the private things he knew about her.

Had she seen the photos on her phone or read their texts? If she had, she'd surely see how happy they'd been together. Or would the images only make her grimace?

She must've heard his approach because her head snapped his way. And just like that her playful expression disappeared and her eyes grew guarded.

He battled disappointment and lifted his lips. "Morning. How are you feeling today?"

"Fine. Just catching up on some chores."

He reached the deck and stopped to pet Graham, who'd come to greet him, his entire back end wagging. "Want some help? I need a break from studying." Did that sound like the pathetic lie it was?

"Thanks, but I've got it."

Lauren was nothing if not fiercely independent. That much hadn't changed. "I thought I'd see if you wanted to go for a bike ride on the rail trail."

"The rail trail?"

Right. She wouldn't remember. "It's an old railroad track they turned into a trail. It runs for twelve miles along lakes and pastures and through the woods. You used to like it. Used to drive me crazy, reading every single informational sign explaining the trail's history."

She didn't return his wistful smile. She didn't remember any of those moments they'd spent together or the laughter they'd once shared. Didn't remember their first kiss at the gorge or the first time he'd professed his love.

Her gaze flickered to her cabin as she put a hand to her throat. "Um, thanks, but I've got a lot of chores to do today."

He was the last person she wanted to spend her day off with. Message received. He pushed past the hopeless feeling welling up inside and dredged up another smile. "I should probably get some stuff done too. If you need anything, I'll be around."

"Okay, thanks." She resumed sweeping.

He gave Graham a final pat and headed back toward the lodge, his steps weighted with despair. They were sixteen days past the accident and she obviously remembered nothing. He kept coming around, trying to show her he cared. But the door to her heart was closed to him. And locked. And boarded over.

She'd let Meg in a little. They'd gone to that bonfire together, had a coffee date last week on her day off. Even his mom and dad had made some headway in regaining her friendship. But she wanted nothing to do with Jonah.

Help me, God. I don't know what else to do. How can I help her remember if she doesn't want to? How can I win her back when she avoids me at every turn?

Could he find reasons for them to work together as he'd done early in her employment? He was afraid, given her current mental state, that she'd only feel pressured and close up like a clam. He couldn't help but feel there was only one solution and it was out of his control.

Please let her remember. I can't lose her for good. I just can't.

He swallowed against the lump in his throat. He hadn't lost it once since the accident. Kept pushing back the emotion, telling himself she'd remember. But he was starting to lose hope.

The lodge was blessedly quiet when he entered. He should study, but he'd never be able to concentrate. He needed something to do. Something that would keep him busy enough to distract him from this miserable nightmare.

Meg glanced up when he stopped by the office. "Hey. What are you doing here?"

"Checking on Lauren."

She homed in on his face, probably seeing everything he wanted to hide. "How was she?"

"Same."

"Her symptoms seem better. She's back to her normal schedule."

"True."

Neither of them said it, but they were both thinking it. Everything was back to normal—except her memory.

"I'm actually glad you stopped by. I've been wanting to talk to you about something."

Her tone warned him it wasn't good news. He sank into his mom's desk chair. "That sounds foreboding and I don't know if I can take more bad news."

"I'm sorry. I know this has been hard. This might not be news to you at all."

"Is it about Lauren?"

"Yes."

Oh, what the heck. How much worse could things get? A lot, if the adrenaline pumping through his veins was anything to go by. "Why not? Lay it on me."

"She said something in passing yesterday when I mentioned her memory loss. She—she implied she didn't want her memories back. That she'd rather forget what happened over the summer and move on with her life."

The words were a sucker punch. She didn't want to remember him? Remember *them*? It was the ultimate rejection. *God, why is this happening? We were in love. We were about to be engaged. She's the love of my life.*

"I'm sorry, but I felt you should know what you're up against."

"For all the good it does me! She won't even talk to me. As far as she's concerned we're over, and that's the way she prefers it. I feel like I'm in waiting mode—and we both know that's not exactly my specialty. I'm just sitting around waiting for her to get her memory back."

"This must be so hard."

"If I don't do something, I might as well throw her a farewell party." The thought of saying good-bye to her made his stomach twist. They'd been about to start a life together, and now it was all gone because of that freak fall. One stupid accident and she was gone to him forever?

His gaze sharpened on his sister. "I have to do something. I can't lose her, Meg."

"I can only imagine how hard this is, honey. But Lauren's not one to be pushed. You should know that better than anyone."

He pounded his fist on his thigh. "Then what the heck am I supposed to do?"

"I don't know. Maybe she'll get her memory back soon and this whole problem will go away."

"But what if she never gets it back?" The question hung in the silence between them.

FIFTEEN minutes later the conversation still plagued Jonah as he dribbled the basketball on the concrete pad attached to the old garage that now served as the laundry facility. He put up a shot and the ball swished through the net. He collected the ball and took it back to the invisible foul line. Shot again. All net. His body went through the motions as he recalled his discussion with Meg.

He felt stuck. He couldn't just do nothing while Lauren moved on with her life alone. But she clearly wanted nothing to do with him, and pressuring her would get him nowhere.

Stuck.

He was gonna lose her.

Memories flittered through his mind. Lauren smiling at him as he rowed them to the cove the first day they'd gone swimming together. The shy way she bit her lip when she was thinking about kissing him but didn't want him to know. The way she sometimes burrowed into his side like she wished she could climb inside him.

He missed the way she felt, her back pressed against his chest as they watched the sun sink below the horizon. He missed her passionate kisses and her contagious laughter. The way she'd quirk a brow at him when he teased her about her shoe collection or the rainbow assortment of nail polish on her bathroom windowsill.

That heat flushed his skin again and the back of his eyes burned. And still he put up a shot. And another. And another.

As luck would have it, the laundry building was clear on the other side of the property. When Lauren had arrived at Pinehaven, Ping-Pong and foosball tables had been crowded in with the washers and dryers.

But Lauren had suggested converting the upstairs of the boathouse into a game room for the teen guests. And at some point over the summer, the Landrys had implemented that idea. Meg had taken her up to the hideout and raved about how popular it had been over the summer. They'd spent over an hour up there playing games that day until they'd laughed themselves silly over their lack of coordination.

Lauren had also suggested renting out pier space to local boat owners, and that idea had apparently netted twenty-four thousand dollars over the course of the season. Easy money for the Landrys. Another of Lauren's ideas that was in the works: resort for a day. Starting next season they would make their property and its equipment available on a limited basis to tourists staying off-site.

It felt great that they were taking her ideas seriously and that they were apparently paying off in spades. Lauren needed that little punch of validation right now because she felt so *off*.

She shifted the laundry basket to her other side, and as she neared the building she heard a thumping sound. Someone was playing basketball on the far side of the building.

She entered the facility and set her basket on the dryer. But before she opened the washer, she headed to the window as if drawn by some invisible force.

Standing to the side, she peeked through the curtains. Just as she suspected, Jonah was making use of the court. He wore only a pair of worn jeans and tennis shoes. Her gaze locked on him as he spun, darted, and pivoted with precision borne from years of experience. He hit every shot as he played imaginary foes. His muscles rippled across his back as he came up for a hook shot, grabbed the rebound, pivoted, and put up another.

Sweat gleamed off the defined ridges of his abdomen and the honed curves of his biceps. He was lean and fit and more muscular than she'd realized. His calves bulged on a jump shot, and his thighs flexed as he juked one invisible opponent, then dodged another. He scrambled toward the basket and jumped for a dunk. The ball went through the net and hit the pavement with a *whump*.

She'd been so busy admiring Jonah's skill—and his physique—she didn't notice anything amiss until he braced his hands on his knees, breath heaving. Until the sunlight, dappling the court, glimmered off his face. At first she thought it was sweat.

But no. Tears trickled from his eyes, running in rivulets down his face. His jaw was clenched, his eyes closed, as if against some unseen agony. She'd never seen him this way. It was so different from the confident, judgmental Jonah she remembered. So vulnerable and . . . broken.

Lauren's heart gave a painful squeeze because she knew without a doubt—*she* had caused this.

It was her fault he was hurting like this.

She couldn't have helped the fall from the ladder or the resulting memory loss. But she'd been so busy worrying about her own problems, she'd hardly given a thought to Jonah's feelings.

They'd been in a happy relationship, and in the blink of an eye he'd lost her. She'd wondered how the feelings could've been real when she felt nothing for him now.

But seeing him out on the court, there was no doubt about it. One glimpse of his suffering removed all questions about the genuineness of his feelings or their previous relationship.

She pivoted from the window, unable to bear the sight anymore. Her chest ached. Was this just empathy, or did some small part of her remember her feelings for him?

Every morning since the accident, Jonah had checked on her with those hope-filled eyes, and she all but brushed him off. He *loved* her, and she'd been harsh and uncaring. Her chest tightened.

She'd been exactly like so many of the adults who'd reigned over her childhood, and she hated herself for it.

Maybe she no longer wanted a relationship with Jonah, but she didn't have to be a terrible human being. Uncertain what to do about the empathy wrenching her heart, she glanced out the window again.

Jonah retrieved his shirt from the ground and wiped his face. He grabbed the ball that had settled near the court's edge and headed toward the parking lot.

A minute later heaviness settled over her as he got into his truck and pulled from the lot. She had to do something to make up for how callous she'd been. For how much she'd hurt him. Something to relieve the pain he was feeling.

But something safe—from a distance.

She withdrew her phone and opened the texting app. Her finger hovered over the thread between Jonah and her. The last entry was September seventh, the day of her accident. She couldn't bring herself to read all the texts they must've sent back and forth.

So she forbade herself from scrolling up and began tapping on the keyboard.

CHAPTER 13

JONAH TURNED UP the music and a driving Jason Aldean song filled the void in the truck's cab. He was emotionally exhausted. He couldn't remember the last time he'd cried like that. Not since he was a child. He'd like to say he felt better, but the ache inside hadn't subsided. The angry, explosive feeling had diminished. But he actually preferred that to this overwhelming despondency.

He'd planned to stay at Pinehaven for the day; he'd told Lauren he'd be around. But it wasn't as if she'd seek him out. And with only one guest, they didn't need him on property today.

He didn't feel like studying. He could see if his friend Javier was free to grab lunch—he flew floatplanes for Air Tours. But Jonah wasn't fit for company today. He passed through town, aimless, not wanting to go home where he'd have nothing to do but think of Lauren.

Ten minutes later the sight of the seaplane base appeared as if out of nowhere. He hadn't even known where he was going until he pulled into the parking lot. He'd only been to the business a couple times, and chances were good his friend was airborne. But maybe he'd luck out and find him in the office. Jonah needed to get out of this funk.

A minute later he crossed the gravel lot and cool air washed over him as he entered the office.

Javier turned from a conversation, his face lighting up at the sight of Jonah. "Hey, buddy. Long time no see." Javier approached in jeans and a blue Air Tours polo. The ball cap that covered his black hair was worn low on a face that never failed to draw female attention. Javier, however, only had eyes for his wife, Allison.

"Good to see you, man." Jonah pulled him in for a hand clasp–shoulder bump. "I was in town and thought I'd see if I could catch you on the ground."

"Good timing. A storm's moving in later. Wanna catch some lunch next door?"

"Let's do it."

The bistro's lake view attracted tourists like flies in the summer. But since it wasn't high season, they had no trouble scoring a table on the deck.

"How are things with you and Allison?" Jonah asked after they'd placed their orders. She was a radiologist at the local hospital. The two of them worked a lot of hours, and she was also caring for her ailing grandmother.

"She's good. We don't see each other as much as I'd like, but things at the base will settle down now that the season's winding down."

"That's a good thing."

"I love her like crazy. I miss her. And I know this is wearing her down too."

"Hang in there, man." Allison was a strong woman. The four of them had gone out a few times over the summer. The reminder that Lauren wasn't his girlfriend anymore weighted his stomach. "It's just a difficult season. You guys are gonna get through this."

"Thanks."

Sensing his friend's need for a change of subject, Jonah asked, "How's work going?" Javier was buying out the owner of Air Tours, who was in his midsixties and looking toward retirement.

"Work's great. Summer was busy and profitable. The buyout is obviously gonna take a while, but Fred's good with that."

"That's exciting. Someday it'll be all yours."

They talked more about Javier's plans for the business. He seemed to understand that Jonah was avoiding the depressing topic of Lauren. But he only let Jonah skirt it for so long.

"How are things going with you and Lauren?" he asked when they'd exhausted the subject of Air Tours. "Any progress?"

"She hasn't remembered anything and doesn't seem open to the idea of getting to know me again." His eyes stung at the words, so blunt, so true. He glanced down at the table where his fingers shredded a napkin.

"I hate that this happened. I can't imagine what it must be like for you."

"She's around all the time, of course, but she avoids me at every turn. Not only does she not love me anymore—she doesn't *want* to love me again."

Javier sat back in the booth, seemingly taking a moment to let that sink in. His eyes softened. "That's awful. I don't even know what to say."

"That makes two of us."

"I'm thinking back to when you got together before. You were showing her the ropes at the resort and she came around. I recall you didn't like her much to begin with either."

"We both know why that is." They'd had more than one conversation about how Lauren reminded Jonah of Monica at first. It had taken a while to sort out his feelings.

"But you got to know the real Lauren, and she got to know you when you opened up to her. Maybe you can go through that process again."

"I'd love to try. But she turns down every offer to spend time together, no matter how trivial. And she already knows how to do her job, so I can't really fabricate reasons to be together. She'd see it coming from a mile away and push even harder."

"There's still the chance she'll get her memory back though, right? It's been, what, a couple weeks?"

"Two weeks and two days. I literally dream about her memory returning. But then I wake up and everything's the same. I can't just sit around hoping and waiting. There has to be something I can do."

"I'll be thinking about that. Something that'll put the two of you together long enough to bring her guard down."

The food was served and Jonah was glad the topic turned to benign subjects for the remainder of the meal. He barely tasted the fish and chips. Maybe this was a lost cause.

"How's she feeling otherwise, her concussion and all?"

"Most of her symptoms are gone. She's back to her full work schedule."

Another thought emerged—one that had been popping up the past few days. Now that her health was stable, it was probably time he told her she'd given up her job at Glitter. She'd be crushed. She'd leave Pinehaven—what reason would she have to stick around then?

Twenty minutes later while they waited for the check, Javier took off for the restroom and Jonah checked his phone. His heart stopped at the sight of a text from Lauren.

I'm sorry for what's happening and that I haven't been more compassionate.

She'd sent the text over an hour ago, seemingly out of nowhere. He reread the sentence three times. Tried to temper his hope. She wasn't exactly asking for a new start, but she'd reached out to him. It was *something*, and something was better than nothing.

Javier slid into the booth. "Is it weird that I like those scented sugar scrubs they have in the restroom? Hey, what's wrong?"

Jonah stared unseeing at Javier. "Lauren texted me. She hasn't done that since the accident."

"Hey, that's great. What'd she say?"

Jonah showed Javier the text.

His friend nodded. "All right, all right. That's a start. Maybe this is the answer you've been praying for."

"If she's open to communicating through text, count me in. That's something. It's a start."

Jonah glanced back at the screen, rereading her text. "What should I say? I don't want to scare her off."

"Yeah, but you don't want to tiptoe around her feelings either. That's not healthy."

"Good point."

"You're a smart guy. You'll figure it out."

The server brought their bills, and they took them to the register and paid. All the while Jonah's thoughts spun. He hadn't felt so much hope since the accident. He could hardly wait to respond to her text. But he couldn't push. He had to be patient with her.

He and Javier parted ways at the office building, and then Jonah settled in his truck. He couldn't even wait till he got home. He had to see where this would lead.

It's not your fault. You didn't ask for this either. He sent the text and waited.

The blinking dots, appeared. He stared at those dots until his vision went blurry.

Then finally her response appeared. *I know, but I haven't been very kind and you didn't deserve that.*

He didn't know what had brought about this revelation, but he was grateful. Maybe Meg had said something to her. He stared at her words. How to respond? She wasn't where he was emotionally. She was still somewhere back in April. He should keep things light.

I remember how things were in the spring. I didn't feel very kindly toward you either. Ha ha.

Her response came quickly this time. A laughing emoji. Then in a separate text. *I really should get on with my chores. I have about eleven million loads of laundry.*

86

That was fast. He fought against the swamp of disappointment—and the urge to remind her to take it easy. But he wasn't her boyfriend at the moment and he didn't want to pressure her. This was a good start. Maybe she'd text him again soon. Or maybe he'd start the conversation next time.

He found a funny GIF of a cat doing laundry and sent it. He didn't start up the truck until she responded with a laughing emoji.

His heart soared with hope. Lauren was communicating with him again. It was something to build on. It was his chance to make her fall in love with him again. And because of that, he pushed away all thoughts of telling her about Glitter.

CHAPTER 14

May 19

EVER SINCE THE ice-out, business had slowly ramped up at the resort. Most weeks at least half the cabins were occupied and Lauren found herself busier. She embraced the work as an opportunity to prove herself. Not that she'd ever get an *attagirl* out of Jonah Landry.

Last week she'd presented her ideas to the Landrys. Tom, Tammy, and Meg had loved them. They'd wanted to build a pavilion for years but couldn't justify the funds. Now that they were renting out boat slips, that would change. Turning the boathouse into a gathering space for teens would cost little more than elbow grease.

Jonah was the only one who seemed less than enthusiastic. But she chalked that up to obstinance. He probably wished the ideas had been his. Plus, he didn't like change—that much was obvious. Heaven forbid they move a Ping-Pong table or change the schedule. The entire world might spin off its axis.

Friday was the first day all eight cabins were occupied, getting the weekend off to a great start. There were two returning couples, two young families, three new couples, and a group of four middle-aged sisters.

On Sunday a fortysomething husband and wife appeared at the front desk to check in. As Lauren pulled up the schedule, it took everything in her to keep the smile from sliding off her face. She'd put the Lawsons down for three nights in Willow Cabin—but it was already occupied.

Her heart skittered across the floor as she met their expectant gazes. "I'm so sorry to tell you this, but I'm afraid we've accidentally over-booked the cabin and we're currently full up. But I'm sure I can find someplace else nearby that will accommodate you."

A frown pinched Miles Lawson's brows as he stepped closer. "Overbooked? That's unacceptable. We don't want to stay somewhere else—this is where we came for our honeymoon twenty years ago."

This wouldn't be easily resolved. The coming conflict wracked her nerves. "I'm terribly sorry about the mistake, Mr. and Mrs. Lawson. I know you must be disappointed, but none of the cabins will be available until Tuesday. We'd be happy to book you someplace else, our com-pliments, of course, and you could return here if you'd like for the remaining night."

"Now listen—"

"Honey." Mrs. Lawson set her hand on her husband's arm.

"This is unacceptable! We left the kids with their grandparents so we could celebrate our anniversary here."

Lauren's cheeks heated. How had she made such a terrible mistake? "Again, I'm so sorry—"

"Sorry does not fix the problem!"

"No, you're right. There are other lovely resorts where we could possibly get you in. I know it's not the same, but we could comp your next visit here if you'd like to reschedule."

He threw up his hands, intimidating her with his six-foot-something height and formidable glare.

"What can we do to rectify the situation?"

"You can get us in the Willow Cabin where we spent our honeymoon! But since that's obviously not gonna happen, I guess we'll be airing our grievances on social media—loud and often."

Tammy slipped out of the office and joined her behind the desk. "Hi there, I'm Tammy Landry, owner of Pinehaven. I couldn't help but overhear the situation." The phone rang and Tammy turned her warm brown gaze on Lauren. "Could you get that, dear?"

Lauren was only too happy to take the call in the office. It was a potential guest with all kinds of questions about the resort. The older woman from Maine didn't own a computer, so after a lengthy discussion Lauren promised to send a packet in the mail.

By the time she got off the phone, all was quiet in the lobby.

Her skin still tingled with embarrassment. This was her second double-booking. But Tammy had caught the first. Lauren didn't know how the woman had resolved the situation, but it would probably be costly, financially if not publicity-wise.

Mustering courage, she returned to the desk and found Tammy restocking the area maps. "I'm so sorry about my mistake. I can't believe I did that. Were you able to mollify the Lawsons?"

Tammy's smile was kind. "I wouldn't say 'mollify,' but I don't think they'll blast us on social media. They'll be staying at the Harborview Resort and I got them in for a couple's massage tomorrow. I think Mrs. Lawson was secretly delighted about the mix-up."

The Harborview was the most expensive hotel on the lake. "I'm so sorry. You can take the cost out of my check." It was more than a week's pay, but this was her fault after all.

"I'll do no such thing. It's the cost of business, dear. We all make mistakes."

"I promise I won't let it happen again."

Tammy patted her shoulder. "You've done a wonderful job, Lauren. Don't let one little mistake bring you down."

Despite Tammy's kindness, the day only got worse. The Drurys got stuck on the lake when Pinehaven's motorboat stalled just as they were coming in from the rain. They finally got it restarted, but they were unhappy when they returned, dripping wet, back to the pier.

The toilet in the Ogdens' cabin overflowed, and by the time Lauren finally managed to clear the plug and clean it up, her jeans reeked of sewage. She returned to her cabin to change, waving at the Gentrys, whose three kids were playing in the sand on the beach. They asked for more paper towels, and Lauren promised she'd bring more by later, even though every cabin came adequately stocked with four rolls. Some guests felt entitled to all the paper goods they could stash in their trunk.

Oh, well. That was the least of her worries today.

She changed her entire outfit, wishing she had time for a shower because the clogged toilet had left her feeling disgusting. But she needed to schedule the repair on the boat's motor. Tom and Tammy were gone for the rest of the day, and Lauren didn't have a truck or the experience necessary to pull a boat from the water or haul a trailer. She would have to ask Jonah. That should be fun.

As she crossed the property heading toward the office, she dictated her task list into her phone. "Schedule boat repair, comma, paper towels to Maple Cabin, comma, gather supplies for s'mores, comma, take dog treats to Oak." The black lab was beautiful—and sometimes it was the little things that made a difference. She was glad the resort was pet friendly.

She'd always wanted a dog of her own, either a Yorkshire terrier or a Maltese, a sweet little pup to cuddle with. She'd enjoyed two dogs in foster care. But they were family pets and she wasn't family, so when she moved she left them behind.

Once she'd aged out of foster care, taking care of herself was enough of a challenge. And by the time she'd gotten on her feet, work and school had kept her away from home for long periods of time. It wouldn't be fair to keep an animal cooped up in an empty apartment, and boarding was expensive.

When Lauren reached the office she scheduled the boat repair for the next day. Then she sent Jonah a text, letting him know the boat would need to be hauled over to the marina soon, please and thank you.

She was about to pocket her phone when he texted back. *That's a two-person job. I'll be over in thirty minutes.*

Ugh. She didn't want to be trapped in his truck with him, not even for the thirty minutes it would require to take out the boat and haul it to the marina. And of course he wanted to do it *right now*.

But he was her boss. *Okay*, she responded.

The bell over the lobby entry tinkled, and she met Mrs. Ogden from behind the counter. The woman was in her fifties with pale skin creased by time and stark black hair featuring a blue streak. She was not smiling.

"Hi, Mrs. Ogden. Is the toilet plugged again?" *Please, no.* She kept her smile propped.

"I'm here about Whiskers. He's not in the cabin and he was there when we left to go fishing."

Lauren frowned. Whiskers was their thirteen-year-old tabby. "Come to think of it, I didn't see him when I was in the cabin. Could he be hiding?"

"He does sometimes get anxious in a new place. But my husband and I have been searching for twenty minutes. He's nowhere in the cabin. He must've gotten out when you left." She delivered the words with the unmistakable tone of accusation.

"I'm sure that's not the case, but let me help you search for him." It was a two-story cabin with lots of nooks and crannies. The cat had to be in there somewhere.

There was nothing but silence between them as Lauren followed the woman to the cabin. Mr. Ogden had already given up on the interior search and was hunting around outside. He sent Lauren a withering look.

Twenty minutes later they were canvassing the property along with quite a few of their neighbors. Dread was a hard pit in Lauren's stomach. Was it possible Whiskers had slid quietly out the door when she'd left? She'd been distracted with her to-do list, but surely she would've noticed.

What a terrible day. She couldn't believe this was happening on top of the booking error she'd made earlier.

When she rounded the laundry building, searching high and low, she almost ran into Mr. Ogden, who was checking the woodpile by the basketball court.

He pulled himself up straight. "If we don't find him, we're suing this place. He's like a child to us. We've had him since he was three weeks old!"

The back of her eyes stung, but she'd never cried on the job and wasn't about to start now. "I'm so sorry, but I truly didn't see him the whole time I was in your cabin."

"But you knew he was there and you were careless when you left, and now he's lost!"

"I'm doing everything I can to—"

"He's an indoor cat—we don't let him wander around outside, and if we don't find him, you're gonna pay for this!"

"What's going on here?" Jonah was suddenly there, towering over her with a scowl.

"This woman lost my cat—that's what's going on."

Lauren's skin flushed under the full weight of Jonah's stare. "Whiskers is missing. I was in their cabin a while ago, unclogging a commode, but I didn't see the cat while I was there."

"He had to have slipped out when she left!" Mr. Ogden's face was red clear up to his receding hairline. "That's the only way he could've escaped."

"You've searched the cabin thoroughly?" Jonah asked.

"We've looked everywhere." Mr. Ogden glared at Lauren. "This is her fault, and if something happens to him, I'm holding this property responsible."

"Mind if I have a go at searching the cabin?"

"Have at it."

Jonah turned to Lauren. "There are some cans of tuna in the lodge pantry. Go get them and set them out around the property. Maybe we can coax him out."

Lauren nodded, then took off toward the lodge. They'd been searching for at least thirty minutes. What if some animal had gotten Whiskers? What if these people lost their beloved pet because she'd been distracted?

Two huge mistakes in one day. She felt like such a failure. Her whole life she'd been champing at the bit to run a business. To run her own life. Was this what happened when she was in charge? What if she was no good at this job? At life? What if she wasn't meant for anything more than the trailer park from which she'd come? What if all the people who'd told her she wouldn't amount to anything had actually been right? Had she been fooling herself all along?

She blinked back tears. She had to focus on the task at hand. She could spiral later in the privacy of her cabin—hopefully after Whiskers had been found.

In the lodge she made her way to the kitchen pantry and found three cans of tuna. She opened them and took them outside, leaving one on the basketball court, one on the edge of the pavilion, and one on the Ogdens' deck.

She joined the search party, keeping her distance from the others. She ventured into the woods, combing the ground and trees for the cat, calling his name.

A lifetime later she heard Jonah's voice calling through the woods. "Found him!"

Her breath released in a whoosh. *Thank God.* The cat was okay. If she'd made a mistake, at least it hadn't ended in disaster. By the time she made it back to the Ogdens' cabin, only Jonah was around.

"Is he okay?" she asked. "Where was he?"

"He's fine. Mr. Ogden found him inside somewhere. He let me know, then slammed the door in my face." Jonah shrugged.

Relief washed over her. "He was inside all along?"

"Yep, hiding somewhere, I guess."

She hadn't been responsible. She tried to let that sink in, but the stress of the ordeal had left her shaken, and releasing it wasn't so simple. However, if she dwelled on it, she'd make a fool of herself in front of Jonah.

She cleared her throat. "Now that the excitement is over, we'd better get the boat over to the marina—hopefully it'll make it to the launch ramp."

"I'll make sure it starts and you can drive it over. Then I'll hook up the trailer and meet you over there."

THIRTY minutes later at the boat launch, Jonah stood in the cool water, helping Lauren guide the boat onto the trailer. Once it was secured, they hopped into the cab and Jonah pulled the trailer out.

Lauren had been quiet since the cat incident and said nothing on the short drive to the marina. Once there, Jonah unhitched the trailer while Lauren went inside to inform them they were leaving the boat for repair.

Soon they were on the road again, and once more the cab was silent.

To Jonah's perspective, their relationship seemed to have shifted over the past month. Ever since Meg had made that claim about their *sparks*. He'd been avoiding Lauren, and when they did come in contact, it was as if they played out the Cold War, personal edition.

But hearing Mr. Ogden verbally attacking her had bothered Jonah. She hadn't deserved that. Nobody deserved to be treated with such disdain. When he'd heard the man yelling at her, he'd wanted to slug the guy.

And yet . . . Jonah hadn't treated her much better. Guilt pinched hard at the thought.

He'd had his reasons. But he'd eventually come to see there was more to her than designer shoes and fussy manicures. She worked well over the required hours and didn't consider herself above any task. He knew firsthand that included some pretty dirty jobs.

He could now admit, at least to himself, that he'd felt those sparks initially—and it spooked him. He didn't want to fall for another Monica, so he put up his guard.

He'd been unnecessarily hard on Lauren. He'd been rude and impatient and even a little mean sometimes. Once his mom had overheard him bossing Lauren around and her eyes widened.

"Jonah." She gave him a look that both admonished and questioned.

His face flushed with heat, but Lauren was already off to the task on which he'd sent her. He gave his mom an apologetic glance, then took off in the opposite direction.

So no, this wasn't like him at all. He was generally known to be congenial and easygoing. But he'd been the opposite with Lauren. No wonder she avoided him at every turn. Smiled at him through gritted teeth.

He glanced at her now. No wonder she was practically hugging the passenger door. She stared straight ahead at the road, jaw clenched, shoulders rigid, hands clasped tightly in her lap.

They were almost back to the resort, but he wanted to ease the tension somehow. "I'll bet Mr. Ogden's feeling pretty stupid about now."

A long pause passed. "Sure."

A minute later he turned into the property. "I'll check on them. Take Whiskers a treat. Maybe you could collect the tuna so we don't draw a bunch of animals onto the property."

"Okay."

She didn't seem her spitfire self. She appeared to have shrunk in on herself, and that wasn't like the Lauren he knew at all. But they'd come to a stop and she'd already jumped from the truck as if she couldn't escape soon enough.

His mind still on Lauren, Jonah grabbed the kitty treats they kept on hand and headed over to the Ogdens' cabin. He hadn't seen their car but knocked anyway. Then he noticed their beach towels, cooler, and fishing poles were gone from the deck. He peeked in the window—no personal effects that he could see.

So he turned the doorknob. "Hello? Mr. and Mrs. Ogden? It's Jonah." There wasn't a peep. And a quick sweep of the rooms revealed none of the personal items that had cluttered the cabin only an hour ago. He frowned at the recliner's footrest, which was extended and sitting at an odd angle. A quick inspection revealed it was broken.

He sighed as he left the cabin, then headed to the lodge to inform Lauren about the departure so she could notify the cleaners. He'd take a closer look at the recliner later and see if it could be repaired.

He removed his muddy shoes at the door and padded to the office, but Lauren wasn't there. So he headed to the kitchen and found her at the sink, facing the window. "Seems like the Ogdens decided to leave early."

She jumped but didn't turn.

"Sorry, didn't mean to sneak up on you."

"That's okay," she said over her shoulder, then busied herself with dishes.

There was something in her voice. She sounded as if she had a cold. But she hadn't sounded like that earlier.

Was she . . . crying? *Lauren?*

He stepped cautiously into the room. "I, uh, think they found Whiskers up inside the recliner and broke the footrest to get him out. I'll bet Mr. Ogden was embarrassed about the way he treated you—he should've been."

"Then why were you scowling at me?"

He blinked. "I wasn't. I was scowling at him."

"Whatever." She sniffed. "I'm just glad the cat's okay."

Definitely crying. Jonah shifted on his feet. He was no good with crying women. You'd think having a mother and a sister would've prepared him better, but no. "It wasn't your fault, you know."

"I know that."

But something was obviously eating at her. She was scrubbing a plate like she might find gold beneath the porcelain finish.

He wanted to do or say something to make her feel better. But what? There were two things that lifted his mood when he was upset—and she probably wouldn't enjoy shooting hoops. "Do you know how to ride a bike?"

She huffed. "Doesn't everyone?"

"Come on then. We're going for a ride."

She set the plate in the dishwasher. "There's nobody to watch over things."

"We won't be gone long."

She cut him a glance. "Since when do you want to hang out with *me*?"

He definitely deserved that. "Since now. Come on."

"Is that an order, Boss?" Her voice held some of that spunk that usually annoyed him.

This time it made his lips twitch. "If that's what it takes. Leave the dishes and let's go."

"Fine." She closed the dishwasher and followed him to the bike shed.

TWENTY minutes later they were riding along the rail trail, pebbles popping beneath their tires. He led the way since he knew the route. The train tracks from 1872 created a bit of an obstacle for bicycle tires. In some places the path ran between the tracks, in other places beside the tracks, and on some portions of the trail the tracks weren't visible at all.

They passed the lake on the right and soon entered the forest's shade. The woods were replete with spring-green aspens that would turn gold in the fall. The temperature was a pleasant seventy. The sun was low in the sky and would set in a couple hours.

He hoped Lauren found biking as calming as he did. Even though he suspected the reason she was upset was because of the way Mr. Ogden had treated her, guilt bubbled up from someplace deep within him. Jonah owed her an apology for the way he'd behaved since her arrival. And it would be difficult to explain without mentioning those sparks.

Along the way they greeted other bikers and pedestrians walking dogs. Soon, off to the right, the lake glimmered in the sunlight, its tiny islands dotting the surface. He took in the view as he drew in the pine scent.

When they reached the turnoff for Albee Beach, he steered into the parking lot. He continued to the far side where dirt pathways cut through a pine grove, leading to the small beach. His pulse raced at the thought of the upcoming talk. Would she reject his apology and continue to hold a grudge? If so, it would be a long seven months—though he could only blame himself.

He stopped at the end of the pavement and removed his helmet.

Lauren pulled up beside him. "Why are we stopping?"

"Thought you'd like to see one of the local beaches. In a couple weeks this place will be crawling with tourists."

She dismounted and set the kickstand, then removed her helmet, her blonde hair falling around her shoulders. He peered at her from beneath his lashes as he removed two cold water bottles from his pack. He was glad the lost-waif look was gone from her expression and posture. He'd take her jutted chin and flashing eyes any day over that beaten-down expression she'd worn earlier.

He handed her a water bottle, then headed through the pine trees toward a picnic table that straddled the woods and beach. They had the place all to themselves today. He sat on the bench, facing the water while she walked out onto the sand and took in the view.

The lush forest flanked the crescent-shaped strip of beach. The water was as smooth as glass at the moment, and the low hills on the other side of the lake rose to meet the late-afternoon sky. A cool breeze blew, refreshing after the ride.

He took a long drink of water. What was Lauren thinking about as she stared across the lake? The wind ruffled her hair and fluttered the sleeves of her pale blue shirt. Her skin was sun-kissed now after spending so much time outdoors over the past month, and her green eyes popped against her tan. It did a little something extra for her legs too.

He jerked his gaze away as she turned and headed toward him. She stopped ten feet from the table. "We should probably head back. We're having s'mores tonight and I need to get everything ready."

"That's not till ten. Have a seat. Let's talk."

Her back went rigid and her chin lifted. That guarded look in her eyes returned. "Are you firing me?"

He blinked. "No, I'm not firing you. You didn't do anything wrong."

"According to you, I do almost everything wrong." She sat stiffly on the other end of the bench, facing the water.

He heaved a sigh. "I know I've been a little hard on you but—" He stopped at the glare she cast his way. "Okay, okay. A lot hard on you. I owe you an apology."

She reared back. "Wow."

"You don't have to act so surprised—I can admit when I've been wrong."

"This is new information."

His lips twitched. "Nonetheless, I'm sorry I've been difficult." He scratched his neck. "It had nothing to do with you personally. It was me. I take full responsibility and I promise to do better from now on."

Her gaze sharpened on his face as a long moment of silence passed.

He let out a wry laugh. "I've obviously shocked you speechless. But I promise I'm not really an ogre."

"You just—you surprised me, that's all. People rarely do that."

He wasn't sure what that meant. People sometimes surprised the heck out of him. *She* certainly had. "You're doing a great job at the resort, Lauren. You've exceeded my expectations."

She burst out laughing. "Well, they were so low, how could I not?"

His face burned even as he chuckled. He'd heard her laugh many times, but this was the first time she'd laughed with him. "Okay, okay, that's fair, I guess. I admit I misjudged you. You just came across a little . . ." How to put this without offending?

She quirked a brow. "Competent? Responsible? Hardworking?"

"Let's just say I thought you might be a better fit for the Harborview."

She waggled her head back and forth as if weighing the comment. "I'll take that as a compliment."

"Fair enough." He took a swig of water. "I have to say, you jumped right in and did the work. I have no complaints."

"I probably shouldn't mention the overbooking mistake I made today, but it'll probably get back to you anyway." She explained what had happened earlier with the Lawsons.

Between that and the incident with Whiskers, no wonder she'd been so down earlier. "Mistakes happen. It's not the end of the world."

"Yeah, but this was a pretty costly one." Her eyebrows popped suddenly. "Hey, now that the Ogdens have left, I can offer the Willow Cabin to the Lawsons."

He added *resourceful* to the list of adjectives describing Lauren. "Great idea."

She jumped up, pulled her phone from her pocket, and seconds later was scheduling an early morning cleaning.

When she ended the call she grabbed her water and headed back through the pine grove. "Come on. We need to get back so I can call the Lawsons with the good news."

Shaking his head, he followed even as a grin tugged his lips. "Anyone ever tell you you're a workaholic?"

"I can think of worse things."

True enough. They mounted their bikes and headed back to the resort.

Jonah felt like a weight had been lifted from his shoulders. He was relieved the apology was over with and that she'd handled it so well.

But as their conversation replayed in his head, he couldn't help but wonder—now that the barrier between them had been removed, what would he do about those sparks?

CHAPTER 15

Present day

THREE DAYS AFTER Lauren had texted Jonah, he was befuddled. There had been no more texts. He'd been busy with schoolwork this week, but he'd seen her in passing. Other than a stiff greeting, complete with an obligatory smile, she treated him no differently than before.

Jonah set his phone alarm and got into bed to wind down. The Patriots game played on TV and he tried to get into it.

A few minutes later his focus fell to the framed selfie Lauren had taken of them at Albee Beach. It had become their favorite place for evening picnics and stargazing. She'd taken the picture one evening in early August, the day before he'd said "I love you" for the first time. She hadn't returned the sentiment right away—but then he hadn't expected her to. Lauren didn't let people in easily, and she certainly wouldn't be quick to divulge her feelings. He was eager to hear her say the words, but she was worth the wait. And anyway, he could see her feelings in the way she gazed at him when they were alone, when her guard was down. She was falling for him, even if she couldn't voice the thought just yet.

His attention flickered back to the TV screen, the fond memories falling away like dust from a centuries-old tome. All of that was gone now. He was starting from scratch and progress was slow, if not stagnant.

He recalled their first trip to the beach, that day she'd been so upset and he'd apologized. And that's when it came to him—

That had happened shortly before Memorial Day weekend—she wouldn't remember his apology or the change in his behavior afterward. The realization sent shivers down his arms. In her mind he'd never apologized for being such a jerk when she'd first arrived.

Excitement buzzed in his veins because this was something he could rectify. Something he could actually *do*. He pushed off the covers, eager to talk to her.

Then he stopped. What was he gonna do, run over there and knock on her door at ten o'clock at night? That would be weird.

It would have to wait until tomorrow.

But then he thought about how distant she was in person compared to how open she'd been with texting. That extra buffer between them felt safer to her. And though he'd rather apologize in person, maybe she'd be more receptive over text.

She was the one who'd opened this avenue of communication, and he was happy to communicate with her any way she preferred, be it texts, letters, or smoke signals.

"Go lie down," Lauren told Graham.

The dog, head hanging low, retreated to his bedding in the corner of the room and lay down with a heavy sigh. Graham kept trying to get into her bed, but it was a twin, and he sprawled out like a starfish. She must've let him share the bed before the accident, but she needed her sleep.

She got comfy under the covers, grabbed her phone, and opened the latest Kristin Hannah novel on her reading app. But ten minutes later she was staring blankly at the screen, thinking of Jonah and the grief she'd witnessed on the basketball court the other day.

At the thought of his tears, her chest hollowed. She'd hurt him to the core with her inability to remember their relationship, with the way she'd treated him subsequently. She'd tried to do better the past few days, tried to smile and greet him as a friend might. But it was so hard to see him in a different way than the one in which she remembered him.

Giving up on the novel, she opened her texting app to the thread she'd started with him the other day. She reread their comments, her lips tipping up at the final GIF he'd sent. He'd been very kind. Which, of course, was so unlike the Jonah she remembered.

Her thumb paused over the screen. She itched to scroll up so she could read all the texts, back to the very beginning. But before she could satisfy her curiosity, her phone buzzed an incoming text. *Jonah.*

She jumped. Her heart raced as if she'd been caught doing something wrong. *Dummy. He can't see you mooning over his texts.*

You awake? he asked.

Her fingers hovered over the virtual keyboard. Finally she replied, *Yes.*

Then she watched those three dots undulate, waiting.

And waiting.

And waiting.

Had he gotten distracted? Changed his mind? Fallen asleep? Restless, she scrolled up to their texts from a few days ago and reread them. Just as she reached the end, his reply popped up.

I'm sorry for the way I treated you those first weeks after you arrived. (Basically for everything you remember before the accident.) I was unkind and judgmental for reasons that had nothing to do with you and I'm so sorry.

Wow. She reared back. Another text came in before she could reply.

I apologized to you in May, but I just realized you wouldn't remember that.

He'd apologized? *You're right. Thank you for apologizing—again.*

I was hard on you when you came here and I shouldn't have been.

She was taken aback by his honesty. By his humility. She read through his apology again and responded. *What reasons?*

What?

You said the reasons had nothing to do with me . . .

While she waited for his response, she reread his apology. Finally his text appeared.

I had a girlfriend awhile back who broke my heart. Let's just say that in some ways you reminded me of her at first. I went on defense to protect myself because—spoiler alert—I was attracted to you.

Another text appeared. *SO glad you didn't ask this the first time I apologized.* 😄

She could hardly process everything he'd just said. She decided to stick to the easier part of the conversation. *Did you ever tell me about this woman?*

Of course. Pretty early on, actually.

Will you tell me about her again?

A minute passed before his reply appeared. *She was an esthetician for Harborview for about a year. We met at the coffee shop and became exclusive after a month or so. Things were getting serious, and then she got a job offer in Manhattan. She couldn't leave town fast enough.*

The guy was apparently no stranger to a broken heart. *I'm sorry. That must've been painful.*

It wasn't fun.

There were no painful breakups in her past she could've disclosed to him. She hadn't dated anyone seriously. Had never been in love. She'd been busy making her education and career her number one priority. But how much had she revealed about her childhood?

How much did I tell you about my past? As soon as she typed the words, she deleted them. She wasn't sure she wanted to know—and she sure didn't want to get into it right now.

Another text appeared. *I'm happy to answer any questions about the past. If you want.*

She typed her response. *Did I do a good job with the resort this summer?* Not the kind of question he was probably hoping for, but she sent it anyway. She didn't want to dig into the romantic relationship she didn't remember and could still hardly believe had ever happened.

You were amazing. The guests loved you. And you've seen all the ideas we've implemented, thanks to you.

I don't recall you thinking they were such good ideas.

Shows what I know. I admit to being stubborn and having an intense dislike for change.

So you're glad about the changes now? Even the pavilion?

Especially the pavilion. We shared quite a few sunset kisses under that roof.

Her breath hitched at his words. But another text popped up before she could respond.

Sorry. Probably shouldn't have said that.

It's okay. But she couldn't help but envision the pair of them sitting at one of the picnic tables, sharing a kiss as the sun sank below the horizon. Was he a good kisser? He had nice lips. His cupid's bow dipping down from rounded peaks, his bottom lip fairly lush. She'd noticed them right off, even though they'd usually been curled in a smirk.

Renting out the slips has been huge for us, he texted when she failed to respond. *Easy money. Brilliant.*

Pleasure bloomed inside at the compliment. *Thank you.*

The barn venue will be another great source of income once it's finished.

She hadn't gone to inspect it yet, but she probably should since the low season would offer more time to focus on it. She wanted to have the work completed before she left at the end of the year. And the exterior would have to be finished before winter set in.

Do you know what my plans were for the remodeling?

We discussed it at great length. You were so excited about it. You even did some sketches. You keep them on the shelf in your closet.

I'll take a look at them. Would you be able to go over there with me soon? She paused before sending it. It would mean spending time with him. But she'd apparently spent a lot of time thinking about what the barn would require, and she needed to implement those ideas quickly if she planned to finish it before she left. She sent the text, and he responded immediately.

Would tomorrow around one work?

It was after checkout and before the weekend check-ins. *Sure. I'll be at the lodge.*

I'll see you then.

Good night.

Night.

Lauren plugged in her phone, shut off the lamp, and settled in bed. If she had the tiniest of smiles on her face, it was only because she was excited about her new venture with the barn.

CHAPTER 16

ALL MORNING LAUREN kept glancing at her watch. She had only two guests to check out. She'd brought the barn binder she'd found in her closet but hadn't found time to review it between tasks.

Meg and Tammy were working in the office and Tom, on Tammy's order, had gone fishing. The three women ate lunch together, chatting about the resort, Tom and Tammy's upcoming travel plans, and town gossip. They carefully avoided the topic of Lauren and Jonah.

Had they approved of her relationship with Jonah? They seemed to like her well enough, but people sometimes hid their true feelings. Maybe Tammy didn't think Lauren was good enough for him. She wouldn't be the first mother to disapprove of her son's girlfriend.

After all, Lauren was leaving at the end of the year. Surely she'd been concerned about the possibility of losing Jonah. Since Tom had all but retired, it would put the future of the resort in jeopardy. But then, Sydney had mentioned Lauren was reconsidering her return to Boston. Maybe they were aware of that.

After lunch Lauren pulled out the binder and scanned her drawings. She was no artist, that was for sure. But she got a vague idea of what she'd envisioned for the final product. Of course, without seeing the barn in its current condition, it was hard to know how much effort would be involved. She had made pages of notes, but many of them were half thoughts, sometimes just a word or two. Even so, she was getting excited about the project—it would be a welcome diversion from her troublesome memory issues. She hoped Jonah could shed some light on her previous intentions.

He arrived five minutes early in jeans and a black tee that did nice things for his form. He wasn't a bulky guy, but he had broad shoulders that tapered down to a trim waist. His arms were muscular—whether from his work at the resort or time in a gym, she had no idea.

His face lit up when he caught sight of her behind the counter. "Hey. You ready to go?"

"Hi. Yeah." She slapped the binder shut. "I was just glancing over my notes."

He held the door for her, then followed her down the steps, awkwardness trailing them like an unwelcome shadow. Why could she text him without feeling weird but being with him felt so uncomfortable? He'd apologized for his behavior—which was now months past. She would just have to get over it.

They treaded across the pine needle carpet, passing the cabins. One of the cleaners was shaking out a rug on Hickory's deck.

Lauren lifted a hand. "Hey, Pam."

"How's it going?" Jonah asked.

Pam beamed. "Hey, you two. Beautiful day. It's so nice to see you two together again."

Lauren's face warmed. "We're just headed out to the barn. Everything okay with the cabins?"

"Good as gold. We'll be out of here by two."

"Perfect."

Jonah gave another wave. "Have a great afternoon."

If the comment had embarrassed him, he showed no signs.

A few minutes later, when they entered the forest's shade on the far side of Lauren's cabin, Jonah broke the silence. "How many cabins are full this weekend?"

"Just three."

He nodded. "It'll get busier as we head toward peak foliage, but not like the summer was." He cut her a chagrined look. "Sorry. I keep forgetting you don't remember the summer."

"I keep forgetting I even *had* a summer."

He chuckled at her wry tone. "This whole thing really sucks, doesn't it? I'm sorry it happened to you."

"Thanks," she said distractedly as the memory of him on the basketball court slammed into her heart. He was suffering much more than she was. How kind of him to consider her feelings when he was the one who was grief-stricken. Heaven knew she'd hardly given his feelings a second thought since the accident.

They came into the clearing and there it stood. The big barn was rustic red and in need of a good paint job. But the stone on the bottom was charming, and the structure appeared sound. At least it wasn't falling apart.

"What do you think?"

"It's got a lot of promise."

His eyes warmed about ten degrees. "How did I know you'd say that? When you first stumbled upon it, it was overgrown with brambles. Took us a week to clear it all. The inside was full of junk that had accumulated over the years."

She wished she remembered that part. How fun to rummage through someone's old things. "Anything old and interesting?"

"You were disappointed to find it truly was just a bunch of junk. Wooden crates, ancient cans of paints and supplies, mechanical parts of machines that probably don't exist anymore. Most of it went to the trash heap."

He unfastened the barn door and it gave a loud creak as he rolled it open. "The plan was to seal the boards, paint the exterior, repair the rock mortar, replace the windows, and reshingle the roof before snow comes."

"Then spend the colder months on the interior."

"Exactly."

She stepped into the barn and stopped. Sunlight seeped through cracks in the siding and through the windowpanes, giving the interior an ethereal glow. The building was spacious, and beyond the thick overhead beams, it opened up to a lofty ceiling. She'd been right in her notes—the space would easily seat a hundred people. She'd catered similar-sized venues for Elite. An old hayloft jutted out on one side of the building, about a quarter of the barn's length.

In her mind's eye, she could see the space finished. Add new wood plank flooring, some fairy lights, and a swath of white tulle draped overhead, and this place would be beautiful. "It'll make an amazing wedding venue."

"That's what you said before. You'd already picked out the flooring, and you'd gotten bids on the exterior work."

"I saw them in the binder."

"Mom and Dad already approved them, so you can schedule the work whenever you want."

"Sooner than later if we're gonna beat the weather."

When he didn't respond, she glanced back where he'd stopped just shy of the loft's shadow. He was seemingly lost in thought, his brows drawn, his eyes downcast.

"What's wrong?"

He blinked up as if just remembering she was there. "Nothing. I just—I haven't been back here since . . ."

The accident. She'd been so swept up in her plans for the renovation that she'd nearly forgotten this was where it had happened.

Her gaze returned to the spot at which he'd been staring. "Is that—is that where I fell?"

"Yeah." He gave her a smile that didn't reach his eyes. "Sorry. Didn't mean to go there. It's probably the last thing you want to think about."

She'd wondered about the incident, but everyone avoided talking about it. And she'd avoided the topic too. But now curiosity got the best of her. "Can you tell me what happened exactly?"

He stared up at the loft and was quiet for a long moment. "We were up there. I was showing you the balcony I'd just cleaned out." A wistful look fell over his face. "You were so excited about how spacious it was. You said we could seat six extra tables up there. You wanted to hang a chandelier and you mentioned the railings we'd need to add. You were excited about the vantage point it would give a photographer. You were practically beaming."

His gaze fixed on the balcony as his eyes glazed over, obviously reliving the moment. "We had a date scheduled that night and you wanted to go get ready. We were going to The Landing." His expression turned sad a beat before his eyes filled with tears.

He pulled his eyes away. Scratched his neck as he tossed her a humorless smile. "Unfortunately, I decided the balcony window needed cleaning right that minute. So I stayed in the loft while you headed down the ladder. I didn't see what happened. But you fell somehow, bringing the ladder down with you." His eyes closed for a long second. "When I looked down you were . . . sprawled on the floor, unconscious." His face went pale. His Adam's apple bobbed. "I thought—"

She envisioned the horrific sight and a shiver passed down her arms.

"I don't even remember getting down from the loft or calling 911. I checked your pulse and—"

Lauren's gaze dropped to his neck, where his pulse fluttered visibly and quickly.

113

"It took forever for help to arrive. Graham was there. He kept whining. He lay down beside you and licked your hand. Then he got up and circled. They told me not to move you, so I just lay there with my fingers on your pulse, begging God to . . ." A sheen of sweat broke out on his upper lip. He ran his palms down the sides of his jeans. "I kept thinking, if only I hadn't stayed to clean that stupid window. If only I'd gone down the ladder first and held it for you."

She hadn't known he was plagued with guilt. She set her hand on his arm. "Hey. It's not your fault, Jonah. It was an accident, that's all."

"I've replayed that moment a thousand times, both awake and asleep."

"You dream about it?"

"More like a nightmare," he said with a wry tone. His arm flexed beneath her fingers.

She drew her hand away.

He gave his head a shake, dislodging the haunted look from his face. "Anyway. That's what happened. When the ambulance got here, they took you away on a gurney and I rode along. You didn't wake until later when they were wheeling you out of the CT scan."

"I don't remember any of that."

"You didn't know what had happened, why you were at the hospital. I told you. Then you asked again a few minutes later. Scared me to death."

"The first thing I remember is Carson coming into the room."

Jonah pressed his lips in a tight line. "Right. He came in and checked on you."

"I was confused about why you were there."

He tore his gaze away. "I could tell something was wrong. You seemed different—guarded. You didn't remember Graham or the barn, but I didn't put it together at first. Thought you were just confused."

"I remember the panic attack."

He cupped his neck. "Yeah. That was about the time I realized my presence was doing more harm than good."

It must've been so hard for him. If he loved her—which he clearly did—leaving her would've been the last thing he'd have wanted to do. But he did it anyway. And stayed away for the remainder of her hospital stay.

No, wait, he'd stayed in the lobby, slept in the chair. She'd forgotten about that. She pictured him huddled in a hard chair, trying to sleep while the woman he loved was just down the hall, having forgotten all about him.

Sympathy compressed her chest. "I'm sorry for what you went through. For what you're going through now."

His lips lifted in a smile that didn't quite reach his eyes. "We've already been through this. Not your fault."

"No, but it's not yours either."

He released a heavy sigh. "I guess it isn't. But it's our reality now, like it or not. We'll get through it."

No doubt they'd do just that. But she couldn't help but ache for the relationship she didn't remember.

And as they turned the conversation back to the barn's renovation, the ache remained, strong and unrelenting. And if she hurt for something she didn't even remember, she couldn't help but wonder—what kind of misery was Jonah enduring?

JONAH handed his menu to the server and settled back in the booth. His family often ate out after church on Sundays. But Meg had made plans with her friends today, leaving Jonah alone with his parents. The buzz of chatter filled the Village Café and the scent of grilled burgers made his mouth water.

Mom's gaze sharpened on Jonah as she leaned onto her elbows. "How are you doing, honey? It's hard to believe it's been three weeks since the accident."

As if he needed the reminder. "I'm fine, Mom. Really. I mean, it's not ideal, obviously, but I'm still hopeful."

"Is she doing anything to help jog her memory?" Dad asked. "Is there anything we can do to help?"

Jonah winced. He didn't want to admit to his parents that she didn't want her memory back at all. He didn't even want to admit it to himself. "Just keep the prayers coming. That's the biggest thing you can do."

"Of course, honey." Mom glanced at Dad, then back to Jonah. "Lauren seems to be excited about the barn renovation."

"She is." Something was up. The two of them were trading glances like undercover cops.

"It's just—your dad and I, well, we were wondering if you're sure you should go ahead with it, that's all."

"With the barn renovation?"

"Right," Dad said.

Where was this coming from? "That's been the plan all along, hasn't it? We approved it months ago."

"I realize that." Mom fiddled with her napkin. "But things have changed since then."

"Not really. We weren't even a couple when Lauren originally presented the idea. We decided the plan made financial sense for the resort. There are the initial costs, of course, but the venue will earn back that money pretty quickly. It's a good investment."

Dad gave him a pained look. "It's not the finances we're concerned about."

Jonah didn't like where this was going. The barn was the one thing Lauren was excited about—minus the dream job she didn't realize she'd given up. "What then?"

"Honey, we're all hoping Lauren's memory will return and we can all go on with our lives as before. But there's a chance that might not happen. And if it doesn't . . . Lauren will return to Boston at the end of the year, and we'll be left to deal with that venue."

"*I'll* be left to deal with it. Come January first, it'll be my problem, right?"

"Well, that's just it, honey. We don't want you to be left with a problem on top of all this heartache."

He pressed his lips together. "Earlier this summer you said it was up to me."

"And we're not going back on that."

"So this isn't about you thinking I don't belong at the resort."

Mom grabbed his hand. "Honey, we never thought that! Of course you belong."

"I didn't mean it like that." Or maybe he had. But he couldn't own up to his real feelings. His parents had been nothing but good to him. Had given him a far better life than he would've had without them. If his mom was disappointed that their family business would pass to him and not their biological child, well, he couldn't really blame her. But it was hurtful nonetheless.

His parents stared at him, waiting for him to finish his thought. "I just meant that you seem to think I might be more fulfilled doing something else."

"We just want to make sure you aren't pursuing the management out of a sense of responsibility or expectation. You're so smart, Jonah. So capable. There are many other things you could do if you wanted."

"You insisted I get a degree, and come December I'll have one. But I haven't changed my mind about running the resort."

"That's not where we were going with this," Dad said.

Jonah stuffed down a flicker of anger. "Then where were you going exactly?"

Mom shifted in her seat, then turned her big brown eyes on him. "If things don't go the way we want with Lauren, we just don't want you to be left with a venue you're not interested in running."

"And renovation debt that requires you to do so."

"She'll be long gone and you'll have that reminder, that's all. We wonder if we shouldn't call it quits before we start investing money in this. Or at least put it off until we see if Lauren's memory returns."

"It's only been three weeks."

"We know that."

"Regardless of if she stays or not, the venue makes financial sense. I want to do it." He wasn't sure if he could tease out his own desire for the venue from Lauren's passion for the project. But he wouldn't take away the one thing that excited her about being here. "Is it still my decision?"

Mom and Dad traded a look.

"Of course," Mom said. "It's your call."

"Then we'll move forward with the renovation."

CHAPTER 17

"HEY, JONAH, COME here," one of the guests from the writers group called as he passed the pavilion on a chilly October day. "We need your opinion."

He'd been heading home to study, but he wasn't opposed to a little procrastination. The romance writers had remained mostly in their cabins by day, presumably working, then brainstorming—boisterously and with lots of laughter—by night.

He approached the group of seven women, ranging in age from twentysomething to midsixties. "What can I do for you ladies?"

"Help a writer out," Donna, the oldest of the group, said. "Cara's working on a romance featuring a rugged type of guy who's attracted to a woman who's a type A personality."

"And since you're a rugged type . . . ," one of the women said.

"Am I now?" he teased.

The women giggled.

"Sit down, sit down," Donna said. "We need a little testosterone in the group."

"We don't bite."

Not so sure about that. He quirked a brow at them, which only provoked more laughter. Over the past few days he'd overheard a conversation or two that would've made a sailor blush.

Cara, the twentysomething brunette, made room for him on the bench, so he took a seat beside her.

"She wants to know what would attract you to that type of woman."

Cara's cheeks bloomed with color as she gazed at him expectantly. "What about that type of woman might appeal to a man like you?"

"Type A, huh?"

"She's very rule oriented but also a real go-getter. She's trying to make partner in her law firm."

"Well, they say opposites attract," he said.

"No doubt," Donna said. "But Cara's looking for specifics."

"Hmm, specifics." It didn't escape his notice that Lauren was just the type of woman they were talking about. "Well, I would admire her work ethic. She'd also be confident and independent, which are appealing traits."

"So you like confidence in a woman?" Cara asked.

"Sure, there's something attractive about someone who knows her place in the world and is comfortable in her own skin."

Cara jotted some notes. "That's good. What else?"

He thought back to the early days with Lauren. She had not been easy! He chuckled. "She'd probably be a bit of a challenge too."

"Is that a good thing?" Cara asked jokingly.

The women laughed.

"Most guys appreciate a little challenge. But like most anything, it can be overdone." Lately gaining Lauren's trust had proven to be an insurmountable challenge. Though she'd been perfectly amicable the past couple weeks, she was resistant to the idea of anything more. "A woman like that would know her own mind too. And she might even be a little guarded."

"Guarded," Donna said. "I like that."

Cara nudged him with her shoulder. "Hey, you're really good at this."

He gave a wry laugh. If he was good at it, it was only because he'd lived it. Was still living it.

"So what kinds of things might get on his nerves?" Donna asked. "Being that they're opposite and all."

That was easy. "He'd admire her independence, but a man also likes to feel useful. So she might make him feel unnecessary sometimes."

"Oooh, good one." Cara jotted that down.

"She'd probably be someone who thought out all the steps before she made a move, and he might be more impetuous."

"That would create some nice conflict," Donna said.

"Also, since she's ambitious, her work might take her in a different direction than he'd prefer." Boy, could he relate. It had been hard putting his heart on the line when Lauren was so determined to make her life in Boston. Especially after the way Monica ditched him.

"Like, to another state?" someone asked.

"Or another planet."

Cara shared a smile with him. "Mai writes romantic fantasy, in case you couldn't guess."

He gave Mai a nod. "Or another planet. Also your character would like to win, so she'd probably be competitive. You could have the hero and heroine shooting for the same goal—and only one of them could win. Sparks would definitely be flying then."

"Ooh," Cara said. "You are so good at this."

"Do me next!" Donna said.

LAUREN took a bite of her grilled cheese sandwich as she sorted through the barn binder in her cabin. In the past two and a half weeks, work on the barn had begun. The mortar on the stones had been fixed and the paint job was already underway. The roof was scheduled for next week.

It was coming along. Her time here at Pinehaven would finish nicely—only two and a half months left. None of her memories had returned, but that was probably for the best.

She saw Jonah often in passing or when he checked on the barn's progress. They seemed to have found a comfortable way to coexist. The awkwardness had faded and a tentative friendship had begun.

What had she been thinking before the accident? A serious relationship with a New Hampshirite shouldn't have factored into her plans. Jonah seemed rooted here at his parents' resort, and Lauren was *this* close to that job at Glitter.

Truthfully, Carson, with his big-city dreams, was a more likely match since once he finished his internship, he hoped to secure that residency in Boston. They'd talked a time or two when they'd gone out as a group. He even texted her sometimes to check on her.

A relationship with him was probably a bad idea anyway—at least for the time being. She wouldn't want to hurt Jonah any more than she already had. Besides, what if they started dating and she fell for him—and then got her memory back? The thought of that romantic quandary made her head pound.

Besides, between managing the resort and overseeing the renovation, she had plenty to keep her busy.

Lauren took her last bite, closed the binder, and checked her watch. They were doing s'mores tonight, but she'd already gathered the supplies. She went to her bedroom, Graham on her heels, and tossed the binder into the top of the closet. The weight of it unsettled a shoebox on the shelf, and the box dropped to the floor, falling open.

She didn't recognize the box, and it didn't have a pair of shoes inside as she'd assumed. Graham sniffed the contents, tail wagging.

"What do we have here?"

She knelt and sorted through the stuff: movie ticket stubs, a rumpled map of Flume Gorge, a pine cone, some notes, a pale pink rock shaped like a heart, and . . . cloth dinner napkins? Three of them in maroon, ivory, and seafoam green.

She unfolded a small piece of notebook paper.

Lauren, here's a coffee just the way you like it (sickeningly sweet and laden with heavy cream). Thought you could use it after the late night. Some of us had to get up early for school.

XO,

Jonah

His printing was small, a little messy, but perfectly legible. She folded it carefully and opened the next.

Found this out by Otter's Pond and thought of you.

XO,

Jonah

She wondered if the heart-shaped rock had accompanied the note. She opened the next message.

Have a great evening, sweetheart. Don't give Dave Jones and his unwife another thought.

No idea what that meant. It was so weird to know that something had happened to her—lots of somethings—that she had no recollection of.

More notes turned up nice little sentiments, all of them alluding to things she didn't remember. In the age of texting it was sweet that he'd gone to the trouble of writing notes. She was starting to see that the Jonah she'd first met was perhaps not the real Jonah. Beneath that long hair and dark scowl lay a sentimental, caring man.

When she'd read them all, she tucked them back into the shoebox with a sigh, feeling a little wistful about a relationship she couldn't even remember. But Jonah had loved her enough to write them, and she'd cared enough to save them. That said something.

As she set the box back on the shelf, the thought weighed on her, leaving her unsettled. With the way those mementos had left her feeling, she was glad she hadn't given in to the temptation to read those old texts or scroll through her photos.

She glanced out the window. It was getting dark outside. Time to get the bonfire going. She grabbed the lighter from the kitchen drawer and glanced at Graham. "You can go with me, but no begging for s'mores. Got it?"

Graham gave a happy bark.

"Good boy." She grabbed the supplies and headed toward the firepit, opposite the pavilion. The night sounds that had seemed so foreign at first had grown on her: the warbling call of insects, the lonely hoot of an owl, the rustling of the wind through the trees.

And soon the sounds of chatter and laughter carried from the far end of the property. The writers group, which filled most of the cabins, gathered for their evening plotting session. It was a friendly, easygoing group that had demanded little of her. She'd done little beyond providing hot chocolate and apple cider for their nightly sessions.

The property lights that came on at dark guided her way. As she approached the cold firepit, she caught sight of the pavilion, lit up with white twinkle lights and hosting the lively group.

A smile curved Lauren's lips as she listened to their lighthearted chatter. She loved managing a property where people enjoyed themselves.

Where she could have a small part in making them feel welcome, making them feel as if they belonged. As if they were part of an extended family. It fulfilled something deep inside her.

A male voice caught her off guard. Jonah. He sat in the midst of the group, quite close to the youngest writer who was about their age, with glossy brown hair that looked as if it didn't know the meaning of the word *frizz*. The group hooted at whatever Jonah had said, and the woman nudged Jonah with her shoulder.

Lauren's smile wilted. She squatted by the logs she'd stacked earlier while Graham, ever the extrovert, charged over to the group to solicit attention. When Jonah caught sight of the dog, he immediately scanned the area and found Lauren by the firepit.

She glanced away before they made eye contact and extended the lighter toward the newspapers she'd stuffed beneath the logs earlier. She flicked the lighter, but it failed to produce a flame.

A moment later the crunch of leaves alerted her to Jonah's approach. "Here, let me help."

"I've got it. You should go back and hang with your friends."

"Guests, you mean. I'll get the supplies."

"I already have them." She gestured to the bag. "I thought you were going home to study."

"I was, but the writers group needed my help with something."

The *romance* writers. "I'll just bet they did."

He cut her a confused look. "What? They were just getting some advice."

"I'm sure they were." She gave a wry chuckle. "I didn't know you were such an expert on romance." Had that sounded catty? Well, she was feeling a little catty. But that didn't make any sense.

"Hey, Jonah," Donna called. "Cara has another question."

The young pretty woman propped her chin on her hand and smiled boldly at Jonah.

Lauren turned her gaze back to him. "Cara has another question," she deadpanned. She stood and set off for the other lighter. What was wrong with her? Was she actually *jealous*? Jonah was only a friend and that's the way she wanted it.

Wasn't it?

Yes, she definitely wanted it that way. She'd been over this. If this whole ordeal with the concussion had taught her anything, it was how much she wanted that job in Boston. She'd worked hard to get where she was. And she wouldn't give it up for any man. She was not her mom, turning her back on what mattered for some random guy.

The thought spawned the childhood memory she'd relived a thousand times. Her mom leaving with a man Lauren hadn't recognized. She'd stood in the window of their trailer, waiting for Mom to turn and wave as she usually did when she left her with their neighbor Miss Sheila. But this time her mom didn't turn around.

This time her mom didn't return.

Sheila kept her for a couple days, and when a woman showed up at the door, it wasn't her mom. The adults talked in hushed tones while Lauren enjoyed cookies in the kitchen. Then the stranger joined her at the table.

"Hi, Lauren. We need to talk, sweetheart." Then she explained what was happening in a soft, kind voice that contradicted her frightening message.

A while later Miss Sheila emerged from the hallway with Lauren's bag. Lauren screamed and cried as the woman took her away. It was the beginning of a very volatile period of her life.

Lauren pushed away the dark memory and rubbed the tattoo on her inner wrist. She was finally in charge of her own future, and she wasn't about to hand that control over to anyone else.

So why had that pretty woman ogling Jonah stirred up these unsettling feelings? Carson had spoken with her about the brain's complexity. Maybe some part of her remembered the relationship she and Jonah used to have. And that part of her had reacted with jealousy.

Yes. That made sense. Giving a satisfied nod, she entered the lodge and retrieved the lighter. Now that that was settled, she could put aside these silly feelings and join the party.

CHAPTER 18

June 7

LAUREN WAVED GOOD-BYE to the Swansons as they exited the lodge, taking their lively tribe with them. "Safe travels!"

The smallest girl waved shyly. "Bye, Miss Lauren."

"Bye, sweetheart. Enjoy the rest of your summer."

When the door closed Jonah entered from the office. "That's one big family. How many kids do they have?"

"Seven. They're so fun though. I think they had a great time. They want to come back next year."

"I saw you shooting hoops with them the other day."

Lauren's face heated. "I'm, uh, not very athletic."

"Really? I didn't notice."

She gave him a mock scowl.

He chuckled, his gaze clinging in a way that made her pulse quicken. "Did you stop by just to make fun of me?"

"I actually thought we'd go check out the barn before the weekend guests arrive."

She'd stumbled across the structure last week and had the idea of turning it into a wedding venue. Another income stream would be very healthy for the family business. But Jonah hadn't seemed impressed with the idea. "Really? You like my idea after all?"

"I just said we'd *check it out*."

"It kinda sounds as if you *like* my idea."

He rolled his eyes. "Are you free or what?"

"For the moment." Tossing him a cocky smile, she went to let Tammy know where they were going. Then she slipped out the door while Jonah held it open. He was a gentleman; she'd give him that.

She had a bounce in her step as she walked. She was thrilled he was giving the barn a look. His parents would never get on board with the idea if Jonah wasn't, since he would soon manage and someday own the place. She'd only peeked through the dirty windows because the door was locked in place.

"Hang on," he said as they passed the toolshed. "Let me grab the bolt cutters."

She waited outside the building, her thoughts returning to the barn. As ideas and questions filled her head, she dictated them on her phone. "Check exterior stone base and roof shingles, period. What is flooring situation, question mark. Is structure sound, question mark."

"Pushy woman with ambitious goals, period."

She whipped around.

Jonah muttered into his phone. "Drags others into folly, period. Won't take no for answer, period."

Lauren scooped a pine cone off the ground and whipped it his way. It smacked him in the eye. She gasped, then covered her mouth. "I'm so sorry."

His gaze locked on her for a long moment, and then he turned away.

"Jonah, seriously, I didn't mean to hit you in the eye." She stepped closer. "Are you okay? Are you bleeding?"

He raised his phone. "Woman has strong arm, period. Atrocious aim, however, period."

JONAH tossed a smirk at Lauren even as she palmed her heart. "Very funny. I thought you were mad at me."

He made a show of squinting from one eye. "I probably would be—if I could see you."

"Maybe if your hair wasn't so long," she teased.

They started toward the far end of the property and were soon enveloped in the shade of the woods.

She gave him a sideways glance. "Seriously, is your eye all right? It looks a little red."

"It was only a pine cone, not a butcher knife."

"Well, it's not every day you bean your boss in the eye with a projectile. I promise it wasn't on purpose."

"No kidding. I saw your athletic prowess on the court yesterday."

"Hey! That's not nice."

He liked this new playful side of her. "It is, however, true."

She pretended to weigh the statement. "Okay, yes, so I'm athletically challenged. I do have other good features though."

"Such as?"

Her chin notched up. "I have great hair."

"Wow, that was fast."

"It's all in the conditioner, my friend."

"I'll take your word for it. But I have great hair *and* I'm athletic." He flung his hair aside with dramatic flair.

She laughed as her gaze flickered over his long dark hair and bushy beard. "You may have a lot of hair, Boss, but that doesn't make it great."

"Ouch," he said through a smile.

"I mean, it's summer and all that hair must get pretty hot. Are you barbershop-phobic or something?"

"I'll have you know I've been very busy."

"Too busy to shave?"

"Maybe." He sent a mock scowl her way. "Some women like the lumber-jack look, you know."

"Is that a fact?"

"That's what I hear."

"Well, some women actually like to see a man's face once in a while."

"Are you saying you wanna see my face, Wentworth?"

A nervous laugh escaped. "That's not what I'm saying at all."

"Okay . . . just making sure." If someone had told him a month ago they'd be flirting, he would've said they were crazy. But here they were, trading quips and sly glances. And if he wasn't mistaken, Lauren was blushing a little.

"So why'd your parents buy this adjacent property if they weren't planning to do anything with it?"

"Years ago when it came up for sale, they were worried about who might buy it. And they didn't want some competing resort or hotel ruining the serenity of the cove."

"They didn't want to put up more cabins?"

"Because of the way the property curves around the cove, there's not a lot of lake frontage. Besides, they figured eight cabins were plenty to handle. It's been a buffer more than anything."

Soon the woods ended at a bunch of brambles. He moved through them, using the bolt cutter and holding branches back for Lauren. "I didn't realize it was this overgrown."

"I can't wait to see the inside."

"Hopefully I can get that ancient lock off."

"Looks pretty rusty," she said when they reached the big barn door.

Moments later he snapped the lock with no problem.

Lauren was fairly bouncing on the balls of her feet. She helped him untangle some vines from the door, and then he gave it a push. It opened slowly with a loud creak.

"Needs new hardware." He stepped inside and it took a minute for his eyes to adjust to the darkness. And oh, jeez. The place was filled with junk.

Lauren swept past him, a rapturous expression on her face. "It's just perfect!"

He gave the place a second glance. Nope. Wasn't seeing it. "Um, have you had your eyes checked recently?"

"See the way the sunbeams flood through the windows? And those rafters—the high ceiling. Ooh, there's a hayloft."

"Also, there's a hundred years of junk in this place."

"Just imagine what we might find."

He'd never seen this Pollyanna side of her. "Like an extended family of rodents perhaps?"

That swept the joy from her face. For all of five seconds. "It needs a grand fireplace over here. And there should be lots of twinkle lights overhead and some draped white tulle to soften the space. The floor is awesome—what we can see of it—but it's pretty uneven, which would make it a tripping hazard. The walls seem good and sturdy, though, don't you think? We'd need a furnace, of course, and air-conditioning. A kitchen and bathrooms."

"Sounds very expensive."

"But do you know what this place could rent for—for one night?"

She named a sum that made him rear back. "Really? That much?"

"People pay a fortune for wedding venues. And this place would seat a ton of people."

"But wouldn't we need someone to run a venue like this?"

"It could really be as simple or as complex as you want it to be. Minimally, you'd just be scheduling the use of it, and the renter would be in charge of everything else. Or you could actually hire someone to oversee it all: the tables and chairs, decorating, catering, all the way up to planning weddings."

He shook his head. "I don't know."

"If that's overwhelming, you could just keep it simple. I checked with a local wedding planner. There's only one other barn venue in a forty-mile radius. She said a lot of people choose to be married outside in the summer, but the winters here are long and there are few options. That's a slow time of year around here. It would give the resort a nice income during low season."

Good point. He hadn't realized she'd already done so much legwork. If the place could rent for as much as she'd suggested, one night would earn more than all eight cabins during high season.

Lauren's phone buzzed an incoming text. "It's your mom. She needs me back at the lodge."

"All right. I'm gonna stay and sift through some of this stuff." He walked her over to the barn door.

"So you'll think about it? The venue?"

"Tell you what. Get a contractor over here to check the structural integrity. If that pans out, you can get some estimates on what this place needs, and we'll go from there."

Her face lit up like a Christmas tree. "Really? Thank you, Jonah!"

If she kept looking at him like that, he might just sign the whole property over to her. Putting a happy flush on her pretty cheeks made his day. But he only said, "Let's not get ahead of ourselves. We're just getting bids."

"I know. But thank you! I'll get back to you with some answers." On the other side of the brambles, she turned, her pretty hair swinging around her shoulders as she beamed at him. "See you, Jonah."

At the sight of her beautiful smile, his heart stuttered, possibly interrupting blood flow to his brain for he went mute for a second. "Uh, yeah. See you, Wentworth. Keep up the conditioner."

With a wave, she was off.

Keep up the conditioner? "Idiot." He thumped his head on the door-frame.

Chapter 19

Present day

"AHOY MATEY!" MR. Cavendish called as he pulled the resort's motor-boat up to the dock.

"Ahoy there!" Lauren smiled at the couple as she walked the pier, Graham at her side, his tail swishing at the new arrivals. Lauren caught the lines Mrs. Cavendish threw and tied up the boat. "Have a good ride?"

"It was just beautiful," Mrs. Cavendish said. "Perfect temperature, and the trees are just gorgeous this morning."

"The boat handled beautifully. We were able to take a couple tributaries back into the woods."

"We felt like Lewis and Clark."

Lauren laughed. She'd discovered some of the tributaries that ran into the lake but hadn't quite trusted her boating skills to maneuver one.

"The gas is below a quarter tank."

"Thanks, we'll fill it up." She helped the Cavendishes onto the pier, where they removed their life vests, then gave Graham the attention he practically begged for.

The sixtysomething couple had come for the fall foliage, and the mid-October display did not disappoint. In the past week and a half, the color had trickled down the mountains into the valley. Vibrant hues now lined the lakeshore, delighting tourists and locals alike.

"We'd better go change," the woman said. "We took your advice and made a reservation at The Landing tonight."

"Have a wonderful time," Lauren called as the couple made their way back to their cabin. She'd never been to the town's most extravagant restaurant, but she'd heard great things. Or maybe she *had* been to the restaurant and just couldn't remember. She gave her head a shake. It was so strange when your brain kept secrets from you.

She gave the boat a glance. The cabins would be full this weekend and someone would want to take a ride. She needed to gas it up but wasn't sure how. Likely, she'd been taught over the summer, but that was no help now. Tom and Tammy had taken their own trip to the mountains to enjoy the foliage and Meg was off-site today. Maybe Jonah would have a moment.

The idea didn't offend her as it would've several weeks ago. At six weeks removed from her accident, she still hadn't retrieved a single memory from the summer. But ever since witnessing Jonah's grief on the basketball court—and his subsequent apology—their relationship had shifted into new territory. They chatted easily and occasionally texted. She was beginning to see what she might've admired in him before—she just wasn't willing to pursue a romantic relationship with him now.

She whipped out her phone and sent him a text. *The motorboat needs gas. Do you have a minute to show me how?*

She stored the life vests under the bench seats, then returned to her cabin for a quick cup of coffee. By the time she was halfway finished, Jonah's text came in. *I can meet you at the dock in five.*

Sounds good. She fixed her ponytail and checked her minimal makeup in the mirror. What was she doing? She was only going to fill up the boat. Giving her head a sharp shake, she donned her shoes.

"You're staying here this time, buddy." She ruffled Graham's fur. The dog had been on the go with her all morning. "You need a nap."

She grabbed her phone and headed outside. The sun shone through the colorful canopy, dappling the ground with golden light. Minutes later she stepped from the shade just as a cloud moved over the sun, chilling the air.

When she reached the dock, Jonah was already standing at the end and staring over the lake, hands braced on his slim hips. She had to admit he cut a fine form in his snug faded jeans and sweatshirt. She could certainly see why that writer had been obsessed with him last week. Lauren had never been so glad for a guest's departure.

Her feelings on the subject were confusing—and not something she cared to explore on this beautiful October day.

The shaking of the pier gave away her arrival. Jonah turned, a welcoming smile curling his lips. "The colors are especially vibrant this year."

"They're beautiful all right. And we have eight cabins full of people coming this weekend to enjoy them."

"They're in for a treat." He assisted her into the boat.

"Sorry if you already showed me how to do this. Hope I didn't interrupt your studies."

"I don't mind showing you again. Good excuse to get out on the water."

They slipped on their vests. Then he took the captain's seat and started the motor. A moment later they were cutting through the choppy water, heading for the gas docks on the other side of the lake. At the steady pace he maintained, the trip would take about twenty minutes.

She was glad she'd put her hair back, though some strands had come loose and now fluttered around her jawline. Jonah's hair was too short to do much more than ruffle a bit. He'd shaved this morning and his jawline appeared as smooth as silk. She could almost feel the softness of his skin, the heat of his flesh, against the pads of her fingers. Her fingers twitched and she chalked it up to the forgotten archives in her brain.

Get a grip, Lauren.

She shifted to the view ahead of them. There weren't many boats out today—surprising since it was a Friday. But then it was only eleven. Anyway, she hardly minded that they had the lake mostly to themselves.

She cut a glance at Jonah, who navigated the narrow pass under the bridge with the confidence of a man who'd been boating his whole life. He was competent and hardworking. She could've admitted that even back in the early days, when she'd considered him a thorn in her side. He clearly loved the resort and anticipated the day he'd run it full-time. This was home for him.

"How's your schoolwork going?" she asked over the hum of the engine.

"Fine, I guess."

She knew from Meg that he was an A student. Learning came easily, but then he'd been raised in this business. He probably knew from experience the things most of the other students were learning from textbooks. "At least you're almost finished."

"December can't come soon enough." Before the words were out, he flinched.

She would be leaving in December, and that must hurt him a great deal. She didn't relish the thought of bringing him pain. He didn't deserve it. But there was nothing she could do—except change the subject.

"So what's up with the dinner napkins?" *That's the subject you choose?*

He glanced her way. "What?"

"I was looking through some things in my closet and came across a few dinner napkins."

His jaw clenched as he stared at the waterway ahead. For a moment she thought he wouldn't answer. "They're . . . souvenirs, I guess you'd say."

"Okay . . ."

His shoulders rose and fell on a sigh. "Our first real date was at Ollie's. When we got in the truck afterward, you realized you'd accidently grabbed the napkin along with your sweater. You kept it as a memento. So the next time we went to a restaurant with cloth napkins, I swiped one of them as sort of a joke."

"You stole a napkin," she accused.

"I left a big tip."

"And the napkin-swiping became a thing."

He gave a wistful smile. "Right."

A chill ran over her arms. But it wasn't because of their conversation. A thick gray cloud had rolled over the sun and the temperature quickly dropped.

Jonah glanced up at the sky, frowning. "I forgot to check the weather before we left."

"I checked earlier, but there was only a small chance of rain." One thing she'd learned though—thunderstorms seemed to crop up quickly around here.

A few droplets splattered her arms. A little rain was nothing to worry about. But the sky was darkening and that cloud coming over the mountains appeared more threatening than she'd like. "I guess that's why no one's out here today."

A low rumble sounded in the distance.

Jonah gave his head a shake, clearly berating himself. "We'd better head for shore." He throttled up and the boat took off, veering off to the right toward the closest shoreline. It was an uninhabited stretch of land. Since there wasn't a house for a good half mile in either direction, perhaps the property wasn't suitable for building.

The rain picked up and she watched the sky warily. A bolt of lightning cut through the clouds to their west.

Hurry, hurry.

But they were already headed full throttle toward shore. There was nothing else he could do. The rain became a deluge, dripping down her face and arms.

A minute or so later they neared the shore. But rather than pull up through the lily pads, he entered the mouth of a tributary she hadn't noticed at first as it was hidden by the draping foliage of a weeping willow. They ducked beneath it and the world dimmed and cooled in the shade of the forest. At least they were somewhat sheltered from the rain now.

He slowed the boat, following the stream into the woods. "There's an old trapper's cabin just up ahead—or at least there used to be. My dad and I came across it years ago when we were fishing."

She tried to wipe the rain from her face, but her hands were soaked. Jonah had fared no better. His sweatshirt clung to him like a second skin, and rivulets of water ran down his neck and under his shirt.

He shifted into neutral and guided the boat to a tiny pier jutting out from the grassy bank. When they neared it Lauren grabbed the line and jumped onto the rickety dock. She secured the boat.

They left their vests and dashed through the clearing to the trapper's cabin. The building was more of a shack, maybe ten by twelve, made of rough-hewn logs and covered with a tin roof. One small window was visible from the front. When they jumped up on the stoop, Lauren was glad for the shelter of a roof.

A crack of thunder reverberated through the valley. She wiped the water from her face and watched Jonah do the same. His hair was plastered to his head, his wet lashes clumped together. She surely looked just as ridiculous. But she was so relieved to be out of danger, she couldn't care less.

Their gazes connected and they burst out laughing.

"You look like a drowned rat," she said.

"I feel like one."

"We might as well have gone swimming."

"The lake water is probably warmer than the rain. At least we're safe." He glanced at her arms. "You're cold. Maybe there's firewood inside."

"If we can even get in."

He tried the door and found it unlocked. It gave an ancient groan as he swung it open. They entered to the smell of must and age and the cacophony of rain on the metal roof. Light from the lone window parted the gloom. The only furnishings were a rustic table with two chairs, a wooden bunk, and a fieldstone fireplace.

"Hallelujah," he said.

She spotted the stack of wood just as he did, her gaze homing in on an old pack of matches. "And a fire source too."

"Thank God. It's been a long time since I've tested my Boy Scout skills."

A smile lifted her lips at the thought of him as a boy earning his badges. "I'll bet you were a good one."

"An Eagle Scout, as a matter of fact." He leaned into the firebox. "Let's hope there's not a nest in the flue."

At the mention of critters she scanned the room, relieved to find no evidence of rodents. "How will we know?"

"The place will fill with smoke."

He looked up the chimney. "Great. Maybe we'll be subjected to all the elements today."

"I see daylight. That's good news." He started stacking the logs.

She spotted an empty cardboard box in the corner and tore it into pieces.

"Good thinking." He lit one of the sections and held it inside the fireplace. "Great news, the smoke's going up."

She handed him the rest of the cardboard. "Since you're the Boy Scout."

"The logs are pine and they're good and dry, so they should light easily." He stuffed the cardboard under the wood and lit them with a match. Moments later the pile caught fire. "Shouldn't take long to warm this place up."

They kicked off their shoes and set them on the low hearth. Thankfully, their socks were still dry.

Lauren glanced around, rubbing her chilled arms. "Who owns this place anyway?"

"It's state property, mostly just set aside to preserve nature. Otherwise, we humans tend to put up buildings on every square inch."

She walked to the gridded window. Outside the trees shimmied under the wind and rain pelted the ground. The sky was a gray abyss. "How long do you think the storm will last?"

"No idea." He pulled out his phone, and a moment later he frowned. "No reception."

She checked hers. "Me either." No surprise. "Everyone has checked in for the weekend except one couple coming from Maine."

"What's the name?"

"George and Alice Chaney."

"Ah, the Chaneys. They're regulars. They'll just head straight to their cabin when they arrive." Since they kept the cabins unlocked, that's what all the regulars did.

"Still, I wish we could get ahold of Meg."

"The guests will be fine. Anyway, I'm sure the storm will clear up soon."

She hoped he was right. The fire was burning strong now, crackling and popping.

"Too bad we don't have dry clothes. I'm soaked to the skin."

A moment later he whipped off his sweatshirt.

Lauren's heart faltered until she saw the T-shirt under it. He stripped off the white tee. "You can wear this. It's still dry."

She avoided staring at his chest. And those abs. How could her brain have forgotten those? Oh, he was holding out the shirt. "Uh, thanks."

He put the sweatshirt back on and turned purposely to face the fire. Right.

She moved back into the shadows of the room before she peeled off her soggy shirt and dropped it onto the bunk. Then she slipped on the dry tee that was still warm from Jonah's body. The raw male scent of him washed over her, triggering something. Not a memory. More like a feeling. Warm and safe and happy.

Home.

She cast a look at Jonah and, finding him still staring at the fire, she pulled the neckline up to her nose and drew in the scent of him. She wished she could bottle it up and take it home with her. How could a scent she'd never smelled before warm her from the inside out?

Feeling shaken at the thought, she grabbed her wet shirt and strolled back to the fire. She hung it from a couple rusted nails someone had pounded into the stone mortar, feeling his appraisal.

"Better?" he asked.

"Much. Thank you."

"You're practically swimming in that thing."

The shirt hung to her thighs, swallowing her. "It's dry. That's all that matters."

"Doesn't sound like it's slowing up out there. Might as well get comfortable." He pulled the chairs over by the fire.

They sat side by side, a warm golden glow lighting the space. The crackling fire and patter on the roof somehow made the room feel smaller. They were alone and she was snuggled up in his warm and yummy-smelling shirt. Lauren crossed her arms over her chest, a flimsy barrier against the intimacy of the situation.

They'd been very intimate at one time, whether she remembered it or not. How much had she told him about her childhood? It wasn't the first time she'd wondered. It wouldn't change anything if she asked the question.

"I've been wondering . . ."

After a moment he glanced her way, patient and waiting.

"Did I ever tell you about my childhood? You know, back when we were . . . together?"

His eyes were steady on her. "Sure. You told me everything."

"Everything, meaning . . ."

"I know about your mom leaving—moving out of state—with some random guy when you were five. That you never heard from her after that." His voice rumbled low and slow. "You told me your mom never knew who your father was. I know about the day you were taken away and put into foster care. You had brief stays in three good homes and four stays in not-so-good homes. I know about the rebellious period that ended when your tenth-grade English teacher convinced you that you were only hurting yourself and that if you wanted to get anywhere in life, you needed to make some changes."

She fought the urge to turtle beneath the collar of his T-shirt. He probably knew about much more than that. Had she told him about the Stinsons, who'd viewed her and their other fosters as a paycheck? About Dillon, the foster brother who'd later bullied her for over a year? And what about Erik Fordham, the foster father whose advances she'd narrowly escaped when she was fourteen?

"You told me all of it."

Shame filled her, forcing her to look away. The shame of having no parents, no family who loved her. The shame of all her belongings fitting into a kitchen-sized garbage bag. The shame of being a year behind in school because of all the moving. It filled her like a heat lamp, burning through her limbs and singeing her cheeks.

She pulled herself tall and jutted her chin as she'd done all those times when she felt less than. "Right."

"And I'll tell you now what I told you then." Jonah waited until she met his gaze. "None of it was your fault. You were just a child and the adults around you didn't take care of you the way they should've."

This whole subject took her back to that feeling of being trapped. Of having no say in her own life. Of being subject to whatever the adults in charge wanted. She would never feel that way again.

"You were powerless." His voice rumbled in his chest. "But you're not now. Look how far you've come, Lauren. I'm amazed by your tenacity and your resilience. I admire you so much."

Her first instinct was to brush off his praise. But she'd been working on that. She recognized the authenticity that shone from his eyes and allowed herself to drink in the compliment. "Thank you for saying that."

He nudged her shoulder. "And since you're probably feeling vulnerable because of what I know about you . . . you should know that I told you private things too."

She gave a wry laugh. "Yeah, but I don't remember any of them."

"So let's level the playing field."

She smirked, imagining his biggest life trauma might be placing second for homecoming king.

"My mother died in a car accident when I was four."

She whipped her head around to him, her smirk falling away. "But . . ."

"Tammy's technically my aunt. My biological mother was Tom's sister."

She reared back. She sure hadn't seen that coming. So much for those dusty archives in her brain.

"We lived in an apartment in Portsmouth, but I barely remember it. I remember a little about my mother, though sometimes I'm not sure if I only think I remember. Mom and Dad have told me so many stories, trying to keep her memory alive for me."

"What about your father?"

"Apparently he took off when my mom announced her pregnancy."

"I had no idea. You Landrys seem like such a close-knit family."

"We are. They're my parents. I'm their son. Meg's my sister. They were well into their thirties by the time I came along and certain they couldn't have kids of their own. When Mom got pregnant with Meg, it was quite the surprise."

Lauren could hardly take it in. She'd thought Jonah had it so easy being raised here in this quaint little town at a family-owned resort. She'd thought him privileged. And maybe that had come to be the case later. But he'd had a rough beginning.

"Was I this shocked the first time you told me?"

He chuckled. "Yes." His smile slipped as his expression warmed. "But it's only fair you know all my stuff too. And I can relate—just a little—to not quite feeling like you belong. Mom and Dad are really the only parents I remember. But Meg is theirs biologically. Sometimes I wonder if they view me different than her."

Lauren shook her head. "I don't believe that."

"I think Mom might've been happier if Meg had decided to take over the resort—it passed down from her side of the family. It isn't *my* family's history."

"But Meg loves what she does. And family is a lot more than blood— trust me, I would know."

"Fair point."

"You should tell them how you feel. Get it out in the open."

He glanced down at his hands. "I wouldn't want to put them on the spot. Or seem ungrateful for all they've done."

Lauren got the feeling he was really afraid of finding out his fears were true. But she suspected they weren't. "The Landrys are your family in every way that matters. They obviously love you very much."

"Oh, I know that. I guess the mind plays games sometimes."

It was true. Right now hers was telling her that Jonah knew her much better than she knew him. She must've trusted him implicitly to have divulged her painful past. Sydney was the only other person in which she'd confided— and that had taken three years of friendship and two glasses of merlot.

What kind of magic did Jonah possess to have worked his way into her heart so quickly?

CHAPTER 20

JONAH WOULD'VE WALKED across hot coals to put Lauren at ease. Relaying his own history didn't cost him a thing. He'd mostly come to grips with his unconventional family long ago. But doing so had seemingly given her the security she sought.

He tried not to stare at her, but it was hard not to when she was so beautiful. And seeing her in his shirt gave him some kind of primitive thrill. The firelight licked her delicate features, giving her face a golden glow. He knew every curve, every slope of that face. He'd traced it with his eyes, with his fingertips. He knew the softness of her fine hair, the taste of her perfect lips, and the sound of her breathy sigh.

And all of that was off-limits to him now.

God help him. He fisted his hands to keep from reaching out and touching her. She'd fly across the room, and the last thing he wanted was to scare her away when they were finally communicating.

Thunder rumbled through the room, rattling the windowpane. He ran his hand through his wet hair. His cowlick was probably sticking up. One of the reasons he'd let it grow out was so that he could control it.

"When did you cut your hair and shave your bushy beard?" Lauren asked, as if reading his thoughts.

"Back in June, I guess." He arched a brow. "Miss it?"

She rolled her eyes. "I was just going to congratulate you on your excellent decision."

He rubbed his bare jaw. He'd stopped shaving when Monica left. Just didn't feel like bothering. Okay, maybe he'd been a little depressed.

She shot him a quick look, eyes teasing. "You did it for me, didn't you?"

"Absolutely not."

She laughed. "You did too."

"Did not."

"All right, Pinocchio, whatever you say. Tell me who the Joneses are."

"What?"

"Mr. Jones and his *unwife* . . . ?"

He chuckled. "Oh, them. Who told you about that?"

"You mentioned them in one of your notes."

He dropped his head back. "Ahh." So along with the dinner napkins, she'd found his notes. He used to leave them on her deck railing, weighed down with a rock or a coffee. What other keepsakes might she have stumbled upon?

"*Hello?* Mr. and Mrs. Jones?"

"They were a couple who came to stay for a few days back in, let's see, I think it was July. He left behind an expensive pair of sunglasses—you knew the brand name—and you called to let him know. You were gonna ship them, but for some reason you didn't have an address on file."

She leaned forward, peering at him, and a damp strand of pale blonde hair fell forward.

He resisted the urge to tuck it behind her ear. "Anyway, when Mrs. Jones answered his cell phone, you explained what had happened." He lifted a brow. "Unfortunately, it wasn't Mrs. Jones who had accompanied him on the trip."

Lauren gasped.

147

"The real Mrs. Jones thought he'd been at a podiatrist convention in Boston."

"Oh no. What did I do?"

"You apologized profusely and promised to smash the sunglasses to smithereens."

Lauren laughed. "I did not."

"You absolutely did. She was pretty upset, but you took the time to talk to her. She'd had her suspicions and it was the last straw for her. She said she was gonna leave him."

"I feel so awful."

"You felt terrible at the time too. But you weren't the one in the wrong."

"Did she ask me about the woman?"

"I don't think so. She probably already knew who it was."

"Remind me to never call a guest about something they've left behind."

"That's actually a good takeaway."

"Did you suspect when they were here that she was his mistress?"

"I wasn't around much that week."

An easy silence passed as Lauren warmed her hands in front of the fire. "How did we become a couple?"

He barely stopped himself from rearing back at the question. She'd been pretty careful to avoid the subject. Maybe she was just tired of not knowing. Or maybe, now that she knew him better, she wondered how in the world she'd ever fallen in love with him.

Currently she avoided eye contact, as if afraid of engaging too much. "Is it painful to talk about?"

"No." A smile formed of its own volition. "It was the best summer of my life. I guess it started when I apologized and started treating you like I should've. Your guard was still up for a while, but it slowly came down as you began to trust me. We became friends, I guess you could say."

"But you're my boss."

"It didn't take me long to see you as much more than a valuable employee," he said dryly.

Her throat dipped with a swallow. "Then what?" she asked, almost reluctantly.

He decided to lighten the moment. "Oh, you know. I used my charm and charisma to win you over."

She snorted.

"You just snorted."

"I don't *snort*."

"I didn't think so either, but I know what I heard."

She laughed. "You need to have your ears checked."

The lilting sound of her laughter made his heart grow two sizes. "Now who's lying?"

She went suddenly still. "Hey . . . listen. The rain stopped."

She was right. Only the sound of the crackling fire was left.

They both got up and went to peek out the window. The gray clouds had drifted away, and the sun was trying to come out. Water dripped only from the trees and from the overhang of the roof.

Jonah glanced around the cabin, a little sad to leave their private little nest behind.

"We should put out the fire and be on our way," she said.

Over the next few minutes they worked together to smolder the flames, playfully nudging each other out of the way. Warmth unrelated to the fire filled him from the inside out, bringing with it a burgeoning hope he couldn't have tamped down if he tried. And he didn't want to. This time alone with her had meant everything to him. She'd dropped her guard and been willing to talk about their relationship. It was a huge step forward.

"It's good to hear you laugh again," he said before he could stop himself.

She tossed a smile his way as they sat to put on their shoes. "You're not half bad to be around when you're not barking out orders."

When her shoes were on, she grabbed her damp shirt and headed for the door while he set the screen in front of the smoldering logs.

"Hey, Wentworth," he called.

On the threshold she turned with an expectant look.

"I did cut my hair for you."

She beamed as she slapped the doorframe. "I knew it!"

Jonah's easy laugher echoed through the cabin.

CHAPTER 21

"I HAVE TO tell her," Jonah said to Meg the minute he returned from gassing up the boat with Lauren. The whole ride back he'd thought about Lauren and their time at the trapper's cabin. She was opening herself to a friendship with him, and while that made him optimistic, it also made him feel guilty.

"You'll have to be more specific." Meg didn't glance up from the computer screen.

"Lauren. I have to tell her she gave up that job in Boston."

Meg's fingers froze on the keyboard as she looked his way. "I was wondering when you'd get around to that."

"It's been six weeks and I have to face facts—she might never get her memory back." Verbalizing the thought caused a physical ache in his chest.

Meg's eyes softened. "But aren't the two of you getting along better? Don't you think maybe . . . ?"

"Getting along is a far cry from where we were before." He glanced upstairs, where he'd tucked away Lauren's engagement ring in his parents' safe. He'd grown tired of seeing it every time he opened his nightstand drawer.

"There's still a chance she'll fall in love with you again."

"I guess. But she's been curious lately about what happened over the summer, and she deserves to know the full truth."

"But if she finds out she gave up that job—which is the only reason she's here—what's to stop her from leaving now?"

Yeah, that was the kicker. She would be devastated about that job. Over the past six weeks she'd gotten comfortable at the resort and excited about the barn renovation. But he wouldn't kid himself. She was a city girl at heart, and without those feelings of love rooting her here, he didn't stand a chance of keeping her till the end of the year.

Much less forever.

"I know the risks. But even though her memory's still gone, her concussion symptoms have faded. I can't justify keeping the truth from her any longer."

"She's gonna be really upset."

"I know." She'd probably blame him. Hate him. All the progress he'd made toward winning her over would be forfeited. He'd be back to square one—if not worse. But he couldn't keep the truth from her any longer in the hopes her memory would return and make the disclosure unnecessary. It wasn't fair to her.

"When are you telling her?"

He should tell her now—just get it over with. But it wouldn't be fair to dump it on her at the start of a busy weekend when they were full up. Better to wait until her day off. "Monday." He swallowed hard. "Do you think she'll go back to Boston?"

"I don't know. I mean . . . she won't have a job to return to. At least she's got this one for now."

"True." It wasn't the way he wanted her to stay, but at this point he'd accept any reason that kept her here. Was that selfish? Maybe. But she'd once been happy here, happy with him. Even if she didn't remember it.

"Heartbreak aside, if she left it would put us in a real bind around here."

That was the least of his concerns. "I'd gladly drop my classes and take over."

"I'm not sure Mom would agree to that."

"Maybe Dad could persuade her. She needs to understand that this is where I want to be."

"You only have a couple months until graduation. She agreed to let you take over at that point, and she never goes back on her word."

"I'm counting on that." There was precious little he could count on right now with his future so up in the air. His nerves rattled as his thoughts turned to that conversation he needed to have with Lauren on Monday.

"I'll be praying it goes well. Is there anything else I can do?"

"Just be there for her, I guess. She probably won't want anything to do with me after this." He wished he'd told her sooner. But he'd been legitimately concerned about her mental health after that panic attack in the hospital. And then he'd foolishly counted on her memory returning.

He might've lost her forever.

CHAPTER 22

June 10

LAUREN'S DAY OFF found her sitting on her deck with her laptop. With her cabin on the far side of the property, the guests didn't wander out her way too often. She might just have to stop by the Hollandsworths' cabin today though. They had the cutest goldendoodle puppy. Maybe she could talk Jonah into getting a resort mascot. Perhaps that was short-sighted since she'd only be here through the end of the year, but it would be nice to have a little company in her room at night.

The early morning's coolness had given way to late-morning heat, but the forest's shade kept her adequately cooled. The tweeting of birds, nattering of squirrels, and occasional drone of a boat motor were pleasant backdrops to her work.

She'd finally settled on a structural engineer to assess the barn. The company had wonderful reviews and reasonable rates, and it would be able to do the job quickly. She was now focused on finding contractors for the renovation—presuming the engineer found the building structurally sound. There were a lot of pieces to the project, and it would be a tight timeline, but she was eager to see it through.

She was researching painters when the sound of someone approaching had her glancing up from her laptop.

Jonah.

She hadn't recognized him at first. His long dark hair had been cropped into a stylish cut, short on the sides, a little longer on top. But as he neared it was his lower face that captured her attention. His jawline turned with masculine angles.

And his lips—he had very nice lips, in fact. The bottom one was almost plump and the indent on the top one was the size and shape of her fingertips. And to think he'd covered all of those beautiful features with that awful mustache and big, bushy beard!

Those nice lips curled into a smile. "I've never seen you speechless before, Wentworth."

"I didn't recognize you! Someone visited the barbershop."

"I had an opening in my schedule."

They'd just talked about his lumberjack look in the barn three days ago. She suspected she had something to do with this sudden change. "Is that right?"

"That's my story." He glanced at her laptop. "What are you up to?"

She allowed the change in subject but had a little trouble pulling her gaze from that newly excavated face. "Pulling some things together for the barn. I found and scheduled a structural engineer and now I'm researching contractors."

"Isn't this your day off?"

"This isn't work. It's fun. But you have to keep paying me. Have a seat if you aren't busy." Meg or Tammy usually managed the resort on Lauren's day off, but Jonah pitched in too.

"Don't mind if I do." The Adirondack chair squawked as he sat beside her. "It's been pretty quiet around here today. I got some wood chopped and fixed the leg on the Ping-Pong table."

"I didn't know it was broken."

"I guess it happened over the weekend."

"Nobody said anything."

"That happens sometimes." Jonah peered at her for a long moment. "So tell me about this job you have waiting for you in Boston at the first of the year. I understand the owner is an old friend of my mom's."

"They went to college together, apparently."

"Ah, right. My mom dropped out after her freshman year when she met my dad."

"Okay. Well, her friend Olivia Stafford is now Boston's premier event planner and the CEO of Glitter. I met her when I worked for a caterer they utilize. She has a planner retiring at the end of the year, and that's basically my dream job. She suggested I get some experience in the meantime, and the job would be waiting for me when I return."

"Event planner . . . Is that corporate stuff mostly?"

"Exactly. They do everything from political fundraisers to corporate conferences."

"I'm starting to see where your passion for this barn venue comes from. What made you want to be an event planner?"

She smiled at the memory his question invoked. "When I was a sophomore in high school, I was invited to a sweet-sixteen party of this wealthy classmate. We weren't close or anything, but the whole class was invited. It was amazing. While all the other girls were going gaga over each other's dresses, I couldn't peel my eyes from the spectacular venue, the amazing decorations, and the acres of food. I'd never been to a party like that. It was quite the production.

"And then I saw this woman in a red wrap dress and realized she was running the whole show. She had a headset on and I just observed her, cool and confident, overseeing every detail from food presentation to service to music and announcements. It was the first time I realized that behind a successful party was a lot of structure and a very savvy person running the whole show."

"And you wanted to run the show."

"I so wanted to run the show! I did some research and found out what it would take to get that job, and that's what I've spent the past seven years of my life doing."

"You needed a bachelor's degree."

"You can become an event planner without a degree. But I wanted to work for the best—and Glitter requires a degree in hospitality management."

"I admire your ambition."

She tossed him a glance and got caught up staring at that face. "Really?"

"It's very attractive. Does that surprise you?"

She huffed. "Most of the men I've been around consider it more of a *de*traction."

"I admire people who have goals and go after them—men *and* women. And speaking of goals, you've been in New Hampshire for three months, and as far as I know you haven't even left Pinehaven. The state might not have much in the way of art museums or theater, but we have natural attractions that are a real treat for the senses. What would you think about heading up to Flume Gorge?"

She'd seen the granite gorge in brochures and had even recommended it to guests. "When?"

"Now, unless you have something better to do."

"Don't you have to oversee things here?"

"Meg's in the office. She won't mind taking the reins."

"Oh." The trail was over an hour away. The thought of spending the afternoon with Jonah made her a little giddy. It was certainly more tempting than the chores she'd been planning to catch up on.

"Do you like to hike?"

"I have no idea."

"Well, it's not too rigorous and the mountains are beautiful. It'd be a shame if you came to New Hampshire and never visited the White Mountains."

Good point. Plus there was that whole giddy thing. The hopeful smile he sent her way was her undoing. "All right. But I'm paying my own way."

"Deal."

AN hour later they were well on their way, chattering about this and that on the drive. Jonah shared a bit about his mom's reluctance to believe he truly wanted to run the resort. He'd also mentioned that Tom and Tammy were actually his aunt and uncle who'd adopted him after his mom passed. He mentioned it so offhandedly, but it surprised her. But then most people probably wouldn't guess she'd been raised in foster care.

That was the goal—to rise above her upbringing, such as it was.

She was becoming comfortable with Jonah. He was easy to talk to. He was smart and funny—and she couldn't stop herself from stealing glances at his freshly shaven face. Who knew there were such attractive features under all that hair? Not that his appearance mattered. They were friends and it had been a long time since she'd had a male friend.

The drive passed so quickly that she was surprised when they turned into the parking lot. After buying tickets they entered the forest, walking side by side on the wide pebbled path. It was quiet back in the woods except for tweeting birds and an occasional rustle in the underbrush. They'd only passed one couple so far. Hemlock trees stretched to the sky above them. The earthy scents of pine and decaying wood filled her nostrils, and soon the distant sound of rushing water reached her ears.

As they hiked down a slope, a red covered bridge came into view and she gasped.

"You can't come to New Hampshire without seeing at least one."

She stopped and snapped a photo. "I have to send this to Sydney. She loves to paint covered bridges."

"Run up ahead and I'll get one with you in it."

She handed him her phone and ran down to pose in front of the bridge. A minute later he met her on the boardwalk where she snapped a shot of the creek running beneath the bridge. The water tumbled over boulders, making the most relaxing sound.

"Just listen to that," she said. "I need that sound effect on my phone."

"Technology can't quite capture it."

As they moved on, past Table Rock, the sound of rushing water grew louder. Then the trail opened to the bottom of the gorge. A narrow board-walk protruded from a granite cliff, ascending from the floor of the ravine. The granite walls shimmered with dampness, and moss clung to their faces like green whiskers. The narrow creek tumbled downhill over boulders, and mist hung in the air all around them, making the boardwalk slick. The roar of the waterfall made conversation almost impossible.

They followed the boardwalk upward, admiring the views. Then finally they reached the upper end of the gorge where Avalanche Falls cascaded some forty-five feet into the ravine below. She snapped shots of the beautiful sight, including one of Jonah leaning on the rails, taking in the panorama.

Once she finished taking pictures, they continued until they reached the top of the gorge. Her thighs were burning, and her lungs struggled for breath, but it had been worth the journey.

She paused at the top and perched her hands on her hips, glad she'd worn her hair in a ponytail. Jonah didn't seem out of breath, but he stopped and took in the scenery.

"That was really cool," she called over the roar. "Now when I recom-mend a visit to Flume Gorge, I'll know whereof I speak."

"We're lucky we practically have it to ourselves today. On summer weekends it's almost as crowded as an amusement park."

They'd only passed a few families along the way, and now not a soul was in sight. She was glad he'd suggested this little outing. She might never find herself back in New Hampshire. She should soak it in while she was here.

They continued on the trail, passing through forests thick with trees and the smell of pine. "I'll bet this is beautiful in the fall."

"The White Mountains are popular that time of year. Did you know the Appalachian Trail runs across the state?"

"I learned that a few weeks ago. We had a couple guests who were planning to hike a section of it. Have you ever been on it?"

"I hiked the New Hampshire portion with some friends the summer after I graduated. My mom was hoping I'd change my mind and go to college."

"I guess she had her way after all."

"She means well."

"Do you like to travel?"

"I love it. My friend Javi and I used to take at least a couple trips in the winter. But then I started taking classes and he got married. We went to Miami, New Orleans, San Diego, Seattle—"

"So you're a city boy at heart."

He gave a wry grin. "Not by a long shot. Love to visit but wouldn't want to live there."

Exactly how she was coming to feel about the backwoods of New Hampshire.

They passed a wooden shelter with a bench and continued on through the forest until they came to an overlook jutting out beside the path. They headed toward it and stopped at the split-rail fence.

Just beyond the railing the ground dropped away, and over the tree-tops below, the distant mountain range hunkered on the horizon. Clouds hovered overhead, casting cotton ball–shaped shadows on the mountains.

"Beautiful." She snapped a couple photos.

He stepped back and took one of her taking a photo. "Turn around."

She did as he suggested and gave a cheesy smile.

He laughed. "Now a real one."

She complied. Then he joined her at the railing and she pocketed her phone and let herself just be in the moment. It was something she'd been working on since she'd been here. She tended to hyperfocus on her job. When she wasn't working, she was making plans. Something about the resort, the slower pace, and the nature surrounding her had made her realize she should stop and soak in the moment every now and then. Live. Breathe.

She feasted on the view. Inhaled the scent of pine. Gloried in the cool breeze sweeping across the valley. It was all so beautiful. Everything in view was God-made, not man-made. Completely opposite of the balcony view she'd had in Boston. A few months ago she might've knocked this rural vista, but she was coming to appreciate nature, coming to have a different perspective.

Oh, she was still a city girl. She loved Boston. But even a city girl could take a trip to the mountains and enjoy the change of pace.

Jonah leaned his forearms on the fence rail. "I think this is the first time I've ever seen you just being still."

"I'm not very good at it."

"Practice makes perfect."

"I had a foster mom who always said that." The words popped out before she could censor them.

He studied her for a long moment.

Her face heated, but she resisted the urge to squirm.

"Foster mom?"

There was no taking it back now. "I was in the system for a while." He wasn't getting any more than that. She never brought up her childhood. It made people see her differently, like some kind of underdog. Some kind of pitiful project.

"Must've been difficult."

"It made me stronger." That's what she told herself. And it was the truth.

He set his fingers on the tattoo at her wrist, his touch stirring every skin cell to life. "Is that what this is all about?"

Most people didn't recognize the fawohodie symbol. They assumed it was some kind of simplified butterfly.

"I looked it up. *The desire to chart one's own course or determine one's own fate.*"

161

"Right." She shifted her weight. She usually just told people it meant independence. His knowing the more specific definition made her uncomfortable. She hoped he wouldn't press her about it. She hadn't much enjoyed her childhood, and she sure wasn't interested in reliving it.

"You're strong and ambitious," he said. "I have a feeling you'll reach all the goals you set for yourself."

Relieved he'd shifted the subject, she smiled at him. "I won't stop until I do."

"I'll just bet you won't."

Their gazes met and clung. They were closer than she'd realized, their shoulders touching. His fingertips lingered on her wrist. In the shade of the trees, his eyes were the color of worn denim. They softened as the moment hung, suspended and mesmerizing. Awareness crackled between them.

His attention dropped to her mouth and her lips tingled with want. She leaned forward.

Or he did.

Somehow they met in the middle and his lips brushed hers, gentle and warm. Her skin hummed at the touch.

He lingered there for just a breath, then brushed her lips again. Testing, searching.

She tilted her head and returned the kiss because she couldn't *not*. His lips were perfect, his kiss drawing her out. It was a giving kind of kiss, not a taking kind. She hadn't realized there was a difference until now.

It was soft and slow and still somehow managed to send her nervous system into overdrive. Her heart was about to leap from her chest and her body buzzed with want. She held herself back—just barely—from drawing closer. She wanted to feel his chest pressed against her. She wanted to touch that freshly shaven jaw and see if his skin felt like velvet.

What was she doing? He was a friend. He was her *boss*. She shouldn't develop feelings for someone she couldn't have. She had a job waiting in

Boston and she was only here through December. The reasons this kiss was a bad idea just kept coming.

As if sensing her resistance, he ended the kiss. But he didn't move away. Their breaths mingled between them.

She kept her eyes closed, unwilling to let go of the magical moment just yet. "I'm leaving at the end of the year."

"December's a long way off. And those were *some* sparks."

She couldn't argue with either of those sentiments. Air stirred between them. She opened her eyes and found his half-lidded gaze as sexy as anything she'd ever seen. But she didn't need a distraction from her work. From her goals. She'd come too far to be thrown off course by an attractive boss. "This is a bad idea."

He blinked and that sexy look was gone, replaced by an expression far less threatening. He put space between them. Turned to lean back against the railing, as casual as a backyard barbecue. "Can I tell you what I'm thinking?"

"Sure. Go for it."

"We haven't talked much about our previous relationships, but my last one was pretty serious and ended with her leaving for greener pastures."

Lauren widened her eyes as she gestured toward herself. *"Hello . . . ?"*

He chuckled. "Yes, but I *know* you're leaving and therefore won't let myself get carried away. The natural deadline will keep us both in check."

"I see."

"So here's what I'm thinking. What about a nice, casual, lighthearted summer romance? We go out to eat, have coffee, enjoy each other's company. It could be fun." He quirked a brow. "You know . . . that state of being that results in pleasure and gratification . . ."

She gave him the side-eye. "I know what fun is."

"All work and no play . . ."

She was catching the drift. Something like he was describing wouldn't be such a horrible thing, would it? She'd been so focused on her goals, and because of that she was terribly lacking in experience. This might be good for her. Jonah, it turned out, was kind, fun to be with, and very attractive. Not to mention quite the good kisser. She could stand more of those kisses.

"I could show you more of New Hampshire, help you make the most of your time here. Plus, I really want to kiss you again."

Her lips twitched. At least she wasn't the only one whose lips still prickled with want. Still, there was that other thing. "There is the little matter of you being my boss."

"I am your boss—when we're working. When we're not, you're the boss."

"Really?"

"Well . . . the boss of you."

She could live with that. Couldn't she? It might be kinda fun to have a summer romance. She hadn't been on a date in almost a year. "Nothing serious though."

"Serious is the last thing I want."

"We'd keep things light and breezy."

"Good words, *light and breezy*."

She thought for a moment, the idea holding more appeal than she'd like to admit. "I suppose we could try it out, do some sightseeing, see where it leads."

He gave her a playful look. "Will it lead to another kiss?"

"Is that all you can think about?"

"What can I say? You have me hooked. But hey, the ball's in your court, Wentworth. I've done enough talking. What do *you* want?"

She liked his style. He was up-front. He'd laid out his thoughts, his hopes, and waited for her weigh-in. To make the final call. It was empowering. It might seem a simple thing, but in her experience, it was not the norm.

Because of that—and because she couldn't get that amazing kiss out of her head—she turned a smile on him. "I guess another kiss wouldn't hurt anything."

"I'll take it." He leaned forward and kissed her again.

He explored her lips while his fingers brushed the sensitive spot on her inner wrist. Then he cradled her face and wreaked havoc on her mouth. Warmth rushed from the middle out like an epicenter. It trickled through her limbs and into her hands.

Oh, he was *good*.

He pulled away too soon. His eyes smoldered a second before they shuttered with a blink. Then they sparkled with humor. "Is that a yes?"

Light and breezy. Natural deadline. Amazing kisses. "I think it is."

His smile widened. "It's gonna be a good summer."

"We'll see about that."

He grabbed her hand and gave it a tug. They started back down the trail, her legs wobbling—and not from the hike. "Before this goes any further, I have a very important question to ask you."

"Sounds weighty."

"The weightiest of weighty."

"Go for it."

"Okay, here goes . . . Would you have kissed me if I still had my beard?"

"I'm not sure I could've located your lips."

His laugher filled the forest.

CHAPTER 23

Present day

HER TIME WITH Jonah at the trapper's cabin earlier had left Lauren shaken. She was beginning to understand how she'd become so side-tracked this summer. He was charming and appealing in all the ways that mattered. She'd taken a misguided step, and before she knew it she was sliding down a slippery slope.

Upon her return to the resort, she poured herself into work. The guests had checked out, leaving the cabins vacant until the weekend guests arrived later today. She double-checked the cabins after the cleaners left and found that firewood needed restocking as well as other odds and ends that kept her on the move. Also, the same storm that had stranded Jonah and her at the shack had strewn debris all over the grounds. She gathered branches and twigs and hauled them to the burn pile. Then she swept the decks of the vacant cabins.

It was late afternoon by the time she finished. She'd missed lunch, so she returned to her cabin with Graham. After filling his dish with fresh water, she fixed herself a sandwich, her future job with Glitter heavy on her mind.

She hadn't checked in with Olivia since her accident. And who knew when she'd last called the CEO prior to her concussion? She checked her watch. Friday afternoon wasn't the ideal time to call a woman in charge of an event-planning organization.

But Lauren needed this. She needed a reminder of her dream. Needed to stay focused on her goals—and not on her all-too-appealing boss. She'd already been close to giving up everything for him once. She wouldn't be so foolish this time around.

She wolfed down her sandwich, eager to speak with Olivia again, then tapped on the woman's name in her Contacts. Her personal assistant, Shayla, answered the phone and notified Lauren that Olivia was in a meeting but that she'd have Olivia return her call.

"Tell her there's no hurry," Lauren said. "I'm just checking in."

"Will do."

Lauren ended the call and gave Graham some affection. She probably wouldn't hear from the woman until next week. "Well, that's a start, I guess. Let's go clean off the deck, huh, boy?"

She grabbed the broom and headed outside with Graham. The mums in her window boxes were bright and happy from the rainfall. She swept the debris from her deck and furniture and decided the chairs needed a good cleaning too. She was almost done with the task when her phone vibrated in her pocket.

It was Olivia. That the CEO was returning her call so quickly made Lauren a little heady. Like maybe she was anticipating Lauren's upcoming employment as much as Lauren was.

She answered the call. "Olivia, hello. How are you?"

"I'm fine, thank you. How are you?"

"Doing well." She wouldn't go into her accident/concussion. The whole traumatic-brain-injury thing was not a good look for a future employee. "The weeks are passing quickly. The job here at the resort is going very well—I think the Landrys are pleased—and I'm certainly learning a lot."

"Well . . . I'm glad to hear it." There was almost a question in her reply, as if she was uncertain why Lauren might be calling.

Maybe Lauren had reached out to Olivia shortly before her accident and it was too soon to call again. "Well, I don't want to keep you. I know you're busy. I just wanted to check in. January will be here before we know it."

A long pause followed. So long, Lauren feared she'd lost connection. "Olivia? Are you still there?"

"Um . . . yes, I'm here."

"As you can imagine, the signal out here isn't the best. You can drop a call right in the middle of town even."

"I'm afraid I'm a little confused, Lauren. When we spoke last . . ."

Trepidation niggled at the back of her neck. She wished she could remember that conversation. "Yes?"

"Lauren . . . I'm not sure why you're checking in with me at all since you passed on the job."

Passed on the job? Lauren's breath tumbled from her lungs. Her grip tightened on the phone. *"What?"*

"Your call back in August . . . You were very clear about staying in Pinehaven."

"I was . . . ?" *No.* She had not given up that job. It wasn't possible. She had to take it all back! If only her lungs were functioning properly. "Listen, Olivia, I should explain. I don't even remember making that call. I had an accident in September that resulted in a concussion. My entire summer is gone. There's a four-month memory gap."

Another long pause followed. "You don't remember calling me?"

"I don't remember anything that happened from May to September seventh when the accident occurred."

"My goodness. I'm so sorry that happened to you. Are you all right?"

"I'm fine now—except for those lost memories. But the important thing is that I still want that job very much. I can't imagine what I must've been thinking to give it up. Have you already found a replacement?"

"Oh dear. What a mess. I've been interviewing for the position, and yes, I've found a capable candidate. I've all but promised her the job."

Lauren grimaced. No, she couldn't lose her dream job this way. "I'm so sorry for the confusion. I have to ask—is there any chance you'd still consider me for the position?" She pressed her palm against her chest and waited, each second drawing out like a terrible nightmare.

"This is very unexpected, Lauren. To be honest I'm a little caught off guard. And I have a meeting in just a few minutes."

"I understand. Would you at least think it over? I have every intention of returning to Boston as soon as I've filled my commitment here. The position at Glitter would still be the ideal situation for me."

A sigh sounded through the phone. "All right, I'll think about it over the weekend and call you back early next week. I can't make any promises."

"I understand. Thank you so much."

Lauren disconnected the call, her thoughts whirling. She'd given up her dream job—and she might not get it back! Sydney had told her she'd been considering it, but Lauren never dreamed she'd actually turned down the job! Positions rarely became available at Glitter, and for good reason. And now she might have burnt her bridge with the CEO of the company.

She sucked in a deep breath, but her lungs wouldn't seem to fill all the way. Her pulse raced. Heart thumped. Panic swept over her, enshrouding her with a sense of impending doom.

She was dying—or something even worse. She paced the length of the deck, trying to distract herself from the awful sensations lighting up every nerve cell in her body. Graham whined, but she couldn't think of anything but the horrible anxiety strangling her like a malignant weed.

Breathe. Just breathe. It'll pass.

This had happened at the hospital. Carson had helped her. She struggled to remember. Slow breaths. Counting.

She slowed her breaths and counted backward from one hundred. Ninety-nine. Ninety-eight. Ninety-seven. Ninety-six.

But still, thoughts crashed in. She was counting on that job. It was the only reason she was here. And she'd already signed a lease for an expensive studio apartment near Glitter's headquarters. Would she be able to get out of it? She wouldn't be able to afford it without that big salary.

"Lauren?" Meg approached from the direction of the lodge. "You okay?"

Lauren nodded but continued pacing and counting. *Please, God. Please, God.*

"What's wrong?"

She finished the inhale. "Pa—panic attack."

"Oh, honey. What can I do?"

Lauren shook her head. The shroud of panic was slowly receding. She continued counting, blocking out Meg and Graham. In two . . . three . . . four, hold two . . . three . . . four . . . out two . . . three . . . four.

It's okay. It's passing. You're gonna be fine.

A few minutes drew out, slow and agonizing. Then finally the anxiety was gone, leaving her feeling like a fruit loop under Meg's concerned gaze. Her face heated. "I'm fine now. It's over."

"Are you sure? Sit down. Let me get you something to drink." Meg passed her and headed into the cabin.

Lauren was grateful for a minute alone. She had to shake that panic attack. While she liked Meg a lot, they hadn't yet returned to the intimate friendship they'd apparently shared over the summer.

Something popped into her mind. *August*, Olivia had said. Lauren had given up the position in August. That meant at least a week—and possibly a whole month—had passed from the time she'd called Olivia until her accident had happened. Surely, if she and Jonah were as serious as she'd been told, she would've informed him. He had to know she'd given up that job.

And he hadn't said a word.

She gritted her teeth. All this time, all these weeks, and he hadn't told her that everything she'd been working toward was gone. Heat flushed through her body until her muscles quivered. She had a few things to say to Jonah Landry. Her boss. Her supposed friend and ex-whatever!

By the time Meg returned with a drink, Lauren was already halfway to her car.

JONAH'S big Friday night plans amounted to a supreme Paddy's Pizza and reading two chapters from his business ethics textbook. Since it was raining again he called in his order. It was a supremely lazy thing to do as the restaurant was right downstairs, accounting for the pervasive aroma of baked yeast bread that filled his apartment. Was it any wonder he subsisted mostly on pizza and subs these days?

While waiting for the delivery he sat at the granite island in his kitchen and read the chapters. Then he signed on to his account on the college website to review the worksheet assignment. He'd planned to finish this earlier today and maybe do something wild and crazy tonight like go out with friends, but there'd been that storm.

His lips curved of their own volition. He didn't regret the storm. He would read a bazillion pages of this deadly dull textbook before he wished away that time with Lauren at the trapper's cabin.

He pictured her drenched and gorgeous in the firelight and wasn't sure he'd ever seen such a beautiful sight. He'd missed the unguarded Lauren. Missed the melodious sound of her laughter, the way her eyes turned to crescents, the way her smile bloomed across her face. Today had been like having her back for just a little while. It made him long for that deeper relationship they'd had. Made him ache for want of it.

God, I miss her so much. Please bring her back to me.

The knock on the door startled him. He glanced heavenward. "That was fast even for You."

When he opened the door his smile broadened at the sight of her, dripping wet on his uncovered stoop. He was about to make a joke about her luck with rain today. Then he noticed the spark of anger in her eyes. The flare of her nose. Her tight jaw and rigid shoulders.

"How could you?" The words were fiery darts, aimed directly at him.

They might have contained poison because a slow, noxious dread trickled through his veins. *She knows about the job.*

Nothing else could make her this furious. A sinking sensation filled him. If he hadn't lost her before, he'd definitely lost her now. Because judging by the fury on her face, there would be no coming back from this.

"I was gonna tell you."

"Sure you were."

Water trickled down her face. Or was it tears?

He opened the door wider and stepped aside. "Come in. Let's talk."

She crossed her arms over her chest, her feet rooted to the landing.

"Come on, Lauren. You're getting soaked. Come inside. Let's talk about this."

She stood immobile for several long seconds. Then finally she stepped into his foyer but not one inch farther.

He shut the door behind her. "Will you have a seat? Can I get you something to drink?"

"This isn't a social call, Jonah. Why didn't you tell me?"

Now that she was under the light, he could see her features more clearly. Her eyes were bloodshot. Those *were* tears. She cried when she was angry, and boy was she angry. Steam practically rolled off her body.

He'd had six weeks to tell her. She deserved an explanation. "I'm sorry. Maybe I should've told you sooner, but I knew it would be upsetting and—"

"Upsetting?"

"Try and see it from my perspective, Lauren. You'd just had a traumatic brain injury. You had a panic attack in the hospital."

"And I just had another when I called Olivia and found out I turned down the job of my dreams in favor of living in Podunk Pinehaven for the rest of my life!"

He winced. "I was genuinely concerned about you. And I thought you'd get your memory back. I kept thinking *any day now it'll come back, and then . . .*"

"And then what? We'd pick up right where we left off? That the job—the one I came here for, the one I would've done anything for—would just be a moot point?"

Well, it would've. But he wasn't stupid enough to vocalize the thought. "I know that position meant a lot to you and—"

"*Means*, Jonah. It *means* a lot to me."

"Right. I just meant—"

"That before I lost my memory I was ready and willing to give up everything I'd worked so hard for? But guess what? I'm not. And if I'm lucky enough to salvage this situation, I'm taking that position."

Relief and dread jostled for first position. Time enough later to unsnarl those feelings. "The job's still available then?"

"She's considering it. But I've probably alienated her, and she's just waiting till next week to turn me down." Her shoulders heaved. Her eyes flashed. A tear trickled down her cheek.

His chest tightened painfully. When she hurt, he hurt.

Her chin notched up. "Even if I get my memory back, I'm taking that job, Jonah."

"Of course. I would never stand in your way, Lauren. That's never been my goal."

Her nostrils flared. "You've had six weeks to tell me about this."

Hadn't he already explained?

173

"You didn't tell me because you knew I would've left, and you couldn't risk that."

"I was worried about you!"

"Maybe that was true at first. But six weeks, Jonah . . . You were being selfish."

He opened his mouth to refute the idea. Then his conscience kicked in. He'd thought about telling her that day he had lunch with Javier. But then she'd texted him, and he was so filled with hope he decided to wait. He *was* afraid she'd leave and he'd lose her for good. He'd admitted as much to Meg this afternoon. So at least part of his reasoning had been selfish. The realization weighed on him like a steel anchor.

He blew out a long, slow breath. "Okay. You're right. I should've told you sooner. I'm truly sorry. I've never wanted you to sacrifice your career. But you got so excited about running the barn venue. If you could remember, you'd know what I'm saying is true."

She dashed away a tear. "Well, I can't remember. And at this point I'm not even sure I can take your word for it."

Ouch.

"Or your family's—they must've known too."

He winced. "This is my fault, Lauren. I asked them not to say anything. They were worried about you too."

A knock sounded on the door.

He sighed at the bad timing. "I ordered pizza. Stay and have dinner with me. Please. We'll talk this out."

Her shoulders went even more rigid. "I think I've heard enough." She opened the door and stepped around the startled delivery boy.

Jonah watched her practically sprint down the steps as he reached for his wallet. After he paid for the steaming box of pizza, he closed the door and set it on the island.

His appetite was gone.

CHAPTER 24

IT WAS SATURDAY afternoon by the time Lauren was able to check the barn's new paint job. The crew had finished yesterday while she'd been stranded at the trapper's cabin with Jonah.

Jonah.

She didn't even want to think about him or the flicker of desperation in his eyes when she'd stood in his doorway yelling at him. She had every right to be upset. She never should've learned about her job like that. He should've told her after the accident when it became clear she didn't remember.

No sense dwelling on it now though. It would only make the hours till Olivia's call drag out. She pushed all thoughts of Jonah and the job away.

Graham trotted ahead on the trail, tail wagging. Then he turned and waited for her, wearing that doggy smile she was becoming familiar with.

"Are you excited to see the barn? Huh? It's just so exciting, isn't it?"

Moments later as they broke through the clearing, Lauren smiled too. The barn was the perfect shade of rustic red, and the white trim set off the windows and new barn doors in just the way she'd imagined.

A crew would be out to reshingle the roof next week, and then the new windows would be installed. The barn would be dried in by the end of

October just as she'd hoped. The kitchen and bathrooms would be framed by then, just in time for electrical and plumbing.

She walked the perimeter of the building, inspecting the work. The crew had done a terrific job. She'd leave a nice review online. When she reached the barn doors again, she slid them open. They glided along the track without a single squawk.

Graham bounded inside the dank space and she followed. Nothing new in here, but she couldn't resist the urge to view it again, to make certain she hadn't forgotten any component of the project. There would be no time for mistakes if it was going to be finished before her departure in December.

If she would even be here that long. If Olivia offered the job to the other woman, would there be any point in staying?

She shut off the negative thought and pored over every square foot of the space, making notes on her phone as she went. Questions for the flooring crew, for the electrician and plumber, the heating and cooling people. There was a lot of work to do in just two months.

Her gaze snagged on Graham who stood near the wall on the far side of the barn. He sniffed the ground, tail tucked low. "What's wrong, buddy?"

The instant the words were out of her mouth, she realized. That was where she'd fallen. She joined Graham, but he continued his incessant sniffing. A dark spot stained the wood. Blood. She envisioned her body lying there on the floor, sprawled and still, as Jonah had described.

Her focus moved to the ladder propped again on the wall near the loft. It stretched upward about twenty feet, and for the first time she envisioned herself falling. She could almost hear the thud of her body hitting the wood floor. The thunk of her head striking the ground.

She winced. A chill swept down her arms. She was glad she couldn't remember the accident. Imagining it was bad enough.

As if he was reliving the accident, too, Graham whimpered. She reached down and comforted him. It could've been so much worse.

She could've died. It happened sometimes—a hard knock to the head like that. She could've died at the age of twenty-six with her whole life ahead of her.

Thank You, God.

She'd been so busy mourning the decisions she'd made over the summer, she hadn't stopped once to be thankful she'd survived that fall. It could've all ended on September seventh. She never would've gotten the chance to realize her career goals. Would've never had the chance to marry or become a mother.

She would've missed the opportunity to have any kind of closure with her own mother, who Lauren assumed was still out there somewhere living her own life. Would Lauren have regretted that? As always happened when she thought of her mother, the boulder returned, weighting her chest.

CHAPTER 25

JONAH AVOIDED THE resort until Sunday afternoon. He knew Lauren well enough to realize she needed space. Even after two days he still wasn't sure how he'd be received. That was how he found himself in the lodge, straightening the brochures, adding oil to door hinges, and vacuuming the floor.

His truck was in the lot. If she wanted to seek him out, she could. If not . . . the lodge could stand a little extra attention.

Someone tapped him on the shoulder.

He turned and found his mom staring at him as if he had three heads. He flipped off the vacuum, ushering in silence. "What's wrong?"

"What are you doing in here? I told Lauren you'd come help her. Didn't you see how many guests signed up for the pumpkin carving?"

Jonah glanced out the window though he couldn't see the pavilion from here. So close yet so far. He remembered the anger sparking in Lauren's eyes on Friday. The flaring of her nostrils. The tears trickling down her cheeks. "Maybe you should help her."

Mom crossed her arms and pinned him with a gaze that made him squirm. "Funny, she said the same thing. What happened between you two? You were getting along so well."

"Lauren found out she gave up the job in Boston."

Mom's eyes lit. "She remembered?"

"No, she called Olivia."

"Oh." Mom's brows pressed together. "I guess she was pretty upset about it."

"An understatement. I should've told her right away." He'd been beating himself up all weekend. "Now she hates me."

Mom put her hand on his arm. "Oh, honey. I'm sure that's not true. She's just angry. It'll pass. At least she didn't leave."

"That's only because she may still have a shot at the position. She's waiting to hear from Olivia."

"That's great. Or not. Oh, phooey, I don't know what to hope for anymore."

Jonah had battled the same emotions all weekend. "If that job is what she most desires, then that's what I want." As much as he longed for her, he wanted her to have whatever made her happy—even if it wasn't him.

Mom squeezed his arm. "Don't give up on her, sweetheart. You made her happy before—you can make her happy again."

He'd thought so initially. He wasn't so sure anymore. "I'd love that, Mom, but it takes two people to make a relationship, and half of us don't want that anymore."

"There must be something we can do. Can't we help her get her memory back? Therapy or hypnosis or something?"

He'd done plenty of research. "There are psychotherapies and cognitive behavioral therapies that can help. And yes, even hypnosis can be effective. So can looking at pictures and experiencing familiar smells and sounds. But all of these require a patient who actually wants to access those memories—and that's not Lauren."

Mom's eyes tightened in a wince. "I'm sorry this is happening to you guys. I keep praying her memory will return."

"You and me both."

His mom regarded him with sympathy for a long moment. "Well, how's school going? Are you enjoying your ethics class?"

"It's fine. My grades are good. Just two months left." He didn't know what he hoped she would say. Maybe something confirming he'd fulfilled his end of the bargain and she knew he was the right person for the job.

"I'm glad it's going well." She glanced out the window and frowned. "Are you sure you don't wanna assist Lauren? It might help clear the air between you."

"I think she'd prefer if I didn't. Besides, these floors won't sweep themselves."

"I'll go on out then. If you change your mind, you're welcome to join us."

A moment later Mom slipped out the door and Jonah turned the vacuum back on, letting the loud drone of the motor drown out his melancholy thoughts.

THE day was perfect for carving pumpkins. Too bad Lauren wasn't in the mood. She was a professional, though, and made sure none of the guests knew she'd rather crawl into bed and pull the covers over her head. Jonah was on property somewhere—she'd seen his truck in the lot over an hour ago. But he had yet to seek her out.

"Those are great eyes, Mia," Lauren told the eight-year-old girl working alongside her father. "Very scary."

"I'm making a friendly jack-o'-lantern," her brother said.

"I love his smile," Lauren said.

"Miss Lauren, can you help me with these ears?" Janae asked. "They're too pointy."

"Of course." Lauren moved down the table and assisted the tween-ager. All the while her gaze kept darting toward the lodge where Tammy had disappeared minutes ago, seeking Jonah. With any luck he'd be busy studying or something.

But Lauren was running pretty low on luck these days. And after their confrontation on Friday, Jonah would probably jump at the chance to help her. He'd made himself scarce this weekend and she was glad for that. She was still angry.

Then there was the anxiety over the job at Glitter. She might hear from Olivia as soon as tomorrow.

At the sound of a closing door, Lauren glanced toward the lodge. It was just Tammy heading back toward the pavilion. When their eyes met, the woman's smile faltered.

So Jonah had told her about their argument—and apparently turned down the chance to help Lauren. Just as well. Maybe Tammy would stop trying to force the two of them together. If Lauren didn't know better, she'd think Tammy orchestrated the whole trapper's cabin episode.

The whole family knew she'd given up her future position and none of them had told her. Lauren couldn't help feeling betrayed and also a little stupid because she'd had no clue. But it had been Jonah who'd made that call. That was the only thing that kept Lauren from being upset with the whole family.

They'd been so good to her after her accident. And really, how could she blame them for trying to protect Jonah's heart after she'd inadvertently stomped all over it? She was perfectly happy to let Jonah absorb all the blame on this one.

Tammy joined the group and assisted the guests, which kept them both busy for twenty minutes or so. Then they found themselves working side by side.

"I'm so sorry about the job, honey," Tammy whispered.

"Are you?" One glance into the woman's puppy-dog eyes and Lauren regretted her harsh tone.

"Oh, sweetheart. As much as I'd love to keep you here forever, I want what's best for you even more."

The woman's authenticity made Lauren feel small and petty. In all the weeks she could remember, Tammy—the whole family, really—had been nothing but kind and gracious. Lauren's background had made her distrustful and cynical. It hadn't been as obvious in Boston as it was here in this small town where people were so nice and accepting.

She glanced at Tammy. The woman had been more of a mom to Lauren than her own mother had been. It wasn't nothing. "I appreciate that, Tammy."

Her arm circled Lauren's waist. "You know, honey, I'd be happy to put in a good word for you with Olivia. She owes me one—the debt goes all the way back to college, and I've just been waiting for the chance to collect on it."

Lauren's heart seized at the thought of securing that position. Surely if Olivia was on the fence about Lauren, she'd listen to her friend. With one simple phone conversation, Lauren's dream job could be salvaged. It was so tempting. And yet . . .

Lauren cleared her throat. "Thank you, Tammy. I appreciate the thought. But if I get that job, I want it to be on my own merits."

Tammy's eyes shone with something like pride as her lips tipped up in a smile. "Very admirable. You're a fine young woman, Lauren, and an excellent manager. She'd be crazy to turn you down."

"Miss Tammy, I can't make the teeth look right."

"Well, let's see what we can do about that." Tammy gave Lauren one last squeeze, then moved around the table to help the younger girls.

Tammy's beaming smile and vitality added a wonderful energy to the affair. And her generous affection with every guest was heartwarming. If she was a little overbearing sometimes, Lauren could forgive that.

She realized belatedly that in offering to rescue Lauren's job, Tammy would've ended up hurting her own son. Did she care that much for Lauren? How was that even possible when her own mother had left her so easily? She wasn't sure she understood that kind of sacrificial love.

The rest of the event Lauren went through the motions, but she struggled to tame her troubling thoughts.

CHAPTER 26

July 8

LAUREN WAS RELIEVED to have the busy Fourth of July weekend behind her. The place had been packed—not only the resort but the entire town. She'd had about one free waking hour the entire weekend, and she'd spent it watching fireworks over the lake with Jonah and his family. At the end of the night, Jonah walked her back to her cabin and kissed her slowly, deliciously. She'd come to anticipate those lingering kisses.

The past four weeks together had been filled with fun and banter. They'd taken short trips on her days off. They'd gone to Laconia for the annual motorcycle week, Weirs Beach for the kitschy atmosphere, and the darling town of Littleton to visit Chutters—home of the world's longest candy counter. She was still enjoying the bags of jelly beans and red licorice he'd bought her.

His family had been accepting and also curious about their relationship. Both Tammy and Meg had tried to pry for information, but Lauren insisted they weren't serious.

Those amazing kisses notwithstanding.

When she wasn't managing the property or kissing Jonah, she was making plans for the barn's renovation. Because, yes, she and Jonah had talked Tom and Tammy into the project. She'd worked hard on her presentation, and the whole family was on board and excited about the additional revenue the venue would bring in. They wanted to start simple—only renting the place for events. Later they might add seating and catering and planning packages.

As eager as Lauren was to get started, it would take a while to clean out the interior and remove the vines and underbrush that practically swallowed the barn. She and Jonah would do that themselves.

But right now Lauren had another job on her agenda. She walked the property with a trash bag, tidying the grounds around the cabins. Most of the holiday guests had checked out yesterday. The afternoon heat made sweat bead on the back of her neck as she worked. She fished an empty water bottle from a bush in front of Willow, then found a Snickers wrapper outside the laundry facility. She was heading to the firepit—a premium trash area—when movement caught her eyes.

An unfamiliar scruffy yellow dog sniffed around the pine log seating. She approached slowly. "Hey there, friend."

The dog didn't stop its sniffing until it found a piece of graham cracker and scarfed it down. That's when Lauren noticed the dog's ribs undulating beneath its coat. "Oh, honey."

The dog finished the cracker and began scavenging again. Burrs were caught in its matted fur. It had been quite some time since this dog had been cared for. A closer inspection turned up the dog's sex.

"Hey, buddy." She held out a hand and the dog sniffed it, looking up at her with brown eyes that told a sad story.

"Let's go to the lodge, huh? We have some food for you there." They kept pet food on hand for guests to use in a pinch. She patted her leg and the dog followed. "Come on, sweetheart. It might not be as good as the snack you just found, but I think you'll be pleased."

He followed her all the way to the lodge, right on her heels, as if he'd been trained. Or maybe he was just that desperate for his next meal. She opened the door and he followed her inside.

"Come on, Mr. Graham Cracker. Let's get you something to eat."

She scrounged up two big bowls and filled one with dog food and the other with water. The dog went for the food first, pushing through it with his nose, hardly coming up for air. "You poor thing. How long has it been since you've had a decent meal, huh? A while, I'll bet."

Meg exited the office, joining her by the supply closet. "Aw, who do we have here?"

"I found him by the firepit, scavenging for food."

"Look how skinny he is. He must be lost."

"He acts like he's starving, poor fella."

"He's so cute." Meg ruffled his fur, but the dog kept chewing. "His fur's a mess of burrs."

"He needs a bath and a good brushing for sure. I think I'll take him to a local vet and see if he has one of those microchips. Someone's probably missing him."

"He doesn't have a collar or anything."

"It might have fallen off." She asked Meg for a vet recommendation and got the name of someone who attended their church. "Would you mind keeping an eye out here while I run this guy over there?"

"'Course not. I hope you find his people."

ALMOST an hour later, the grandfatherly Dr. Nolan glanced up from the scanner. "He doesn't have a chip. He wasn't wearing a collar or tags?"

"Nothing. I found him just like this sniffing around our firepit." He'd already given the dog a brief examination. "He has to belong to someone."

"I hate to say it, but it's likely someone dumped him on the side of the road. That happens sometimes."

She wanted to cover the dog's ears. Instead she gave him some affection and he licked her hand.

"Well, he seems healthy enough, other than being emaciated and dehydrated. Time and good care will take care of that. I'd put him at about three years old. I suspect he's a Jack Russell terrier mix underneath all that matted fur. Once he's cleaned up and fed, he'll make someone a good little pet."

If only there *was* a someone. She so wished she could keep him and, when her time expired at Pinehaven, take him with her. "I don't suppose you know anyone looking to adopt a dog?"

His bushy eyebrows pulled together. "Sorry, no. Seems there are always more pets than people searching for one. You can't keep him yourself?"

"I live at the resort." They'd already covered their connection with the Landrys. "And the Landrys turned down my suggestion for a mascot weeks ago." With all the regular chores that went with running a resort—plus the guests' pets—Tom and Tammy didn't want the extra hassle of a dog.

"That's too bad. We have a bulletin board out front for animals seeking adoption. It's already quite full, but you never know. There's a shelter in town, but I'd make that a last resort."

"Right." Maybe Meg would take him or Jonah. No, Jonah's apartment didn't allow pets.

She attached the collar and leash Dr. Nolan had given her and checked out at the front desk, even though the kind doctor hadn't charged her for the visit. On the way out of the office, she frowned at the overflowing bulletin board filled with photos of cute puppies and kitties. That wasn't promising.

"Don't you worry, Graham Cracker. We'll find someone who wants you." She walked the dog out to the harbor and around the patch of grass while she searched for the local shelter on her phone. She searched for some kind of promise they didn't terminate animals. Nothing.

She closed the website and called Meg, filling her in on the situation. Then she jumped right to the question. "I don't suppose you'd like a cute little doggy to come home to at night?"

"Oh, I wish I could. He's so sweet. But my roommate's allergic to dogs and just about everything else under the sun. If I so much as pet a dog without washing my hands, she goes into a sneezing fit."

Lauren's stomach sank. "That's too bad. Can you think of anyone else who might be willing to take him in?"

"Gosh, not right offhand. I guess I could ask a couple friends. You never know."

"Would you? Because the only other option is the local shelter and it's not a no-kill kind of place."

"I'd hate to see him go there. I'll try a few friends right now and get back to you."

"Thanks. I'll check with Carson."

She got Carson's voice mail and left a message. "Hey, Carson, this is Lauren. I found this sweet little stray dog who apparently doesn't belong to anyone, and I was wondering if you might be willing to take him in or know anyone who might foster a dog until I can find someone. Maybe Carina would be willing? I'm kinda desperate here. Call me back."

She disconnected. Even if Carson couldn't do it, maybe he knew someone who could. Or maybe one of Meg's friends would come through.

Forty-five minutes later, Lauren was officially out of luck. None of Meg's friends had come through. Carson was gone too much to have a pet, and his girlfriend was afraid of dogs after having been bitten as a child. He'd promised to ask around the hospital but didn't seem too optimistic.

Lauren could feel walls closing in around her—which made no sense at all since she was outside. She sat on the curb in front of the harbor and the dog sat beside her, his nose resting on her thigh.

It was getting late. She couldn't leave Meg filling in for her at the resort forever. But what was she supposed to do? She couldn't take this sweet little guy to the shelter. Sure, it was possible he'd find a home— but it was also possible they'd exterminate him before week's end.

She couldn't even think about that possibility. She petted the dog's head, her fingers catching in his matted fur. "It's gonna be okay, fella." But was it? She knew what it was like to be unwanted. Not to be chosen for adoption because you weren't a cute little . . . puppy.

She peered into the dog's sorrowful eyes until her own began to sting. "I know, honey. But you're so sweet and special. Even if I can't keep you, you should know I really want to. I'd be your mommy if I could." Her last words wobbled in her throat.

"Lauren?" a voice called.

"Jonah." She stood as he approached. "What are you doing here?"

"I was just—Hey, who's this?" His gaze swung back to hers, his smile slowly slipping as his eyes filled with concern. "What's wrong, honey?"

At the endearment, tears dripped down her cheeks. "I found him at the resort and he was starving, so I took him to the vet, but he doesn't belong to anyone, and no one will take him in—not Carson or any of Meg's friends, and the local animal shelter kills dogs!"

"Hey . . ." He tugged her into his chest and wrapped his strong arms around her. "It's gonna be okay. We'll figure something out."

She snuggled into his warmth, soaking up the comfort. His embrace felt so nice. She couldn't remember the last time she'd been comforted in someone's arms. And she loved that he didn't discount her feelings. But all the understanding in the world didn't solve her little friend's problem.

She sniffled. "Do you know someone who might take him in? Maybe Javi and Allison?"

"They've got their hands pretty full right now. But I think I have another idea."

She leaned far enough away to meet his gaze. "What? Tell me."

He searched her eyes. "Would you like to keep him?"

"Of course I would, but your parents already turned down my mascot idea, remember?"

"Let me see what I can do, okay? Where's your car?"

She gestured across the town square. "Over at the vet's office."

"Take the dog back home and I'll track down Mom and Dad."

"But what if they——?"

He gave her chin a soft pinch. "They're not monsters. They'll at least let you keep him until we can find a home for him."

"Really? You think so?"

He swept her tears away. "Of course. If all else fails, I'll hide him in my apartment for a few days. Now head on home and I'll give you a call in a bit."

"Okay." She gave him an extra tight squeeze. "Thank you, Jonah." She started for her car, tugging the leash. "Come on, Graham Cracker."

"Graham Cracker?"

JONAH tracked down his parents at the town hall. He waited on the steps until the Chamber of Commerce meeting adjourned, then pled his case before they could even reach their car. He didn't even mention fostering the dog until it could be adopted. Remembering Lauren's tears and the way her voice had wobbled, he went straight for the big ask.

He used all the persuasive tactics he'd learned in speech class to convince them.

"The guests will love having a pet around, and he'll be no extra work for us. And you know Lauren—he won't distract her from her work. Besides, she'll be leaving at the end of the year and taking the dog with her, so it's just a short-term situation."

His mom had been the first to waver, and then his dad crumbled like a crooked Jenga tower.

Later Jonah arrived at the property, then traipsed across the grounds toward Lauren's cabin. He couldn't wait to tell her the good news. To see her face light with joy, her eyes curve to half-moons.

He took the steps to her deck and knocked on her door. It was after dinnertime as it had been a few hours since they'd parted ways.

The door swept open and Lauren gazed at him, hope in her eyes. "Well?"

He beamed at her. "The dog can stay."

"Oh, Jonah! For how long? I don't know how long it might take to—"

"He's yours for keeps if you want him."

Her mouth gaped. "What? Really? I can keep him here? He's mine?"

Jonah chuckled. "He's all yours."

She threw herself into his arms so hard he had to brace himself to keep from stumbling backward. "Thank you, thank you, thank you!"

"It was nothing."

"It was everything. I can't believe I get to keep him! I have a dog. He's *mine*."

He held her tightly, his heart kicking up a few extra notches at her nearness. She felt so good against him, so right. She'd quickly become a constant in his life. When he was at home he texted her often. He made mental notes to take her to this place or that. When he wasn't with her he craved her. It had been harder and harder to tear himself away when they said good night. And when he woke up, she was his first thought. Those initial sparks had ignited a fire.

You're getting in deep, Landry.

Who was he kidding? He was already over his head. Just making her happy was the best feeling in the world. Well, next to having her pressed up against him like this.

He kissed the top of her head just as the mutt jumped up on his legs and barked. "I think someone wants our attention."

Lauren grinned down at the dog. "That's the first time he's barked."

Jonah petted the mutt. His coat was now soft and fluffy. "You gave him a bath."

"And a good brushing—remind me to get myself a new hairbrush. I wanted him to make a good first impression on your parents. You're sure they're okay with this arrangement?"

"I promise. He turned out pretty cute under all the matted fur. What will you name him?"

"Graham," she said quickly. Then she told him how she'd found him scarfing down a graham cracker left over from last night's s'mores.

He gazed down at the cute pup. "Well, Graham, welcome to the Pinehaven family."

CHAPTER 27

Present day

GEOFFREY CHAUCER HAD been right: All good things must come to an end. Lauren finished blowing leaves off the last cabin's deck and pushed the pile into the forest. Graham barked at the loud hum of the blower, chasing leaves as they tumbled through the air.

The foliage around the lake was still beautiful, but it was apparent by the crisp carpet of leaves that peak season had passed. She was sorry to see it go. Sorrier still that the cold winter was on their doorstep. Already, even though it was two in the afternoon, the air was chilly.

Blower still running, she pulled out her phone and checked for missed calls. Nothing. The weekend had dragged like the last five tread-mill minutes. What if Olivia didn't bother calling her back? Lauren drew in a deep breath, letting the earthy smells of pine and decaying leaves soothe her soul.

Funny that she would even find those scents soothing. When she'd first come here, this level of nature was foreign and intimidating. The smells, the night sounds, the lack of modern amenities . . . She'd been reluctant to part ways with the city, but she was glad she'd learned to be content in the country.

Lauren waved to one of the cleaners as she left the last cabin. Then she finished driving the leaves into the woods and shut off the blower. She still had an hour before check-ins would begin. She'd head to the barn.

The roofers had started bright and early this morning and the window installers had come soon after. The place would be dried in by the end of the week. She couldn't wait to complete the interior. To see her vision fulfilled.

Construction noises carried through the forest, the sounds of progress making her almost giddy. "Come on, buddy!" She patted her leg and Graham left some fascinating scent in the leaf pile to trot alongside her through the woods. "What did you find back there, huh? Some treat from Saturday's bonfire?"

Graham gazed adoringly up her, making her go soft inside. "I wish I could remember finding you." Meg had told her about the day Lauren found him all matted and scrawny. And about how Jonah had gone to bat for her with their parents. Hearing that had made Lauren go all soft inside.

"You must've been a pitiful sight, but you'd never know it now." His coat was soft and shiny, his nose cool and damp, and his eyes were bright with curiosity. He was devoted to her, following her around like a delighted shadow, ready and willing to do whatever she asked. Over the past couple months Lauren had fallen in love with him quickly and easily.

Her phone vibrated in her pocket and she checked the screen. Olivia. She stopped in her tracks. *Oh, God. Please, please let me get this job.*

She took a steadying breath, then accepted the call. "Hello, Olivia. How are you?"

"I'm doing well, thank you. How was your weekend?"

"It was busy. We were fully occupied for the weekend. All the peepers arrived to enjoy the fall foliage."

"Sounds lovely. We had a storm over the weekend that took most of our leaves down. Winter's right around the bend."

"I was thinking the same thing a few minutes ago." *Come on.* This small talk was about to kill her.

194

"Likewise, the beginning of the year will be here before we know it. Losing Ella will be difficult. She's really poured her all into the company."

"I'm sure that's true. If you're willing to give me another chance, I'll be just as devoted to Glitter. As you know, it's always been my dream to work for your wonderful organization."

"Yes, of course. I did a lot of thinking over the weekend. The other applicant I'm considering for the position has considerably more experience than you."

Well, Lauren was fresh out of college—*everyone* had more experience than she. "I see."

"She has enthusiastic references and turning the position over to her would be very easy for me."

Lauren waited, breath held as she sensed a *but* coming.

"I like your passion, Lauren. I like your grit—you've worked your way through college, holding down a full-time job for a demanding boss. I sense you've got what it takes to be a successful event planner for Glitter."

"Thank you." Lauren sensed another *but* and this was a terrible place for one.

"But your indecisiveness makes me a little hesitant. When you reached out back in August, you gave up the position—reluctantly, but you gave it up. And then suddenly weeks later you want to be considered again."

"I assure you I'm not normally indecisive. It was the accident." She could hardly be blamed for her memory loss!

"I understand and I even sympathize with your situation. But for whatever reason you gave up the position *before* the accident. You didn't exactly give an explanation and it's really none of my business. But you conveyed you were staying in Pinehaven indefinitely."

Her dream job was slipping right through her fingers! "I can't even tell you what I was thinking at the time, Olivia. But I promise I have every intention of finishing well at Pinehaven and returning to Boston at the end of the year. I've enjoyed working here—and as you said I would, I've learned a lot. But I want that position with your company more than ever."

"I can't help but wonder if that might change if you get your memory back—there is that possibility? That you'll remember exactly why you passed on the position?"

Lauren wasn't getting into her private life, but there was zero chance she'd find herself in love with Jonah again. Zero chance she'd give up her career for him again. "It's been more than six weeks. I haven't had a single memory return and I don't expect to. Regardless, I can't envision being so foolish as to refuse such a great career opportunity for the second time."

A long silence had Lauren squeezing her phone so tightly she feared she'd shatter the glass. Had she lost the signal? "Olivia? Are you still there?"

"I'm here. I'm just thinking." A heavy sigh followed. "I didn't become CEO of this company by accident. It took hard work, determination, and reliable gut instincts. And my gut feels good about you, Lauren. I'd like to extend that offer one more time."

Her breath rushed out. "Thank you, Olivia. You won't be sorry."

"I hope you're right."

"I'll finish well here in Pinehaven and I'll check in regularly if you'd like."

"That's a good idea. Let's keep in contact."

Lauren kept her cool all the way through the good-byes and until she ended the call. Then she let out a whoop that could be heard over the sounds of construction, and she might have even danced a little jig with Graham.

CHAPTER 28

AS THE DAYS on the calendar sped by, Jonah's anxiety ratcheted up. Somehow it was the last week of November, and he and Lauren were still barely on speaking terms. He'd hoped that since she'd recovered her dream job, she might let him off the hook. But no.

In the five and a half weeks since she'd confronted him on his doorstep, she avoided him whenever possible. When she did speak, it was with that overly polite tone he remembered from her early days at Pinehaven. Her smiles were downright frosty.

He'd already apologized multiple times in person and via text. She had a right to be upset. But the longer it dragged on, the more he suspected her anger was just a convenient shield. She'd gotten a second chance at that position, and she wasn't about to risk it by allowing him back into her life.

His bruised heart gave a pitiful thump. Sure, she couldn't recall what they'd had before, but it hurt just the same. Surely there was some part of her, deep down, that remembered the love they'd shared. He couldn't imagine all those amazing feelings and wonderful memories being completely eradicated as hers apparently had. It was impossible not to take it personally.

Especially when she seemed to have drawn closer to the rest of his family, Meg in particular, during the impasse. He could hardly resent her for it though. On the contrary—he was glad she had people here who loved her—people she could care about in return.

He arrived at the resort, stepped from his truck, and dashed through the blustery cold. The deciduous trees had shed their fall flesh, revealing skeletal fingers that pointed skyward. Already a few inches of snow had fallen, though it had soon melted away.

As he entered the lodge, a crackling fire and the strains of "Winter Wonderland" greeted him. His mom started with the Christmas music the second Halloween passed. She also went over the top with decorations, though she wouldn't put them up until the day after Thanksgiving since she used live garlands and trees.

Yes, *trees*. A giant one in the lodge and a small one in each cabin. She loved when the smell of pine permeated the lodge, and their regular December guests anticipated seeing the decked-out property each year.

After hanging his coat on the rack, Jonah peeked in the office and found it empty. His parents' SUV was outside, but they were probably upstairs in their living quarters. He headed through the lobby and toward the kitchen for a snack. Sustenance before facing his long-lost love.

But as luck would have it, Lauren was in the kitchen.

He stopped on the threshold, words jamming his throat.

She glanced up from the sandwich she was making on the island and smiled—an eight on the frosty scale. "Hello."

"Hi." He stuffed his hands into his jeans pockets. An awkward silence ensued. "How's your week going?"

"Pretty slow. Only two cabins occupied."

"It'll pick up in December." She would leave on the twentieth, less than four weeks away.

"That's good."

"How's the barn coming along?" It had always been a favorite topic, and he longed to see her eyes light up the way they used to.

"Fine." Her eyes were as flat as a skipping rock. "We're on schedule."

In other words, it would be finished before she hightailed it out of Pinehaven. And then he would be left with a ginormous red reminder of the one who got away. "I'd love to see it." Yes, he was fishing for an invite. He was that desperate. If they could just hang out awhile, surely he could lower those walls yet again.

She capped the mayo. "Be careful of the wiring. The electrician isn't finished yet."

Well. No invite then. She wasn't taking any chances, was she? Heaven forbid she let him in even a little. She might end up stuck here in Pinehaven for the rest of her life.

He dredged up a smile. "Anything you need?"

"Don't think so."

Okay then. He tried to think of something else to say. Something work related, just to keep her talking. Wow, he'd sunk so low. *You're pathetic, Landry.*

"Hi, honey." Mom entered the kitchen, slipped her arms around his waist, and gave him a squeeze. "What brings you out today? Don't you have a class?"

"Just finished. Came to check out the barn's progress." And also to see if he could eke a few words and a brittle smile out of Lauren.

"Oh, it's coming along great, isn't it, Lauren?"

She aimed a tropical smile at his mom. "I'm very pleased with the work so far. I can't wait to see the floor finished. They're starting it next week. Fingers crossed the electric and plumbing will be complete by then. The ductwork is finished. Did you see the size of that furnace?"

Wow. That was more words than she'd said to him in all of November.

"Well, it's a huge space. I love the ceiling fans you picked out. And the chandeliers! You have exquisite taste. I can't wait to see them hung."

"Thanks. They were a real bargain." She'd gotten them secondhand from a hotel on Squam Lake that had gone out of business. He'd extracted that bit of info from Meg.

"We appreciate the way you watch every dime as if it were your own."

Lauren's smile warmed another ten degrees. "I enjoy scavenging for deals. It's second nature to me."

Mom headed to the freezer and opened the door. "Your dad's craving ice cream. If I keep it upstairs, he'll eat the whole container when I'm not looking." Ever since his heart attack Mom monitored his diet—a service to which his dad reluctantly submitted himself.

She grabbed the container, shut the freezer door, and headed from the room. At the threshold she turned, meeting Lauren's gaze. "Oh, honey, I almost forgot to ask. Are you busy tomorrow?"

"Not really. Only two cabins are occupied and no one is checking in or out. Why? I was gonna scout out some white gauzy material to drape from the barn ceiling, but that could wait."

"Oh, good. I have a lady near Colebrook who's painting some Christmas decorations for me and they'll be ready tomorrow. I'm so eager to see them, but in the morning Tom and I are heading to visit friends in Bartlett, and I want to put them up Friday." The day after Thanksgiving.

"I'd be happy to pick them up for you. Just text me the address."

"Thank you, honey. I'll see if Meg can work from the office tomorrow in case one of the guests needs something or we have a last-minute check-in."

Lauren beamed. "Perfect. I can't wait to see this place all decked out for the holidays."

"I just love Christmas. Oh, Jonah, you'll need to tag along with her—you don't have classes tomorrow, right? Those decorations are gonna be heavy."

Jonah perked up. *Way to bury the lede, Mom.* He would've grabbed this opportunity even if he'd had to ditch a final. "No problem."

Lauren's smile had faltered. "I'm sure I can handle it. I'm stronger than I seem."

"Oh, they're much too unwieldy for one person, dear. They're large wooden cutouts: Mr. and Mrs. Claus, cute little elves, Rudolph, a sleigh, and a toy factory. She's making me a nativity too. They're so darling. Meg found her online, and since we had such a great year, I decided to go all out. The kids are gonna love it!"

"Oh. Okay."

"I'll send you both the address. You can take the property truck or Jonah's, whichever you prefer. I'll leave the check in the office tonight." She glanced down at the container. "I'd better get this ice cream to your dad before it melts. Have a good afternoon, kids."

As soon as she cleared the doorway, Lauren glared at him.

He held up his hands, palms out. "Don't look at me. I didn't have anything to do with this."

There was no smile on her lips, frosty or otherwise, as he slipped from the room, following his mom. He had an idea to run past her.

He found her at the foot of the steps. "Real smooth, Mom."

She blinked at him with her innocent brown eyes. "What?"

"You're not fooling anyone with this spontaneous field trip—not that I'm complaining."

"I don't know what you're talking about."

"Okay. Well, listen, I was thinking about the barn venue. What would you think of having a New Year's Eve party out there for the community? It might be an effective way of getting the word out about the venue if the locals see it firsthand." Not to mention distract him from the fact that Lauren was gone.

"That's a great idea. You should run with it. Let me know how your dad and I can help." She started up the stairs again.

She seemed on board with the idea. But even though he was graduating next month, he still sensed she was less than thrilled about his taking over the resort. Maybe it was time to settle this once and for all. Get it out in the open like Lauren had suggested weeks ago. He was tired of carrying this weight.

"Hold up, Mom." He caught up with her midflight where she stared at him expectantly. "You're okay with me taking over the resort at the first of the year as we agreed—right?"

"Sure, honey. You do a great job around here, and if that's what you really want, your dad and I are on board."

"Do you really mean that?"

"Of course I do!"

"Because I've been telling you for years it's what I want. If you're not concerned about my ability to run this place, then either you don't believe me for some reason or . . ."

Mom tilted her head, her gaze sharpening on him. "Or what, honey?"

The words caught in his throat. The ones that had taunted him as he labored through seven years of college, fitting classes around his work schedule. "Is there some other reason you don't want me running Pinehaven?"

Thought lines creased her forehead. "Like what?"

"Like . . . like maybe you hoped Meg would change her mind someday?"

"*Meg?* She's perfectly happy with all her numbers. Why would we be hoping for that?"

"I just thought maybe you wanted to—" His throat tightened, strangling off the words.

She put her hand on Jonah's arm. "Wanted to what?"

"It's just . . . This place was passed down through your family, Mom. I thought maybe you wanted your real child to take it over."

Mom's expression turned stricken as tears glazed her eyes. "*Jonah.* You are my real child. You're my *son.* Honey, what have I done to make you think this?"

His own eyes stung. "You haven't—I just wondered, Mom, that's all. You and Dad want to retire, yet you insisted I get a degree. It felt like you were just drawing things out, like maybe you'd really hoped Meg would take over."

She cupped his cheek. "My sweet boy. I just didn't want you to take on this responsibility because you felt we expected you to, especially once Meg dropped out. You're so smart and gifted—you could be anything you want to be. We just want you to be happy, that's all."

"This resort makes me happy, Mom. I love this work. I *belong* here."

She smiled through her tears. "Yes, you do. You belong here in every way possible." She wrapped an arm around him.

He drew her into an embrace, and a wave of relief washed over him as she held him tight.

"Jonah Landry, I love you more than words can say. You're gonna do a wonderful job with this place. I trust you completely with its legacy, and your grandparents would approve 100 percent."

"Mom . . ." He tried to pull away, but she held him tight.

"Real child." She whacked him on the back of the head. "Don't you ever say something like that ever again. Don't you even think it!"

His lips twitched. "Mom. The ice cream's melting."

"What?" She pulled back and glanced down at the container smooshed between them. The lid had come askew and ice cream was trickling down Jonah's shirt. "Oh. Sorry, honey. I'd better get this up to your dad before he ends up with a milkshake." She palmed his face again. "I love you. Please don't give this another thought."

"I won't. Love you too, Mom."

So much had gone wrong this fall. But as he turned and headed back down the stairs, Jonah felt lighter than he had in months.

CHAPTER 29

LAUREN COULD NOT believe she'd been suckered into this errand. Tammy had sent the address last night, and only then did Lauren realize the town was way up north and practically in Vermont—three hours away. Darn that Tammy!

She got into the driver's seat of the old GMC and fastened her seat belt while Jonah slid silently into the passenger side and buckled in. They'd barely said hello, which was just fine by her. The less said, the better, to her way of thinking. It would be a long three hours. Six, really, when you counted the return trip. She sighed.

"Sure you don't want to take my truck?"

"Yep." She turned the key and the vehicle rumbled to life. Sure, Jonah's truck was newer and nicer. But she'd had enough of sitting in the passenger seat. Moments later she pulled from the resort lot and onto the main road, his presence filling the vehicle like noxious fumes.

That probably wasn't fair—and not quite accurate. But clinging to her righteous indignation felt good. Safe. Especially when his presence seemed to fill the cab, his masculine scent tickling her nose.

Minutes later they exited town and the quiet swelled until she feared the whole truck would combust from the vacuum. She turned on the radio and the sounds of Christmas music filled the air. She wasn't a big fan of the holiday—it had largely disappointed. As a child she'd believed in Santa for about two seconds. Her first Christmas with a foster family quickly dispelled any belief in a benevolent stranger who bestowed gifts on every child.

She found another station—Taylor Swift crooned "Midnight Rain." Anything was better than Christmas music. Lauren's feelings about that particular holiday were eclipsed only by her disillusionment about birthdays.

Case in point.

Because, yes, today was her birthday and she was trapped in a rattly, old truck with the man who threatened her peace of mind. Typical.

"Are we gonna talk about this?"

He speaks. She supposed a nice, quiet drive was too much to hope for. "About what?"

"Lauren. You can't stay mad at me forever."

"Are you sure?"

His sigh rose over the chorus's crescendo. "Well, you can't be mad at me on your birthday."

He remembered. A small bubble of joy swelled inside. She took a mental pin and popped it, then aimed a scowl his way. "This isn't exactly the way I wanted to spend it."

"Why not? You don't even celebrate your birthday, so what does it matter?"

She kept forgetting he knew so much about her. She squirmed in her seat, then jabbed a button, turning off the heat. "Then I guess it doesn't matter that I'm mad at you today after all."

"You're not really angry anyway, are you? You're just scared."

She snorted, though his words hit a little too close to the mark.

"You like having a nice little wedge between us, don't you? It's a lot less scary than a friendship that might morph into more."

"You don't know what you're talking about."

"You gave up that job for me. For *us*."

"Which you lied to me about."

"Only by omission. And I've already apologized for that—numerous times."

"Whatever. The only way I would've given up that job is if you'd manipulated me into it."

He turned wide eyes on her. "Is that what you think happened?"

His surprise made her waver. But no. She must've been backed into a corner to have given up that job. "It's what I know," she said with far more certainty than she felt.

He gave a wry laugh. "You go on kidding yourself. Maybe one of these days you'll get up the courage to ask me how it all went down."

"You're really ticking me off."

"Thought you were already mad. And just so you know, we had the kind of love people die for, Lauren. We were happy. You lit up like the sun when I kissed you and squirmed with want when I touched you. It was pure magic."

Her knuckles blanched on the steering wheel as her internal temperature rose ten degrees. "Shut up, Jonah."

"You'd like that, wouldn't you? You don't want to hear the truth because you're scared to death of giving us another chance. Scared it'll lead you right back to the same place."

"Not happening. I don't know how you tricked me into it before, but it won't happen again. You hear me?"

"There was no trick, sweetheart. It was just love, pure and simple."

"I'm done with this conversation." She turned up the radio and let the intro of "Cry Me a River" fill the cab.

THIS trip wasn't going the way Jonah had hoped. Confronting Lauren had been a miscalculation—not that it was actually a decision. The anxiety of the past few weeks had swelled into irritation and he just snapped.

Bad idea. Lauren wouldn't be pushed into anything, certainly not a relationship. She had to do everything herself—the decisions, the driving, even the navigation apparently.

Fine, he'd just sit here like an idiot. Just as he had for the past two hours and fifty-seven minutes of this trip. Thank God they were almost to their destination located in a residential area outside a tiny town he'd never been to. The area's amenities included only an old-time gas station, an antique shop, and a pizza place.

Lauren slowed in front of a two-story, white-sided home and backed into the driveway. Once past the house, a big outbuilding came into view. Above the door a beautifully painted sign read *Santa's Workshop*.

After she parked they exited the truck, and when they approached the door, Jonah ushered her in first. A bell tinkled upon their entry.

He stepped onto the pristine cement floor and took in the space, which was filled with unpainted wooden cutouts: Frosty the Snowman, sleighs, Santa, nativities, snowflakes. The smells of sawdust and paint mingled in the air.

A gray-haired woman, clothing splotched with paint, emerged from a room in the back. She looked all of five feet and a hundred pounds. Crow's-feet gathered at the corners of her eyes as she smiled. "Hello! I'm Clara. How can I help you?"

"Hello, I'm Lauren and this is Jonah. We're here to pick up Tammy Landry's order for the Pinehaven Resort."

The woman's face fell. "Oh dear. I'm just finishing those up now."

"We don't mind waiting," Jonah said.

"Well, I'm afraid they won't be fit for travel till tomorrow. They have to dry, you know, or they'll get all messed up in transit. I could've sworn I told Tammy tomorrow."

Jonah glanced at Lauren, taking in her wilted smile. "There must've been a misunderstanding."

"We've driven three hours," Lauren said. "Maybe you have a rack or something we could use to protect them?"

"I'm afraid not. You wouldn't want road dust and whatnot settling into the finish anyway. I'm so sorry for the trouble."

He could see Lauren's wheels spinning for ideas and coming up blank. See her shoulders going rigid at the thought of more time with him.

"Thank you, Clara," he said. "We'll come back tomorrow. Will morning be suitable?"

"Yes, of course. Come by any time after nine. Again, I'm so sorry about the mix-up, but I think you'll be very happy with the pieces."

"I'm sure we will. We'll see you in the morning." He ushered Lauren outside.

As soon as the door closed, she turned a glare on him. "Are you gonna tell me this was a mistake? Because I'm not buying it."

"I have no idea, but if it was, I had nothing to do with it."

She crossed her arms, steam practically rolling off her flesh. "I'm not doing this all over again in the morning."

"Of course not. We'll find a hotel and stay the night."

She snorted. "I didn't exactly spot a Holiday Inn on the way into town."

"We'll find something nearby. We're not making that drive again." He was already tapping away on his phone. There was service, but it was very slow.

Lauren strode toward the truck and got in, shutting the door with more force than necessary, because, yes, his mom was no doubt up to her tricks. Sometimes she interfered, but her heart was in the right place. At the moment he wasn't sure whether to be thankful or resentful for the extra time with Lauren—he was leaning toward resentful.

The map finally opened, showing nothing in a twenty-mile radius except for a place called the Timber Ridge Motel. He clicked on the lone photo as he headed toward the truck and grimaced. Beggars and choosers . . .

He put on a good face as he got in the truck. "Good news. There's a place four miles away. It appears they have vacancies." Mainly because, who'd want to stay there?

Scowl in place, she started the truck.

"Go north out of the drive."

She stopped at the end of the drive and gave him a withering look.

Right—she didn't do north and south. "I mean left. Then right at the stop sign. And that'll take us into the next town."

He glanced at his phone. There were no reviews of the motel. But that was good, right? People usually left them only when they had something negative to say.

Minutes later Lauren slowed in front of a one-story motel that squatted on a slab of concrete. It boasted—and he used the verb lightly—about a dozen exterior rooms. The sign protruding from a rusted pole appeared to be from the seventies and advertised color TVs. A fenced-in pool sat in the middle of the paved lot, but it was dry and seemed to be sprouting a garden.

Lauren pulled into the lot and parked in front of the office. "Well. Happy birthday to me."

CHAPTER 30

"THIS HAD BETTER not be one of those stupid only-one-room-left scenarios," Lauren snapped as they approached the motel's interior service window. She inhaled, filling her lungs with the nicotine from a lifetime supply of smoked cigarettes.

"There are only two cars out front."

"That's not making me feel better." She couldn't believe Tammy had done this. It had to have been on purpose. She certainly wouldn't put it past the woman. And maybe Jonah had been culpable, too, despite what he'd claimed. After all, he'd lied to her before. Sure, by omission, but whatever.

"Two rooms, please," she said to the bleached-blonde woman behind the glass, whose black roots were half grown out.

Deedee (according to her name tag), who was probably approaching forty, eyed Jonah with a lecherous smile. "Sure thing, honey. I'll need a credit card."

He reached for his wallet. "I've got this."

"Better believe it," Lauren mumbled. She sure wasn't paying for this debacle. Her gaze skittered around the lobby, afraid to stare too closely. *Please, God, no bedbugs.* And would a Keurig be too much to ask? "Is there coffee in the room?"

"Just in the lobby."

Her gaze stopped on a half-filled pot of ink-black coffee that had likely been sitting since this morning. Hard pass.

Three minutes, four lingering gazes, and two sultry smiles later, the transaction was complete.

"Thanks, Deedee," Jonah said.

"You're welcome, hon." The gust of wind from Deedee's fluttering lashes nearly knocked Lauren over.

"Is there a place nearby where we can grab a bite to eat?" he asked.

"Nice of you to ask, but I don't get off till morning." Deedee winked as she handed him the keys. "Just kidding. There's the corner bar down the street on the right."

"Thank you." Lauren would definitely be looking that up first. "What's it called?"

"The Corner Bar." Deedee said the words extra slow while bestowing a condescending expression on Lauren.

"Right," Jonah said. "Well, thank you so much for your help."

"I'll be here all night if you need anything." She pinned Jonah with her gaze. "Anything at all."

Lauren rolled her eyes. "We get it—you're single and available. Thank you." She and Jonah exited the building.

"Somebody's a little jealous," Jonah singsonged as soon as the lobby door closed behind them.

"*So* jealous. Thank God for fresh air. That lobby reeked of smoke and desperation."

"You hungry?" He flashed his phone screen. "The bar doesn't look too bad. They have wings."

Lauren glanced at the screen, then toward the motel rooms, where God only knew what awaited her. "I need proper fortification before I go in there."

"That's the spirit."

Two and a half hours later—because service had been just that slow—Lauren and Jonah stood in front of their respective hotel room doors.

"Here goes nothing." She slid the old-fashioned key into the slot and twisted.

"May the odds be ever in your favor."

She opened the door and flipped the switch, lighting a sole lamp beside a double bed covered with a hideous floral blanket.

Jonah peeked into his own room. "Let me know if you need anything."

"A gallon of hand sanitizer and a hazmat suit would be just swell."

Instead he gave her a wry grin. "Lock your door behind you."

"As if I'd forget."

"Good night."

"Very optimistic of you," she muttered as she stepped onto the olive-green sculptured carpet. Once inside she shut the door and twisted the lock. She was definitely keeping her shoes on. She moved to the air-conditioning unit and flipped it on, not because it was hot but because of the weird odor she didn't care to identify.

She hung her purse from a hook by the door. Inside it was a bag from the local drugstore that contained a toothbrush, toothpaste, and deodorant. At least she didn't have to worry about anything crawling into a suitcase.

Timidly, she walked past the bed and dresser to the speckled Formica countertop, circa 1974. She peeked into the bathroom, complete with a stained toilet, a tub with a plastic shower curtain, and the distinct odor of mold. She zeroed in on a squiggly black hair near the tub drain and grimaced. So no morning shower then. After closing the door she returned to the living area.

A text buzzed in from Jonah. *Whatever you do, don't turn on the bright overhead light.*

She thumbed out a response. *My tub has a hair in it.*

Only one? Lucky. The sheets seem clean at least.

She peered at the polyester spread. Who knew when that thing had last been washed. *You're very brave.*

Get it off there, quick.

He had a point. She pinched the cover and gave a tug, sending the thing into a heap at the foot of the bed. The sheets were Pepto-Bismol pink but seemed clean enough, and not a hair in sight.

The sound of a TV came through the wall on Jonah's side of the room. She stilled and listened as he flipped channels for a while, then settled on a news channel. It was only eight o'clock—too early to settle in. And she wasn't quite ready to submit to whatever might be in that bed. Her head itched at the thought.

She took the lone chair at the table for two by the window. Might as well read—nothing too scary, given her current situation. She opened the reading app on her phone. She preferred physical books, but these were desperate times. She shopped online and treated herself to a new women's fiction novel she'd been wanting to read—it was her birthday after all.

Several minutes into the book her nose began to itch. Because she was allergic to mold and it was clearly on a first-name basis with this place. A sneeze built and escaped.

Her phone buzzed with a text. *Bless you.*

LAUREN awakened, her bladder begging for relief. So much for avoiding that bathroom. A glance at her phone showed it was only 10:21. She'd gone to bed out of boredom at nine. She flipped on the lamp, then slipped from the bed, straight into her shoes, and went to the bathroom. She was just returning when something scuttled across the floor.

"Aaaahhhh!" She jumped onto the bed and screamed again because, *mouse!* It had to be. It had been too big to be anything else and it had gone behind the dresser. Ick! The bed trembled as she did a little heebie-jeebie dance.

What now? It would come out eventually—it couldn't stay there forever. She could never sleep in here now. What if it crawled over her? A full-body shudder passed over her. Her gaze toggled from one end of the dresser to the other, waiting for the rodent to make its escape.

Someone pounded on the door. "Lauren! You okay?"

Jonah. "It's a mouse! There's a mouse in here!"

"Oh, for crying out . . . I thought you were being murdered in your sleep."

"Did you not hear me? I am trapped in this room with a mouse!"

"You're not trapped. Just open the door and come out."

"*Just open the door,*" she mocked. "I can't get off the bed!"

"Why not?"

"Because of the *mouse!*"

"Well, you can't stay there all night."

She was not stepping one foot on that floor. She took in the layout. There was that chair not too far from the bed. She could jump to that, maybe, then step onto the table, and from there she could reach the lock. Maybe.

She moved across the bed to the other side, watching for the mouse. Then she eyed the distance to the chair.

"Lauren?"

"I'm coming!"

She made the leap and caught her balance, just barely, on the rickety chair. She stepped up onto the center of the table, which wobbled precariously. Then she braced her weight on the window frame and stretched for the lock.

The second it twisted, Jonah pushed through. "Where is it?"

With a grateful squeak she fell onto him, wrapping arms and legs around him. "Who cares? Get me outta here!"

TEN minutes later Lauren sat on Jonah's bed. Because, yes, Jonah had offered to take the floor. He was currently fetching a tarp from the truck.

214

She wasn't sure she'd be able to sleep at all the way her pulse still raced. Also, this whole place was probably infested with mice. There was still no guarantee one wouldn't come crawling over her in the middle of the night.

The door opened and Jonah returned, tarp in hand, and pinned her with a look. "Stop thinking about it."

"I can't help it. It almost got me."

His lips twitched as he spread the tarp on the floor beside the bed. "They don't eat people. Not live ones, at least."

She scowled at him. Then she remembered the way he'd held on to her when she clung to him like a monkey. The way he whisked her from that room in two seconds flat. She went soft inside. "Thank you for the rescue. And for the bed. Here's a pillow."

He took it and tossed it onto the tarp. "Want me to turn off the lamp?"

Were rodents nocturnal? She wasn't taking any chances. "Can we leave it on?"

"Sure." He paused, shifted his weight, seeming to have something else to say.

"What's wrong? Do you want your bed back? Because if you do, I'm gonna sleep in the truck. I'm wide awake and probably won't sleep anyway."

"It's not that. I just—I have something for you. I wasn't sure if I should give it to you."

A birthday gift? Though not a fan of birthdays, she welcomed the distraction. "If it's a respirator, what took you so long?"

"No such luck." He reached under the tarp and retrieved a poorly wrapped box, topped with a red bow. "Happy birthday."

The package was the size and shape of a shoebox. Quelling the soft feelings already stirring inside, she hiked a brow. "You got me shoes?"

He shrugged, cheeks flushing.

215

This uncertain side of him was kind of adorable. She tore into the paper, shooting him a wry grin. "Please, God, black suede Louboutins."

"If that's the kind with the red soles, you're fresh out of luck."

"Darn. They'd go so great with my new——" Her hands stilled as the paper she'd ripped away revealed part of the box. The part with the logo.

Heelys. He'd bought her Heelys.

And just like that her thoughts flashed back to her seventh birthday when all she'd requested from her foster parents were a pair of Heelys. She needed new tennis shoes anyway. Her old ones squeezed her toes. Their two sons had Heelys and all the neighborhood kids did too. Once when Brandon had left his lying in the foyer, she'd slipped them on and tried to skate around the driveway. But they were much too big.

She'd been so excited about getting her own, about being able to skate to the bus stop and back again like the other kids. But when she'd opened her present on the morning of her birthday, she found a pair of regular tennis shoes instead.

Now, as her gaze homed in on the logo, her heart swelled two sizes. She pushed back the emotions and forced herself to tear away the rest of the paper. She'd relayed the story to Jonah—she'd never told anyone else—and he'd bought her the shoes.

She didn't even know Heelys still existed, much less in adult sizes. But he'd hunted them down for her. She couldn't seem to catch her breath or tear her stinging eyes from the package.

"Lauren?"

He was being so nice to her after she'd given him the silent treatment for weeks. What was wrong with her? Why did she push away everyone who cared about her? Her throat ached with unshed tears.

The bed sank as he sat. "I hope I didn't—I hope you don't mind me giving them to you. I got them back in August and figured you might as well have them."

She swallowed the boulder in her throat. "It was very thoughtful. Thank you." It wasn't the shoes. The Heelys craze had come and gone. The disappointment had faded. But these shoes represented everything she'd never received as a child: real parents, family, stability. And maybe Jonah wasn't perfect, but she knew in her gut, if he could give her all those things, he would.

"Really, Jonah. This was very sweet."

"You should've gotten them when you were seven. You were as deserving as anyone else."

That was true. Every child was deserving of love and consideration. She was still working on believing that she was too. Jonah made her believe it when he gazed at her like this—like he adored her. When he made her feel safe. He seemed to be an expert at that.

She zeroed in on the picture of the little girl on the box, her face lit with a smile as she skated in her Heelys. Lauren's own lips lifted as she popped off the lid, grabbed a shoe, and put it on.

CHAPTER 31

August 5

THE SUN SETTING over Loon Lake was the prettiest thing Lauren had ever seen. Luminous shades of pink streaked boldly across the sky as the fluorescent globe melted into the horizon. She didn't understand why, but sunsets seemed more glorious in Pinehaven.

The boat bobbed gently in the water where Jonah had anchored it for their onboard picnic. The food she'd prepared was long gone, the remnants packed away. Conversation had flowed easily, but now, almost in reverence, they watched the sun set in silence.

They hadn't had much time alone lately as Sydney had come up for the weekend, staying in Lauren's cabin. She'd taken one look at Graham and fallen head over heels. And by the end of the weekend, she seemed to think Jonah hung the moon. The man did have his charms.

Lauren leaned back onto Jonah's chest, head resting on his shoulder. Graham curled up at their side. He'd gained weight in the month since he'd become hers. Whenever he saw her, his eyes sparkled with joy and his tail wagged gleefully. It was a wonderful feeling to be so desired. So *needed*.

Lauren curled her fingers around Jonah's hand as they watched the last of the sun slip away. A wonderful feeling, indeed. Who knew she could be so compatible with a country boy? Though she'd seldom dated, she always fancied the city slickers with their styled hair, freshly shaved faces, and designer suits—Starbucks in hand as they dashed to their next meeting.

Jonah was nothing like that—though he had begun shaving daily, much to her delight. She loved running her fingers over the sharp turn of his jaw. So sexy.

She did so now because he was right *there* and lately she couldn't seem to get enough of him. She drew in the scent of his soap that had become as familiar as her own reflection in the mirror.

He stared at her now, affection in his eyes as they roved over her face. "You're more beautiful than the sunset."

"You say the nicest things."

"I haven't even begun."

"Do tell."

He dragged a finger down her nose. "You have the cutest nose I've ever seen. I noticed it right away, the way it flares gently and ends in a cute little button."

"My *nose*? That's what you like about me?"

"Patience, I'm just getting started." His attention shifted to her eyes. "When you smile and your eyes curve, it just about makes me crazy. And your grin . . . Those luscious lips of yours just about do me in."

"Now we're getting somewhere."

He leaned down and brushed her mouth, making her insides go warm. "But your laugh . . . That's my favorite. I can't hear you laugh and not smile."

"Is that why you tickle me so much?"

"What can I say, I'm addicted."

"As far as addictions go, it's not so terrible."

"Right? But I have another addiction that might be worse."

"I knew it. You were too good to be true. What is it, gambling? Shopping? You've lost all your savings and now you're after mine?"

"It's not your money I'm after, sweetheart. It's those delicious kisses." He dragged a thumb over her lower lip, watching its slow journey. "It's all your fault. You shouldn't kiss me like that."

"Like what? Like this?" she whispered as she reached up and brushed his lips with hers.

He growled as he took the kiss deeper. She didn't know how to break it to him, but it wasn't her making these kisses addictive. But if he wanted to give her the credit . . . She yielded happily to his explorations. He cupped her neck and worked his magic until she shimmered and melted just like the sun.

A boat must've passed nearby because the dinghy began rocking like mad in the wake. The kiss ended with laughter as they held each other until the rocking subsided.

Once still again, their gazes locked and their expressions turned serious as the moment drew out. Those eyes of his were stormy blue beneath sleepy lids. And the way he stared at her—with such desire and affection. Every woman should be gazed at this way. It was the headiest feeling in the world to be adored by such a wonderful man.

Something welled up inside her, something powerful and moving. It swept over her like a tidal wave, taking her along for the ride.

But before she could put words to the emotion, Jonah spoke. "Sweetheart . . . We need to talk."

A weight dropped like a cement block in her stomach. Nothing good ever began with those words. She should've known better. This thing between them was too good to be true. She'd let her guard down and now the proverbial *other shoe* was about to drop. Panic took her by the throat. She pushed away from him.

Jonah grabbed her arms, preventing her escape. "Hey, wait. What's wrong?"

"Nothing. Just say it."

"Say what?"

"Whatever you were gonna say."

"I can't say it now. You've gone all prickly on me."

"Well, what did you expect? 'We need to talk' is practically an omen."

He sighed, giving her that patient look. "Poor choice of words. Come back here, Wentworth. It's nothing bad, I promise." He coaxed her back into his arms.

She leaned there rigidly against his chest. Maybe she had gotten ahead of herself. She could've misread the situation. Guys didn't talk in that gentle voice or gaze at you this way when they were getting ready to break up. Did they?

"Sorry," she squeezed out.

"It's okay." He always seemed to understand when she acted like an idiot.

Well, that made one of them.

He kissed her forehead and they sat in silence while he caressed her shoulder. Gradually, she relaxed in his arms.

"You deserve good things, Lauren," he said minutes later. "I hope you know that. You're so special. I know back in June we just set out to have a little fun. I was determined not to fall for you—and now look at me. I'm a complete goner."

She lifted her gaze to his, searching. Goner? What did that mean exactly?

"I just couldn't help myself." He pinched her chin gently, his eyes softening. "I've fallen in love with you, honey."

She sucked in a breath. Blinked up at him. Had he really just said that?

"You don't have to say anything. I know it's kind of quick." He chuckled. "That's the way I tend to do things. You've turned me upside down, inside out. I thought I knew what love was, but I didn't have a clue until I met you."

She was breathless. Wordless. "I—I don't know what to say."

He put a finger over her lips. "I just wanted to tell you how I feel. I certainly couldn't hide it anymore. I was about to burst. My heart's in your hands, sweetheart."

His declaration made her almost giddy. His love was a wonderful and precious gift. She wanted to hold it close like a beautiful, fragile butterfly.

But how could this ever work? They lived in different states. She had a job awaiting her in Boston, and he was destined to stay here and run Pinehaven. He was *made* for this place.

Did he expect her to give up her dreams? To forfeit the job she'd worked so hard for? "Jonah . . . I won't be here forever. I have a life in Boston."

"I know. I get that. But I thought you had a right to know how I feel. And if there's any possibility you could feel the same way eventually . . . Well, I guess we'll have some things to work out."

Eventually? Judging by the way her heart pummeled the walls of her chest, she felt that way *now*. Which begged the question: How had this happened? They were supposed to be having fun! There was nothing fun about the fear flooding her veins.

"Hey . . . listen, it's gonna be okay. I didn't tell you that to worry you. That's the last thing I wanted. We'll work this out."

In her experience things didn't usually work out in her favor. But no, that was her childhood speaking. She was in charge of her life now, not some well-meaning caseworker. She wouldn't let anything bad happen. Although she seemed to have let herself fall in love. Was that a bad thing? It kind of seemed like it.

"Have a little faith, honey. It's barely August. Let's just see how it goes." He smiled gently as he cupped her cheek. "If you want that, too, that is."

She should probably tell him how she felt about him. Own up to the fear that roiled in her gut. But the words seemed to be lodged in her throat. "Sure. Let's just see how it goes."

He kissed her then, so softly and reverently she couldn't imagine anything more breathtaking. But the worry coursing through her took control. How would this ever work out? And what would become of her when it all came to a crashing halt?

HAD Jonah thought he was in love with Monica last year? Ha. His emotions hadn't come close to the overwhelming, consuming feelings of love and devotion he had for Lauren. He couldn't be with her enough. Couldn't kiss her enough. Or touch her enough.

His grades had fallen off a bit this summer, and he couldn't even bring himself to care. What did his GPA matter when compared to time with the woman he wanted to spend the rest of his life with? Because it was becoming apparent that Lauren was the only woman for him.

In the couple weeks since his declaration, they'd continued working together and exploring the area on her days off. They'd gone out to dinner a few times, the mood inevitably turning romantic, serious.

She still hadn't returned his proclamation. It didn't surprise him that she was hesitant to voice her feelings. But she didn't have to say the words—her feelings were obvious in every lingering gaze, every affectionate touch.

But even while he sensed her feelings for him had grown exponentially, he also detected her trepidation. And who could blame her? It was hard laying your heart on the line when the future was so ambiguous. Hard enough for him with the whole Monica fiasco in his past, much less for someone like Lauren whose past was rife with uncertainty.

She might be the strongest, most capable woman he'd ever known, but she wasn't without her vulnerabilities. He hurt for all the horrible things she'd been through as a child. He wanted to make it up to her somehow. To love her better. To help her see how much she deserved to be adored. He wanted to give her the stability she'd never had along with the freedom to chart her own course.

Ultimately, it was that line of thinking that made him realize what he had to do. So on her day off, exactly two weeks after his profession of love, he invited her to his apartment for dinner. He wasn't much of a cook, but he cobbled together a meal: a simple salad, grilled steak, and baked potatoes with all the toppings.

They ate at the small table on his balcony as daylight waned and shadows lengthened. He'd lit the only candle he could find and used the cloth napkins his mom had given him as a housewarming gift. The balcony faced the town park, but if you craned your neck a bit, you could see the evening sun shimmering on the lake's surface.

Lauren complimented his grilling skills and said it was the fluffiest potato she'd had in ages. Conversation flowed well as it always did between the two of them.

But as the meal wound down he became nervous about the upcoming conversation. What if he'd read her wrong? What if she wasn't in the same place he was emotionally? Would his offer be perceived as too much, too soon? What if he only pushed her away?

". . . and then the frog leaped on her head and she ate it."

The lengthy silence clued him in. He shook away his heavy thoughts and replayed her words in his head. *What?*

She chuckled. "So you are listening. You had that blank look—plus you've just about pulverized that potato skin."

He glanced down. So he had. He pushed back the plate. "Sorry. Guess I'm a little nervous."

"Oh yeah?" She arched a brow. "What's up?"

He loved when she arched that brow. It made her look so saucy. *Focus, Landry. This is too important to screw up.* He gathered his courage and broached the subject. "I'd like to circle back to the conversation we had on the boat a couple weeks ago."

She froze for a fraction of a second. And then that saucy expression was back. "Yes, we should definitely resume our debate about whether or not white chocolate is *real* chocolate."

"That's not up for debate. I clearly won that argument."

"*Au contraire.* Further research has revealed white chocolate is made from cocoa butter. I believe this revelation strengthens my argument."

He tipped his lips up. He loved it when she got fired up over minutia. "I should've come more prepared. I guess I'll just have to concede."

She beamed. "I was hoping you would."

He gazed at her beautiful face, his heart too small for all the feelings it held for her. He would move to Timbuktu if she'd have him.

Lauren's countenance sobered, no doubt a result of his lovesick expression. "I guess you have more than cocoa on your mind."

He hadn't said he loved her again since that first time. He hadn't wanted her to feel pressured to return the sentiment. "I know we're still months away from December. I don't want to rush things, but I sense you're a little hesitant since I brought up the L word."

She placed her napkin on her plate. "That's a fair statement, I guess."

"Okay . . . So what I'd like to know is, are you unhappy that I've fallen off the proverbial cliff? Or are you worried about what might happen if you fall off it too?"

She gave a nervous laugh. "Those cliffs . . . treacherous little buggers."

"Maybe so, but the fall is pretty exhilarating."

"No doubt." She shifted in her seat. Picked some lint off her pants. "The truth is, Jonah, my hesitation doesn't exactly stem from either of those scenarios."

"I see." His nerves began fraying at the edges. "Or, I guess, I don't see. I don't know what you mean by that."

She took a sip of her drink and her hand trembled a bit as she returned it to the table. "I'm not worried about falling off the cliff"— her gaze met his, fear flashing in her eyes—"as I seem to have already fallen."

The air whooshed from his lungs. Relief swallowed him whole as his lips turned up. "You have?"

"I have."

He was laughing. He couldn't help it. He was just that happy. "I've been so worried. I thought maybe—I'd hoped. But you're hard to read sometimes."

"You were right about what you said before though—I can't help but be a little hesitant. I live in Boston and you're rooted here in Pinehaven. I can't quite bring myself to feel happy or even content with that obstacle in our way."

He leaned forward and grabbed her hand. "Will you feel better if I offer a solution?"

She angled her head to the side, eyes narrowing. "Depends what it is."

"Don't look so suspicious. I've been giving this a lot of thought. It's been eating me up inside. I know it's awfully early to talk about this like forever is at stake, but Lauren . . ." He pinned her with a stare. "You're it for me, honey. I know it happened fast, but I love you so much."

Her eyes glazed over and she blinked against tears.

"Is it too early to talk this way?"

She swallowed. Shook her head.

"*Phew.* Under different circumstances I wouldn't rush this conversation. But I don't want you holding back because you're worried about the future. So I just wanted you to know . . . I'm willing to leave Pinehaven."

Her lips parted. She seemed to search his face for some hidden code that wasn't there. "You're willing to move to Boston?"

"I'm willing to move to Boston."

Her expression filled with joy and maybe even hope. "*Jonah.*"

"I was thinking I could get a management position at a nice hotel. I have plenty of experience in hospitality, and come December I'll have a bachelor's in business."

"Really?"

She seemed so surprised. As if she'd never believed he would give up so much for her. He pinned her with an accusatory look. "You thought I was going to ask you to move here."

Her cheeks flushed. "It crossed my mind. But what about your parents? They're expecting you to take over the resort. They're wanting to retire. I don't want to cause a problem between you and them."

"They can either put off retirement for a while or hire someone else to run the place. It's nothing they haven't talked about before. They've always wanted me to do what was best for me. And if you're in Boston, that's where I want to be." He would never choose any job over Lauren. She meant way more to him than that. And he would never ask her to give up her dreams. She'd been given so few advantages in life—had to claw her way to the top. He admired her spunk and resilience more than he could say.

Her eyes grew intense. "Maybe we should give it a little time before you tell them. I mean, are you sure you're willing to do this? You'd be giving up so much."

"We can wait a bit if you want. But I'm certain—this is what I want."

"But you love the resort."

It was true. Running the resort was *his* dream job. He'd never envisioned doing anything else, despite his parents' insistence that he explore other options. He tugged her hand, pulling her from her seat and guiding her to his lap, where she melted into him.

He wrapped his arms around her and brushed her lips with his. "I do love the resort. But I love you even more."

Her eyes went teary again as she palmed his cheek. "But how can I ask you to give that up for me?"

He kissed her perfect nose. "You didn't have to ask, sweetheart."

CHAPTER 32

Present day

LAUREN RETURNED FROM the road trip tired and yet, somehow, content. She flopped into bed that night and caught up on texts, periodically petting Graham, who sat conveniently beside her on the floor. She kept reliving those moments at the motel when Jonah had given her that present.

Her gaze flashed to the top of her closet where she'd stashed the Heelys. That gift had warmed her heart. If she was honest, it had also opened her heart. Their easy and fun conversations on the way home resonated with her. Perhaps enjoying his company in a way she hadn't since the accident had opened some familiar pathway in her brain. Or maybe it was like those time-loop movies: no matter where they were in time or space, no matter what they did, they were destined to fall for each other.

Staring at her phone, she was unable to resist the temptation to peek into the past and see what being with Jonah had been like. She opened their text thread and scrolled way back to the very beginning. She skimmed past the perfunctory texts she remembered. They were short and to the point, all revolving around resort duties. Her replies were direct, sometimes abrasive. She couldn't help smiling, remembering how he'd pushed all her buttons.

Then sometime in May the tone of their exchanges shifted. Sometimes Jonah would bring up things that weren't work related. He sent a couple funny gifs. Their texts were short and sweet. She began joking with him, using her sarcasm as she would with a friend. And then there was this entry.

Thanks for inviting me to Flume Gorge. I had a nice time.

Just nice?

Fishing for compliments?

Always. ☺

I agreed to see you again, didn't I?

We have a great time together. Those sparks. Whew.

Not denying that.

You're worrying again. Live a little. You work too hard.

My boss is telling me I work too hard?

I'm just unselfish like that. Or maybe I'm being selfish. Hmm.

She'd sent him the emoji of a brain exploding and he laughed at that. Their exchanges continued on, sometimes business related, most times not.

In early August he sent a text late one night. *I like you.*

I thought we established yesterday that you love me.

Oh, I do. But I like you too. ♥♥

She'd known he'd loved her. But knowing he also liked her implied a different kind of intimacy. It implied that she was someone he chose to spend time with because of who she was. That it wasn't all about sparks and chemistry. He liked her for who she was, good and bad. He enjoyed her company.

The only texts that followed were of the housekeeping variety until she reached the one she'd sent in September, apologizing for not being more compassionate after the accident.

She skimmed the rest of the texts. She now had a fuller picture of their relationship prior to her accident. A more complete picture of Jonah. Post-accident, she knew him as a patient and caring man. He'd treated her with all the respect in the world. Had given her the time and space she'd asked for—a big ask given the kind of heartbreak he must be going through.

The Jonah in the text thread was decidedly more gregarious. More forthcoming with his thoughts and feelings. Though since her accident she hadn't exactly encouraged him to express himself. Doing so would've made her uncomfortable. Would've put pressure on her. He seemed to know that and responded in a way that let her off the hook.

Seeing the contrast of Jonah before and after her accident only strengthened her respect and admiration for him.

She glanced at the photo app, her heart booming in her chest. No doubt there would be many pictures of them, of Jonah, of memories that had been erased. But she'd seen enough for one night. And given her vulnerable state, she wouldn't risk opening herself to him any further.

LAUREN had never experienced the kind of Thanksgiving the Landrys put on. They set up a huge table in the lodge and fed not only the family but also welcomed guests and stragglers from town who had nowhere to go. All told, twenty-seven people were sitting around the tables in the lobby.

The day after Thanksgiving they set up the cutouts she and Jonah had picked up two days before. Lauren couldn't think of that trip without remembering the Heelys he'd given her and the fun she'd had circling the motel's potholed parking lot with Jonah egging her on. She hadn't laughed so hard in years.

Business picked up the first week in December as the town's Christmas on the Lake Festival got underway. Light displays featuring holiday scenes lit up the shoreline. People came from miles around to view the magical display, visit Santa in his makeshift cottage, sample the local hot chocolate, and listen to the symphony performing classical Christmas music.

At the resort the barn was coming along. The flooring was installed that first week of December. It looked just as Lauren had envisioned it. And as she gazed at the beautiful venue, so close to completion, she couldn't help the little bubble of sadness that bloomed at the thought of leaving it behind. At the thought of leaving Pinehaven and the Landrys.

And yes, Jonah.

Since that fateful road trip they'd come to a sort of truce. He was busy finishing the last of his classes. However, that didn't stop Tammy from setting up jobs for the two of them to tackle together. Her interference hardly escaped Jonah's notice either, but they complied with Tammy's requests. And Lauren found herself enjoying the tasks all the more. Jonah was fun and easygoing. He let her take the lead, set the pace. She would miss him when she left.

She would miss him most of all.

She brushed the thought away as she traipsed across the property only two days before her departure. She huddled into her coat as she made footprints in the newly fallen snow.

She'd been in contact with Olivia about her job, which would start January second. That gave her almost two weeks to settle into her new studio apartment.

When thoughts of her dream job failed to produce the usual infusion of adrenaline and excitement, she shrugged it away. She had a lot on her plate—a lot to wrap up here before she left. The barn was finished except for the twinkle lights, but there were a million of those. She'd wanted to hang them herself, but after her fall the Landrys insisted on hiring someone to do it. A small crew was coming tomorrow.

The fully occupied property required a good deal of her attention and she still had to pack her things. The cabin felt like home after so many months here.

The sense of sadness at leaving swept over her again. She'd become so close with the Landrys. They were the kind of family she'd always wished for. And the rustic resort—which at first had turned her off—had grown on her in ways she couldn't have foreseen. She would miss the nightly sunsets over the lake, the colorful guests, the frequent sightings of deer in the woods and loons on the lake. She would miss the sense of community and the feeling of belonging in this family.

She brushed away the melancholy thoughts as she neared the lodge.

When she reached the steps, Tammy exited the building. "Hi, sweetheart! Oooh, it's freezing out here."

"You need a heavier coat."

"I'm stubborn—I refuse to take the winter coat out of storage until after Christmas."

Lauren laughed as they passed on the steps. "Suit yourself."

"Oh, shoot! I forgot our passports and I'm already late for my appointment with Ellen." Ellen was her travel-agent friend. Tammy was surprising Tom with a spring cruise for Christmas.

"If you tell me where they are, I'll take pictures and send them to you. Will that work?"

"Oh, you're a doll. They're in our little safe upstairs in the entry closet. The passcode is 5489. Thank you, honey!"

"No problem." As Tammy rushed to her car, Lauren headed inside, instantly grateful for the warmth of the fireplace. She'd come to clean up the mess one of the families had made in the lobby. The pieces of several games and two puzzles were scattered haphazardly around the seating area. It would take a while to sort it all out. But she passed the clutter and headed upstairs so she could allay Tammy's worry.

The lobby held the comforting scent of pine and looked like a Christmas wonderland with the sixteen-foot Fraser fir, decked out with ornaments, garland, and white lights. Ropes of lit garlands topped the mantel and wrapped around the wooden banister. Tammy sure knew how to make a place welcoming. She had a gift, both with décor and demeanor. She had the ideal personality and skills for the hospitality business.

At the top of the stairs, Lauren twisted the doorknob and found it unlocked. Tom had left with Meg to get supplies for the property, so she helped herself to the entry closet and found the safe situated on a shelf at eye level. She put in the passcode and levered the door open.

Her gaze skittered over two shelves, passing a small hanging-file box, a manila envelope, boxes of blank checks . . . Ah, there they were. The passports were stacked toward the back, just past a blue velvet jewelry box. She withdrew the passports, snapped photos of the picture pages, and set the documents back inside the safe. Then she sent the photos to Tammy.

She was just about to shut the safe door when she spotted the jewelry box again. Perhaps it contained an heirloom ring once belonging to Tom's mother. Or maybe a lovely pair of diamond earrings Tom had gifted Tammy for one of their anniversaries. That was probably more likely since the jewelry box looked newish. Her curiosity got the best of her. She scooped up the box and lifted the lid.

She gasped at the sight of an oval diamond engagement ring. The glimmering central diamond was rimmed by a halo of smaller sparkling diamonds. It was beautiful—and obviously new!

Why would the Landrys have a new engagement ring in their safe?

Even as the question formed she knew the answer. It was Jonah's. He had bought it for *her*. The ring was just to her taste. It was exquisite. Breathtaking.

She clutched her chest. Jonah had been planning to propose—and then she'd fallen and lost her memory. Her heart ached for him all over again. She wanted to find him immediately. All these weeks he'd been so sweet, so patient with her. He was an extraordinary man and he loved her enough to spend the rest of his life with her.

The ache inside bloomed until she couldn't even look at the ring anymore. As if the jewelry box was burning a hole in her hand, she snapped the lid closed and shoved it back on the shelf. Then she slammed the door closed and yanked the lever until it locked with a heavy clank.

If only she had locked her heart so thoroughly. Because seeing that ring and feeling his pain, she realized now what she hadn't known only a moment ago.

She'd fallen in love with Jonah Landry.

Her eyes burned with unshed tears. How had she allowed this to happen, not once but twice? The first time she'd given in to the feelings and surrendered everything she'd worked so hard for.

Only now did she realize how that had happened. The feelings roiling through her were as powerful as a riptide. But undertows were dangerous and so was love. It was seductive and spellbinding. It held the power to drag you away from what mattered most.

Hadn't her own mother taught her that very lesson? Hadn't Lauren suffered for years because of her abandonment? No matter how hard it might be to leave Jonah behind, Lauren would not make the same mistake.

CHAPTER 33

FROM THE MOMENT Jonah awakened at dawn, he was filled with dread. He lay in bed feeling miserable. Lauren was leaving Pinehaven around nine o'clock. He'd have to leave soon—he'd insisted on coming at eight to help pack her car because he was just a glutton for punishment like that.

He glanced out his bedroom window, hoping for an unforecasted snowstorm to delay her departure. No such luck. Just a dusting. Less than two hours from now he'd be saying his final good-byes. He didn't know how he would hold it together. It felt like his heart was being ripped from his chest.

Lauren had been a little more guarded the past couple days. Had even avoided him on a few occasions, possibly hoping to put some distance between them before the actual separation. That sounded like her. He'd tried not to take it personally.

His stomach was churning with acid—had churned all night, in fact, and the familiar pain kept him tossing and turning. He got up and went to retrieve his heartburn medication. He chewed up three tablets and hoped they helped more than they had yesterday.

His last class was complete, finals taken. He was all set to assume management of the resort. And somehow his future had never seemed so bleak.

JONAH had a long pep talk with himself on his way to the resort. He would put on a good face. It wouldn't be fair to burden Lauren with his heartbreak. It wasn't her fault she didn't love him anymore. She deserved the bright future awaiting her. She deserved that dream job for which she'd worked so hard. She deserved to have the life she wanted.

Even if it didn't include him.

He clenched his teeth against the rising tide of anguish. He would send her off well if it killed him. And it just might.

He pulled into the resort drive, the happy faces of the Christmas cutouts mocking him. He couldn't see them without remembering their road trip—that dilapidated motel and the mouse that had sent her soaring into his arms. Her beaming smile and melodious laughter as she sailed across the parking lot in those Heelys.

A band tightened around his heart until he feared it might strangle him to death. How could something hurt so much and not kill him? He didn't know it was possible to feel this much pain and go on breathing.

All these weeks he'd been telling himself she could still get her memory back. But it had been more than three months now and not a single memory had resurfaced. He had to let go of that fantasy or he'd drive himself crazy, hoping. It was time to accept reality and learn, somehow, to be okay with it.

He pulled into the lodge parking lot ten minutes early. He would gather himself on the walk to her cabin, then distract himself by loading her belongings. And then afterward, the good-bye . . .

He glanced in the rearview mirror and tried to assemble his features in a way that didn't betray his every feeling. "This is what she wants," he said to his reflection. "What she's earned. She deserves your support."

Loving her before the accident had been so fun. So easy. Falling for her had felt like the most natural thing in the world. He wanted her, he wooed her, he won her. Of course she'd wanted the relationship too.

That was what made this so hard. She didn't want it now, but that didn't erase his love for her. This kind of love—the sort that involved letting go—felt unnatural and impossibly difficult. But he loved her enough to do just that. Through this trial his love for her had grown and stretched, like the roots of a scorched plant searching for water.

The realization didn't feel like much of a parting gift.

It was time to see her off. He schooled his expression. There would be time for grieving once she was gone. He exited his car, his footsteps weighted with dread as he started across the property.

LAUREN gave the room one last glance. She had everything, she was sure of it. But a part of her dreaded leaving this cabin for the final time. It had been her home for nine months. Even if she didn't remember four of them, they seemed somehow deeply ingrained in every cell of her body.

Late last evening she'd walked to the barn with Tom and Tammy and gone over last-minute details. It was Lauren's first time seeing the place lit up at night, the way it would be for most of their future events. The twinkle lights and draped white tulle softened the interior just as she'd hoped. And the towering stone fireplace was a magnificent focal point.

The whole room was downright magical. Any bride would be thrilled to be married or host her reception here. So many happy memories would be made in this building. She just wouldn't be here to see them. The thought sent a pang of regret pinging through her like a pinball through a machine.

She shook away the melancholy thought as she slipped on her coat. Then she grabbed the box, her purse, and laptop bag. "Come on, Graham. Time to go."

Tail wagging, the dog followed her outside.

She shut the door behind them and it latched with a cold click of finality. She'd pulled the car right up to the cabin to load it, remembering like yesterday when she'd moved in. Who could've known this place, these people, would have such a big impact on her?

Don't think about that right now. Just get through this—you can mourn later.

She had to stay strong. It was time to drive over to the lodge and say her last good-byes to Tom, Tammy, and Jonah, who should be arriving shortly.

She'd parted ways with Meg last night after she'd met up with their single friends from church one last time. The woman had clung to her for a long moment, telling Lauren in a husky voice that she'd better keep in touch. Lauren wanted that. Meg had become like a little sister to her these past couple months. But Lauren wondered if staying in touch would only make it harder to let go of Jonah.

She opened the passenger door. She just wanted to get this over with and get on the road. Then she could focus on her new job. On her new life.

She was putting her things inside when Jonah's voice called out, "Good morning."

She backed from the car's interior. "Morning."

Graham greeted Jonah as if he hadn't seen him in months.

Jonah seemed somber despite the grin plastered across his face. His breath fogged in the morning air. He looked so handsome as he offered Graham some affection. He'd barely made eye contact with her, which was probably why his gaze settled so quickly on the car. It was hard to miss the back seat, piled high with all her things.

Jonah straightened, the semblance of a smile wilting from his lips. "You're all packed up?"

"I was awake early this morning and decided to go ahead and get loaded." She glanced back at the cabin. "It's all clean and ready for you."

At the end of the month, Jonah would be moving onto the property to assume the management position.

"You're all ready to go?" His voice held a ragged edge.

Her throat constricted as if someone had tightened a corset around it. She shrugged. "No sense dragging this out."

He winced.

She wished she could call back the insensitive words. But this good-bye would be hard for all of them. She had to somehow keep her composure.

She was an old pro at that. She opened her driver's door. "We were just heading over to the lodge to say good-bye."

Jonah stuffed his hands into his coat pockets. "Right. I'll walk over with Graham and meet you there?"

"Sure." She got into the car and started it up, watching Jonah take off across the property, Graham on his heels.

Two minutes later she was parking in the lot, her heart beating out a steady tattoo at what lay ahead. As she exited the car Graham bounded over.

Jonah had grabbed a snow shovel. "You can go on in if you want. I'm gonna clear the walk."

There was barely an inch of snow and it would likely be gone by noon. "Okay."

She headed inside where a fire was already crackling in the fireplace. The strains of "Silent Night" carried softly through the lobby speakers.

The stairs creaked as Tammy and Tom descended from their apartment, and Graham rushed to greet them, nails clicking on the wood floor.

Tammy's gaze fixed on Lauren. "We thought we heard you pull up. You can't already be packed and loaded."

"I got an early start."

Her brow furrowed. "But Jonah isn't here yet."

"He's outside shoveling the walk."

They reached the bottom of the stairs and headed her way, Tammy with her small, quick strides and Tom with his lumbering gait.

Tammy made a beeline for Lauren and wrapped her arms around her, holding tight. "You can't leave. You just can't."

"*Tammy,*" Tom said.

"Well, she's part of the family now. We're just supposed to let her go?"

"She has a life in Boston. It's her choice. Let loose of the girl, sweetheart. You're gonna squeeze her to death."

Tammy drew back, her teary gaze clinging to Lauren. "I wish you'd at least stay for Christmas, honey. It just won't be the same without you."

"I hate to miss it, but I should get settled into my apartment before my new job starts." Lauren hadn't planned to say anything touchy-feely. Her emotions were on edge and she didn't want to chance it. But they'd been so good to her and it wouldn't be right to say good-bye without letting them know how much they meant to her.

She swallowed past the lump in her throat. "Thank you for everything, both of you. You've been wonderful and I'll miss you all so much."

"Oh, honey . . ."

Tom stepped forward for an awkward hug. He gave her back a few pats and drew away. "You've been a joy to have around, Lauren. We sure do wish you the best of luck."

"Thank you. That means the world. And please take care of yourself, Tom."

He grumbled.

"Listen to your wife—she loves you." Lauren moved to more comfortable ground. "And if you have any questions about the barn or anything else, feel free to reach out."

"We will," Tammy said. "We're so grateful for everything you did here—all the improvements and ideas, and the barn. That Olivia is getting quite the deal. I'll make sure she knows it."

"Thank you."

"You're welcome here anytime, sweetheart. If you just need a place to get away for a couple days, you come right on up. We'll make room for you."

Lauren couldn't see that happening. But it was sweet of her to offer. "Thank you, I appreciate it. Well, I guess we'd better get on the road." She turned for the door, calling for Graham.

The dog trotted to the door, oblivious that he was about to leave this place, these people, for the last time. She was so jealous of his ignorance.

Tom and Tammy stayed put, probably wanting to give Jonah and her a chance to say their farewells in private.

With a final wave and a wobbly smile aimed their way, Lauren exited the lodge.

She didn't even have time for a deep, steadying breath because there was Jonah scraping the shovel across the patch of walkway closest to the lot. His cheeks were flushed, his hair windblown. He tossed the snow aside, then leaned the shovel against a tree trunk and turned her way. He tried for a brave face but didn't quite get there—his eyes betrayed his struggle.

She knew the feeling. The lump in her throat grew into a boulder as her feet carried her toward him, seemingly of their own volition. And then she was in his arms, trembling inside and praying he couldn't tell how very much she didn't want to let go of him.

He held her tight, his breath warming the top of her head, his lungs expanding against her chest.

Keep it together. Now is not the time to lose it.

"I'll miss you," he whispered.

That didn't even begin to cover it. "Me too. Thank you for"—*befriending me, being patient with me, loving me*—"everything."

"You're gonna do great at your new job. They're lucky to have you—don't you forget that." He drew away too soon, that brave smile propped in place, his jaw like granite. "I don't want to hold you up."

"It's pretty cold out here." She emphasized the thought by huddling awkwardly into her coat when she would've gladly stayed in his embrace for hours.

He opened the passenger door for Graham, who hopped in. Jonah gave the dog a final scratch. Then he shut the door, came around the car, and opened the driver's side door for her.

She brushed past him, not allowing herself to make eye contact, because her emotions were bubbling dangerously close to the surface.

"Drive carefully."

"I will."

He shut the door as Lauren buckled up. Then she started the car and put it in Reverse. She didn't glance his way until she'd put the car in Drive. He looked so stoic standing there, shoulders rigid, jaw tight. Her Jonah. Pain unfurled in her chest, overwhelming, unrelenting.

Tearing her gaze away, she accelerated. She barely made it to the end of the driveway before hot tears trickled down her face.

CHAPTER 34

LAUREN HADN'T MEANT to drive straight to Sydney's apartment. But when she looked up from her musings, that's where she was. The drive home to Boston had seemed long and wearying, and she'd entered the city to find the highways congested and construction everywhere.

Her initial crying spell had lasted for miles, and after she was spent of emotion, she determined to put Jonah from her mind and focus on her new job. She even placed a Bluetooth call to Olivia, and they went over the January events already on her calendar.

Now she pulled into the apartment lot and Graham stood on the passenger seat, nose pressed to the window.

"I guess we're stopping here. Would you like to see Aunt Sydney again?" Maybe Lauren didn't remember the two of them meeting, but Graham would.

He turned, tongue lolling from his mouth.

"I'll take that as a yes."

After letting Graham relieve himself, they entered the building. The dog trotted up the interior steps ahead of her. After two flights Lauren stopped at apartment E and knocked.

The door swung open almost immediately. Sydney's brown eyes widened at the sight of Lauren, and she grabbed her in a hug. "You're back! I was hoping you'd stop by."

"It's so good to see you."

Sydney withdrew. "You've been gone too long! Don't you go away again."

"It seems like forever."

"Come in, come in." She petted Graham on his way past. "Hello again, little friend."

Lauren followed her inside. Sydney's short and sassy black hair stuck out every which way. She wore a chic sweat suit in hunter green that complemented her olive skin tone.

Once inside, her friend squatted down to greet Graham. "I missed you, too, puppers. No doggies are allowed here, but we'll just keep that to ourselves, won't we?"

Graham licked her cheek, smiling the way only dogs can.

"Oh, you're such a charmer. We'll soon be besties." She cut Lauren a glance. "Maybe then you'll tell me why your mommy looks so rough."

"Gee, thanks."

"I was just getting ready to make a grilled cheese sandwich. Want one?"

"Sure," Lauren said. The sound of food made her slightly nauseated, but it was lunchtime.

"I can't believe you're finally home. We have massive amounts of catching up to do."

"I know. You have a boyfriend I haven't even met. I haven't seen my new apartment yet—I came straight here."

"Good girl. We can go over later and get your things from storage." Jeff had offered his help and the use of his truck. The two of them had met several weeks ago at the restaurant where she worked.

While Sydney got lunch underway, Lauren filled a dish with water and set it on the floor, but Graham was more interested in sniffing every square inch of the place.

They caught up, Sydney telling all the things she and Jeff had been up to since they'd last talked. They reviewed their Christmas plans—dinner here at Sydney's with a few friends—the restaurant's upcoming expansion, and Sydney's recent promotion to manager.

As Lauren set the table she told Sydney about her phone call with Olivia and the events already on her schedule for January. "I hope Ella left some good notes. I can't wait to throw an event I planned from start to finish."

"That'll happen soon enough." Sydney sent a smile Lauren's way as she moved the sandwiches to plates. "Do you realize you've attained your dream job—and you're barely out of college? You lucky girl."

"I know. Somebody pinch me."

"Well, it's hardly *luck*. You've worked hard for this, putting yourself through college while working full-time." Sydney studied her friend a long moment while Lauren straightened the napkins on the table.

Her friend's stare was like a heat-seeking missile. Then Sydney approached with the food, and they sat across from each other at the breakfast table and dug in.

At least Lauren did.

Sydney was still searching Lauren's face. "So are you ever gonna tell me what's going on?"

"What do you mean?"

"Come on. It's me you're talking to. I can see right through that fake smile of yours."

"I'm just tired from the drive, that's all."

"Uh-huh."

Lauren rolled her eyes. "Fine. It was harder leaving Pinehaven than I thought it would be."

Sydney pinned her with a disbelieving look. "Leaving Pinehaven or leaving Jonah?"

"It's one and the same, isn't it?"

"Not really."

Lauren lowered her sandwich as her throat thickened with that stupid lump again. It was just too fresh.

"I've never seen you like this. I thought you'd be over the moon about starting at Glitter. It's all you've been able to talk about since January."

"I am excited about it." She tried to infuse some enthusiasm into her words.

"Are you? 'Cause it seems like you're about to cry."

Lauren blinked back tears. "It was hard leaving them—all of them. I got attached to the Landrys. They're—they're so wonderful."

"They're warm and welcoming people."

She could almost feel Tammy's arms around her. Feel Tom's awkward pats on her back. But who was she kidding? It was Jonah she felt wrenched about leaving. Jonah she would miss most of all.

Lauren squirmed under Sydney's direct gaze. "I think I fell in love a little."

"I think you fell in love a lot," she said softly. "Did you tell him?"

"*No.*" Lauren dabbed at her eyes. "Why would I do that to him? Jonah's firmly rooted in Pinehaven. He's finally taking over the resort for his parents. And my life is here."

"Are you sure it's worth the sacrifice you're making?"

If only her mother had asked herself that before gallivanting off to New York with a man who probably lasted two minutes! Heat infused her face. "It's not just another job—it's my *dream* job. And I refuse to throw away my dreams for any man." She gave a hard sigh. "I don't want to talk about this anymore. It is what it is and there's just no point in wallowing in it. I'll get over it soon enough."

Sydney's expression softened. "All right, honey. Sorry for pushing. I'm here if you need to talk."

Lauren took a few deep breaths. She hadn't meant to get so riled up. "I appreciate that." But talking wouldn't fix anything. Talking wouldn't take away these feelings and it wouldn't give her everything she wanted. She'd feel better once she immersed herself in her new job. Until then she just had to be patient.

CHAPTER 35

LAUREN SLOGGED THROUGH Christmas feeling numb. She was all set up in her new apartment, which was situated on the third floor of a large brownstone. The neighborhood was charming, the house only two blocks from a nice park where she could walk Graham.

If the windows were a little thin, she could live with that. She would get used to the street noise and wail of sirens again. The floors must've been well insulated because she couldn't hear so much as a peep from her neighbors, whom she'd met only in passing. It was so quiet she often turned on the TV for company.

New Year's Eve passed with a fizzle. Sydney had tried to talk Lauren into going out with her and Jeff. She'd even offered to find Lauren a date. But the thought of being a third wheel or trying to make conversation with a stranger sounded exhausting. She begged off and spent the evening binge-watching *Gilmore Girls* and eating apple pie left over from Christmas.

New Year's Day came with five inches of snow, but that was okay. She spent the time preparing for her first day at Glitter. She steamed her outfit—a dove-gray Michael Kors suit that flattered her complexion and build. It projected a confident professional appearance, which was exactly what she needed for her big first day.

On arrival at the office her heart shimmied in her chest as Olivia showed her around the twentieth floor of the skyscraper located in the

Central Business District. The offices and lobby were sleek with glass and steel, and everyone was friendly enough, if not exactly warm.

But this wasn't a family resort—it was a prestigious corporation.

The place was a hive of activity and Lauren was eager to get going. Her office was small, but if she leaned just right, she could see Boston Commons, now covered with snow, and sidewalks where tiny people bustled to and fro.

Lauren sailed through her first day, keeping appointments and making certain the preparations for the upcoming parties Ella had planned were all on track.

BEFORE she knew it, Lauren had weathered her first three weeks and two events relatively unscathed. She loved engaging with new clients—so far she'd scheduled a June fundraiser for Four Paws International, a corporate training event for Fidelity Investments, and a retirement party for the CEO of City Sports. It was a good start and Olivia seemed pleased.

Each day she worked until her stomach growled for dinner—usually around seven—grabbed a quick bite on the way home, then worked from her laptop until almost bedtime. She was determined to impress Olivia.

Staying busy also staved off thoughts of Jonah and the Landrys, who'd recently been buried under nine inches of snow. Because, yes, she checked the resort's social media regularly for Meg's updates. It was Lauren's one guilty pleasure.

But after seeing photos of the resort's pine trees draped with snow and the frozen lake, hosting a smattering of ice shanties, she felt so homesick that she snapped her laptop shut. She dropped a tip on the table and left the restaurant.

All the way home her mind spun with thoughts of Jonah and the resort. What was he doing right now? How many cabins were booked? How had the first booked event at the barn gone Saturday?

Once parked in front of her building, she pressed her palm to her chest where the ache still resided. How long would it take to forget? She almost wished someone could thump her on the head so she could lose all memory of him and the love that often felt like a vise around her heart.

No such luck.

She'd just get home and get back to work. If she was busy planning her future, she couldn't focus on what she'd left behind.

She exited her car, huddled against the brittle wind, and made her way up the brownstone's steps. The entry was warm and cozy, even if it did have that musty, old-building smell. She went to the mailboxes, opened the box with her key, and grabbed the bundle—it had been a few days since she'd checked.

When she shut the box, one of the pieces fluttered to the ground. As she reached for the postcard advertisement, a sense of déjà vu swept over her.

Then she froze. Because this wasn't just an uncanny sensation that this had happened before. It was the flash of an actual memory.

The late-August sun beat high overhead as Lauren approached the resort's mailbox, a full day's schedule on her mind. Graham sniffed around the edges of the woods, tracking a squirrel or chipmunk. He'd filled out nicely in the month and a half since she'd found him. He'd become her little sidekick, following her everywhere, gazing up at her with admiration.

She was smiling as she reached into the box and retrieved the mail. But as she slid the bundle out, a piece fluttered to the ground. She stooped to pick it up, her gaze sweeping over the personal letter. It was addressed to her and had been forwarded from her Boston address. Her eyes caught on the sender's name, written in a familiar scrawl.

A cold chill swept down her spine. After twenty-one years of silence, her mother had written her a letter.

Lauren's hand trembled as her focus locked on the envelope. The return address was Boston. Her mother lived in Boston again? The zip code was a district only fifteen minutes from her apartment.

Fifteen minutes!

The thought made her pulse pound in her temples. What could the woman have to say for herself after all these years? Did she seek forgiveness? Did she think an apology would suffice?

Mentally whirling, Lauren started back down the drive, barely aware of Graham. Her legs wobbled beneath her.

Her mother had written her.

She couldn't quite digest the thought. She wanted to tear up the letter, unread. Her mother didn't deserve anything from her.

But the thought of that return address plagued her. Not only was her mother back in Boston, but she knew where Lauren had lived.

She had to find out what the woman wanted. Lauren stopped in the middle of the driveway, ripped open the letter, and unfolded sheets of notebook paper. The same familiar scrawl filled the pages.

Dear Lauren,

It's taken me many months to get up the nerve to write this letter. I looked up your information last fall and have started to write you so many times. I've even thought of knocking on your door. But I don't have the right to enter your life that way, and I realize you might not want to hear from me at all. I wouldn't blame you.

I'm writing to tell you how sorry I am. I don't expect your forgiveness. But I hope the deep regret and sorrow over my choices—

Lauren didn't want to hear this! She tore her eyes from the page. Couldn't get the letter out of her hands fast enough. She wadded the sheets of paper into a tight ball and threw them into the woods. That boulder was back, sitting so heavily on her chest, she could hardly breathe.

Her mother was in Boston. Her mother knew her former address—had considered knocking on her door!

Lauren's childhood rushed at her like a tsunami, threatening to swallow her. The feeling of being abandoned by the person who was supposed to love her most. The sensation of being moved like a chess piece in some cruel game where she always came out the loser. The feeling of belonging nowhere, belonging to no one. The uncertainty that hung over her like a cloud. Never feeling settled because her circumstances might change overnight, precipitating another move, another family, another school.

Her heart was like a jackhammer in her chest.

A terrible sense of dread crawled over her. She was having a heart attack. She would drop dead in the driveway and no one would find her for hours. Sweat trickled down the back of her neck.

Graham was there suddenly, nudging her hand with his wet nose. She took hold of his fur like a lifeline.

She slowed her breaths. Breathed more deeply so she didn't hyperventilate. *Think about something else!* She looked up and focused on the canopy of trees, their green leaves shimmering in the summer breeze. The squirrel nattering on the limb. A robin fluttering to her nest.

Breathe.

Just breathe.

Long minutes later she emerged from the encroaching darkness. Her breaths came more easily and her galloping heart rate slowed to a trot. Maybe she wouldn't die after all.

On shaky legs she continued down the drive, her head spinning, the past casting a long shadow over her soul. The thought of returning to Boston—where her mother now resided—seemed impossible. What if the woman came to see her? The sight of her would break Lauren into a million pieces. She was sure of it.

All these years she'd buried the hurt and animosity down deep. But now it all shot to the surface. She couldn't face her mother or even the fear that she might show up at any moment. Living so close, Lauren could run into her on the street. That was the last thing she wanted. But she had to return to Boston.

Didn't she?

She loved the city. Had a dear friend and a wonderful job awaiting her. And she had Jonah. Jonah, who was willing to leave his life, job, and family behind for her.

But why should he do that when the very thought of returning to Boston—to her mother—now made her feel sick inside?

If she stayed here, he wouldn't have to leave everything behind. Couldn't she stay and manage the barn venue instead? Perhaps turn it into a full-scale operation, offering wedding packages, complete with planning services? It had been on her mind since the beginning. She'd been sad at the thought of leaving it behind. Of leaving Pinehaven and the Landrys behind.

If she stayed, she could still have Jonah and a wonderful job that offered the independence she'd always sought. She could have all of that—and never have to face the possibility of seeing her mother's face again.

Darcy Wentworth would never find her in Pinehaven, New Hampshire.

All of this flashed through Lauren's mind as she stood in the brownstone's lobby, the mail quivering in her hands. So many realizations all at once.

After all these years, her mother had written her.

Jonah had not cajoled her into giving up the job. She'd done it willingly. She'd done it out of fear. The letter from her mother had shaken her to her core, and she'd chosen to run from all the feelings it stirred up.

Had she told Jonah about the letter? Surely it would've come up if she had. She recalled their conversation at the trapper's cabin. He'd said that Lauren had never heard from her mother after she'd left.

She couldn't believe she'd made such a monumental decision about her future—about *their* future—without telling him the real reason why.

She was running so hard from the past, she hadn't bothered giving him all the facts. The man had been about to propose to her based on her half-truths.

These discoveries so captured her thoughts that it took a moment to see an obvious, important detail: after all these weeks, a memory from the summer had finally resurfaced.

Perhaps more would follow. But she couldn't even think about that right now. Since she'd lost her memory she'd been processing everything all wrong. She hadn't given up her job for a man as she'd assumed. All these weeks since the accident she'd been so guarded, so afraid she'd lose herself in Jonah again and give up her dream.

But that wasn't what had happened at all.

Back in September she could've died, falling from that ladder. If she had, she never would've had the chance to find out why her mother had abandoned her. Never would've had the chance to confront the woman. Because she'd been too scared even to read the rest of the letter. Too scared to face the woman who'd caused her deepest wound.

But she wasn't too scared now. She wanted answers.

She jogged up the stairs, her thoughts spinning at these revelations.

She tried to remember more—like telling Jonah she wanted to stay in Pinehaven. But try as she might, she couldn't budge the cement wall that guarded the rest of her memories.

Moments later she let herself into her apartment. Graham ran to her greet her, happy and excited to have her home. She ruffled his fur. "Hey, boy. How you doing, huh?" She was glad the dog-sitting service had let him out only two hours ago because now she was in a big rush.

After giving him some affection and checking to make sure he had water, she strode to her bedroom. Once there she whipped open the closet door and grabbed her computer bag. The letter was just where she'd shoved it after she'd retrieved it from the woods—deep inside a pocket she never used. She perched on the bed and smoothed out the creases. Then she began reading where she'd left off two weeks before her accident.

I don't know how much you remember about our life before I left. You were so young. When you were three I had an accident at work involving a forklift. It resulted in a broken tibia and a lot of pain. And prescription pills.

Over the course of months I became terribly addicted to them, and before I knew it I was getting pills wherever I could. I became a drug addict. I was a terrible wreck, Lauren. I don't remember much of those years. I left you for a man who was little more than a promise of my next high. And you, my sweet baby girl, deserved so much more.

By the time I finally got help, I was alone and you were twelve. According to Social Services, you were being cared for by a nice couple that had children of their own. You had two parents and a brother and sister. You were attending a good school and lived in a nice suburban neighborhood.

I wanted to demand you back. I wanted to show up at that undisclosed location and haul you out of there, beg your forgiveness, and keep you with me forever. When I settled down I realized my foolishness. Instead I decided to start the long process of going through the system to regain custody of you.

But one day I took a hard look in the mirror. When I was at my lowest, I abandoned you. Even as far as I'd climbed from that pit, I only had a minimum-wage job at a car wash. I lived in an apartment in a rough area of town and had to have two roommates to make that financially feasible. I had no degree and a criminal record associated with the drug use. What could I possibly offer my darling girl?

For once it was time to think of what was best for you—and I was not it.

It ached to the marrow of my bones to realize that. To know you were better off with someone else. Better off without me in your life. But I was determined to put you first this time.

And so I did.

I hope that was the right decision. Every day I pictured you growing up in that happy family. Having your first date. Getting your driver's license. Going to prom. While you celebrated all those firsts with your new family, I celebrated them from afar, with tears in my eyes but hope in my heart that, for once, I'd done right by you.

I almost reached out on your eighteenth birthday. But I figured you probably didn't even remember me by then. You were so young. I didn't second-guess that decision until last summer when a coworker of mine (I work at an insurance company now) confided in me about the birth father who'd abandoned her. It had left her with insecurities and deeply rooted anger, and for the first time I feared my decision to stay out of your life had been a mistake.

I pray my terrible choices haven't caused you irreparable harm, Lauren. You don't deserve that. You were always such a sweet, open child with a warm, tender heart. I'm sorry for not loving you the way you deserved to be loved. I'm sorry for leaving you. I'm so deeply sorry, my sweet girl.

I'm here if you ever need me for anything. Even if you only want to unleash some justified anger or ask me hard questions. But I also understand completely if you want nothing to do with me at all. All I want is for you to be well and happy.

I love you,
Mom

Lauren didn't realize tears were streaming down her face until she set the letter aside. She had a good cry, then dashed the tears away and went for the tissues in the bathroom.

The woman has no right to profess her love. Parents who love their children don't abandon them. They don't track them down years later only to desert them again.

The family she'd described in the letter had been the Warrens, and yes, they were great. Lauren was happily ensconced in their family for over a year. And then Greg Warren's job had transferred him to California. At first Lauren thought she would go with them. But apparently Social Services didn't work that way. And the Warrens, for whatever reason, had never offered to adopt her.

So Lauren had been moved into another home in a different part of town, a different school. New friends. New foster parents. This one with a man who leered at her whenever his wife was absent.

She hadn't had the happy childhood her so-called mom had imagined. And she wasn't sure she could forgive the woman for the choices she'd made and the repercussions they'd had on Lauren's life.

She returned to her room, stuffed the letter back into her laptop case, the heavy weight of her past riding her shoulders like a freight train.

She didn't know what to do with all this new information. But she knew one thing. She was finished running from her past.

CHAPTER 36

FOR THE NEXT week Lauren was on autopilot. The content of that letter had shaken her world. She had few memories of her mother or her life before foster care. She only remembered feeling safe and loved, and then that terrible sense of the rug being pulled from beneath her.

She didn't remember her mother's work-related accident. Knew nothing of her addiction. Just that one day she was there and the next she was gone.

But as the days passed, her emotions swung from anger to sorrow and back to anger again. She reread the letter until it was soft with her tears.

And then she opened up to Sydney.

"My mother wrote me a letter," Lauren blurted the moment her friend answered the door.

"Oh, honey." Sydney grabbed her hand and pulled her inside. "You're shaking. Go sit down. I'll get you a drink."

Lauren settled in the living room and her hands trembled as she reached into her coat pocket to retrieve the letter. When Sydney rejoined her, Lauren handed it over. She didn't think she could relay the contents without melting into a puddle on the floor.

She waited as Sydney brushed away a tear or two, flipped to the second page. Lauren had a knot in her throat the size of Texas. She'd sat on this for a week, trying to process. Her job had become little more than a distraction, and she'd made some mistakes this week. Given a caterer the wrong dates, missed an appointment with a client. She couldn't even bring herself to care much.

Finally Sydney lowered the letter. "Wow, Lauren. I can't even imagine how you must be feeling."

"*I* don't even know how I'm feeling. It changes from one moment to the next. I've been a hot mess this week. I didn't know she was an addict. I didn't know about the accident. They didn't tell me any of this. I only knew she left me for a man because he came to our door and off they went and she never returned."

"Oh, Lauren. How awful for you."

"Sometimes I'm so angry I want to slap her. And other times, when I'm reading that letter, I start feeling sympathy for her, and then I don't *want* to feel sympathy because her actions caused all of this—everything that transpired afterward."

"I can only imagine that mixed emotions are completely normal under the circumstances. She abandoned you and you've gone without answers for all these years and now here they are."

Lauren's eyes filled with tears and overflowed. "I was just a little kid."

Sydney wrapped her arms around her. "It was so unfair. I'm sorry that happened to you. It's truly a miracle you turned out to be such a wonderful person."

"I have these little flashes of memory from when I was really young. I feel safe and loved in all of them."

"I guess she gave you a good start at least. Maybe that was enough of a foundation to get you through the tough stuff you had to face. I admire you so much for overcoming all those challenges."

Lauren leaned back and fixed her gaze on Sydney. "But have I really? When a letter from her rocks me like this . . . have I really overcome my past?"

"Look at you, honey. Your chances of being a successful adult probably weren't that great, statistically. Yet you're a good person. Kind. You're strong and resilient. You put yourself through college and now you're working for a prestigious company. I'm so proud of how far you've come."

And yet that job wasn't exactly feeling the way she'd expected it to. Maybe she'd just been too overwhelmed by the letter. Once she got past this, she'd feel more like herself.

Wouldn't she?

"I think I need to go see her." The words blurted out, releasing a weight from her chest.

After a moment of silence, Sydney nodded. "Okay. Let's talk about that. What do you hope to get out of a meeting with her?"

"I don't know." Lauren collected her thoughts. "I guess I need to tell her how I feel. Maybe I need more answers. But I can't go on like this, wondering and feeling angry. I've hardly been able to do my job."

"Well, no wonder. This is traumatic stuff. If my long-lost dad resurfaced, I don't know what I'd do."

"Would you want to see him?"

Sydney paused as if considering the thought. "I don't know. I think I'd be too mad at first. But later . . . maybe. Take some time if you need it. Or go see a counselor and talk things over. I went to that good one a couple years ago—Liz. I could get you her information."

"I might do that. But I really think I need to see her." Her heart quivered at the thought.

Sydney squeezed her hand. "Whatever you need to do. I'll go with you if you want company. Just know I'm here for you."

It was two days later, a Saturday and the first day of February, that Lauren got up the courage.

She pulled her car to the curb in the run-down neighborhood. The two-story apartment building was made of faded red brick, but someone was trying to keep it up. The paint on the black shutters and front door seemed fresh, and even though it was barely eight in the morning, the walkway had already been shoveled. The yard boasted a few nice trees, and shrubs crowned with snow crouched along the exterior walls.

She stared at the face of the building, her hands wrapped around the cold steering wheel. Which of those apartments was her mother's? Apartment B, so the bottom floor probably. The one with the dead hanging plant on the patio? Or the one with the covered grill? She didn't know anything about her mother. Probably wouldn't even recognize her.

She'd searched for her on social media this week and found nothing. Her mother apparently kept a low profile. *Like mother, like daughter*, she mentally scoffed. The woman had probably given up on hearing from Lauren since she'd sent the letter months ago.

She watched as a young woman exited the building with a toddler. Maybe Lauren shouldn't have come here. Maybe she should've reached out by letter instead. But she was so unsteady, her emotions raw. The element of surprise would give her an advantage, and she needed that. Would her mother even know her?

She drew a deep breath and blew it out. Time to face this head-on. She turned off the engine and exited the car. Huddled against the cold, she rushed toward the building. A plane roared past overhead. Down the street a garbage truck beeped, then emptied a can into its depths. The smell of freshly fallen snow filled her lungs.

When she reached the building she opened the door, stepped into the well-lit entry, and wiped her feet. She'd worn her Prada suede ankle boots—she needed all the bolstering she could get—her matching leather moto jacket, and a pair of gold hoop earrings. She wasn't going into this feeling like that foster kid in someone else's castaways.

She snorted at the thought because in actuality she'd bought her entire outfit secondhand.

And then there it was. A black door with a big gold *B* on the face. She stopped, but her heart thudded ahead like a galloping horse. She wet her lips. Swallowed hard. Then knocked.

As she lowered her hand, she scrambled to remember what she'd planned to say. But everything seemed to have vanished from her mind.

A noise sounded from behind door. Someone was home. And then a lock clicked and the door swept open to reveal a woman with wavy light brown hair worn just past her shoulders. "Can I help you?"

Darcy Wentworth. Her mother. Lauren saw herself in that petite face, in those green eyes fixed on her.

Her mother must've seen it too. Her lips parted. Her eyes widened. She covered her mouth. "Lauren?" she asked softly. "Is that you?" Tears erupted and streamed down her face.

Words caught in Lauren's throat, jumbling together like a twenty-car pileup.

"It is you. Oh, honey! Come in." She opened the door wider. "Will you come in? Please?"

Lauren stepped tentatively forward, her pulse racing, her lungs working to keep up. She passed her mother and the door clicked shut behind her. She glanced around at the homey living room, complete with area rugs and plants and candles.

I'm standing in my mother's apartment.

A yellow tabby cat slinked forward and wound around Lauren's legs.

"Sorry." Darcy snatched the cat away. "He—he's a very curious little guy. Have a seat. Can I get you something to drink?"

"No, thank you."

Her mother stared while Lauren perched on the closest seat, an armchair. Then she covered her mouth again with trembling fingers. "I'm sorry, I just can't believe you're here. I'd given up all hope."

It helped a bit that her mother was more shaken than she was. It seemed only fair. "I got your letter."

As if losing a war with gravity, Darcy sank onto the sofa across from Lauren. It was so strange seeing her familiar face again. She looked older. Her eyelids were hooded, and thought lines creased her forehead. She got by with little or no makeup.

"I hope it didn't . . . make things worse for you. I prayed so hard that I was doing the right thing. I didn't want to disrupt your life. And then when I didn't hear back, I feared I'd made yet another mistake."

Lauren wet her dry lips. "I don't think it was."

"Oh, I'm so glad." Darcy's eyes seemed to drink her in as her face softened. "You're so beautiful. Far prettier than I ever was. Lauren, are you happy? Has life been good to you?"

Lauren thought of her disjointed, unsettled childhood, and anger burst to the surface. A snort erupted. "No, it really hasn't."

The light extinguished in Darcy's eyes just before she closed them. "Oh no. No. I'm so sorry to hear that."

"You apologized in your letter. It doesn't make everything right."

Her mother swallowed hard. "No, it doesn't. How can I help you, honey? What can I do for you?"

There was a question. What could her mother do for her? Did she want to rail at her for leaving? Curse her for the string of events that came afterward? She searched the face of the woman across from her. The woman who was wringing her hands and staring bravely, eyes full of regret.

The woman who'd been ensnared by an addiction she'd acquired from an accident. She'd been only twenty when she'd had Lauren. And a year younger than Lauren was now when she'd left. She'd missed out on most of her daughter's childhood. Was now in her midforties and had little to show for her life but regrets.

The sympathy the letter had conjured up bloomed once again. Darcy Wentworth had already paid a high price for her mistakes.

"You can yell at me if you want. I wouldn't blame you for hating me."

"I don't hate you." Lauren wasn't sure what she felt. But the negative emotions were draining away as if someone had pulled a plug. She didn't want to throw her tattered childhood in her mom's face. Maybe she'd wanted to earlier, but not now. Not seeing her and looking into her war-torn eyes.

"How can I help you then? I'll do anything you want."

Lauren thought a moment. Thought about those happy little flashes from her earliest years. They were short and vague and left so many gaps.

"I'd like you to tell me about when I was little," she said.

CHAPTER 37

LAUREN SLIPPED INTO the grand kitchen to check on the champagne.
Mr. Carrington was just about to offer congratulations to his daughter
and future son-in-law, and everyone needed a glass.

A young server passed with a tray of champagne, and a dozen more
trays were loaded and ready to go. She'd hired her previous employer as
caterer, and Mercy was doing a great job.

"Speech in five minutes," Lauren told her.

"We're on it."

Lauren stepped back into the fray of the party. Glitter didn't ordinarily
do private events, but Mr. Carrington had been one of Ella's big corporate
clients. He'd approached Lauren about the event in early January, after
his daughter's Christmas engagement. Olivia had agreed that they should
cater to the client in this case.

It had been a quickly planned affair, but since the event was to be held
in their home, she didn't have to secure a venue last minute. The party's
atmosphere was beautiful and inviting—the bayside mansion didn't hurt
matters—and the event had gone off without a hitch so far.

Moments later Mr. and Mrs. Carrington gathered the attention of
their guests—about a hundred of their closest friends and relatives—
and congratulated the couple.

The bride- and groom-to-be, who were about Lauren's age, flushed happily as they gazed into each other's eyes.

The toast was made, glasses were raised, and Lauren smiled as Mrs. Carrington gathered her daughter in for a heartfelt embrace. The two were very close, you could just tell. She took Cassandra's face in her hands and said something that made her tearful daughter laugh.

Lauren wondered if she and her mother could ever have that kind of intimate relationship. Perhaps too much time had passed. Time they'd spent apart, each living their own lives. But her visit to the woman's apartment last week had gone better than she'd hoped. She'd stayed for two hours and left completely drained.

But hopeful. They were meeting for coffee next week. It was a start.

Lauren turned her attention to the happy couple. The announcement finished, people gathered to offer their own congratulations. She zeroed in on the groom's face. He looked quite ordinary really, with brown hair and an average face. But his beaming smile and the light in his eyes when he gazed at Cassandra made him extraordinary. His love for her was written all over his face.

Would anyone ever look at her that way again?

"You did a fantastic job with the party, Lauren." Mrs. Carrington approached, tucking a dark, curly lock behind her ear. "And on such short notice. I was worried when Greg told me Ella was retiring. She's been handling his events for years."

"Thank you. I'm glad you're happy. Your home is so beautiful and inviting, it really didn't take much."

"Oh, you're being too modest. I've had to throw a party or two myself—enough to know it is not my forte." Her head tilted as she studied Lauren, brown eyes twinkling. "I don't suppose you plan weddings, do you, dear?"

Lauren laughed. "I think Glitter would draw the line there."

"Oh, well, it never hurts to ask." The woman squeezed her arm. "We'll be sure to recommend you to Greg's business associates. You've got a real talent for this."

"Thank you. That's very kind of you."

Mrs. Carrington waved at someone across the room, giving a broad smile. "You'll have to excuse me. My great-aunt is about to tell me why my dress doesn't suit my coloring and complain our chairs are uncomfortable." She winked.

After she left Lauren began collecting empty flutes. While she worked she took stock of her emotions. She was feeling a bit unsettled, which made no sense. This event—the first one she'd planned start to finish—had gone off without a hitch. Her clients were pleased. She would soon be recommended among a very elite set of corporate types. And still she was feeling vaguely—there was no getting around the word—*depressed*.

She thought back through the past few minutes when her mood had taken a hit. The toast, the happy couple, the mother-daughter moment. All of it had stirred up a bit of melancholy. But it was Mrs. Carrington's question about planning a wedding that had stolen the air from her party balloon. The comment had dredged up thoughts of the barn venue she'd worked so hard on. Of Pinehaven. The Landrys.

Jonah.

She thought of that engagement ring tucked away in a safe on the lodge's second story. The ring he'd bought for her. Her gaze drifted to the happy couple across the room, chatting with another couple their age. She and Jonah could've been engaged right now. She could've been wearing that ring on her finger. But she'd fallen and hit her head and now she was here in Boston, alone.

She turned her hand over and traced the fawohodie symbol on her wrist. Freedom and independence. She had officially achieved both. She was her own boss and her salary provided the kind of upscale studio apartment she'd only dreamed about as a girl. So why wasn't she happy?

She kept sweeping away the glasses until they were all in the kitchen. There was really nothing else for her to do here. Her part was finished. The caterer was in charge of cleanup.

She waited for Mercy to finish speaking with a server. "I'm gonna take off now unless there's anything you need from me."

"Nope, we're all good here. Go home and get some rest. Thanks for the business."

"Of course. Thanks, Mercy. Your crew did a terrific job."

"I'll see you next time."

Lauren slipped from the party and handed the valet her ticket. Vehicles were parked in a long string down the curving road. As she waited for her car in the makeshift shelter, Mercy's words repeated themselves in her head: "*next time.*"

Lauren gave her head a sharp shake. Why was she feeling so gloomy? She should be celebrating her first event. She was proud it had gone off so well. But . . . the triumph of success wasn't quite living up to the hype.

What was wrong with her?

When the valet arrived with her car, she tipped him, then drove toward her apartment. And the longer she drove, the more she realized that she didn't just feel gloomy. She felt homesick. She missed Pinehaven and the resort.

She missed Jonah.

It had been seven whole weeks since she'd last seen him. How long would it take to stop missing him? For these feelings to dull?

What if they never did?

The drive home took forever as traffic was awful on Friday nights. It was almost eleven by the time she let herself into her apartment. Graham acted as if he hadn't seen her in a century. She took him outside and he did his business quickly as he didn't enjoy the cold any more than she did.

Back in the apartment she changed into leggings, fixed herself a drink, and settled in her favorite recliner, Graham curling up at her feet. She grabbed her laptop and went straight to the resort's Facebook page, hungry for news. Meg only posted every so often during the winter.

She had texted Lauren a few times with questions, and Tammy had checked on her twice. But nothing from Jonah. Not that she'd expected anything. Still, a part of her had hoped.

The page opened and a photo caught her eye. Jonah stood in plaid flannel, faded jeans, and work boots in front of the lodge's fireplace, warming his hands. The fire cast a golden glow on his skin as he stared into the flames, wearing a pensive expression. His hair had grown out a bit and his beard was back, although it was nicely trimmed.

The sight of him stole her breath. Her stomach squeezed. She ached for him. She reached out and touched his face. But the screen was cold and flat and lifeless.

She read the caption below the photo. *Even our resident handyman needs to warm up by the fire occasionally. Come stay in one of our picturesque cabins on beautiful Loon Lake and take advantage of our bargain winter rates. Ice fish, snowmobile, and ski to your heart's content!*

She skimmed the thirteen comments below, three of them written by guests she'd met this year. It had been fun meeting people from all around the country, making them feel at home, having a small part in making their vacations special.

She glanced at the photo of Jonah again and remembered she had a whole cache of photos on her phone she hadn't let herself pore over. But now she couldn't seem to stop herself. She opened the app and scrolled backward to her early days at the resort.

She'd taken beautiful shots of the sun rising or setting over the lake, inviting shots of cabins draped in snow, smoke curling from their chimneys. Then came the photos she recognized, only through the brochures, of Flume Gorge. The bridge, the tumbling creek, the falls, and then a mountain vista.

Then there was Jonah, standing on the end of the resort's main pier, staring out at the water. Jonah chopping wood. And another, apparently taken moments later as he spotted her, a playful grin flashing on his face.

There was a sequence of at least ten goofy selfies Jonah had taken at a restaurant when she'd apparently left him alone with her phone.

The two of them snuggled up in the motorboat. A selfie with the sunset in the background. Jonah at the coffee shop, white mug to his quirked lips, his piercing blue eyes staring straight at the camera's lens. They seemed so happy. So relaxed. So in love.

There were dozens more, some with Meg and the whole Landry clan. She soaked in each one. For the first time since her accident, she wanted her memory back. She wanted all the memories attached to these photos. To this man.

That was out of her control. But she still had the ability to make new ones. Her heart did a slow roll. She wanted to be back at the resort right now. She wanted to be with Jonah.

She wanted to be *home*.

Her breath left her lungs in a sudden rush. She wasn't sure when Boston had stopped being her home, but it had. And the so-called dream job for which she'd fought so hard . . . It had only left her feeling empty. There were things here she cared about. People she cared about.

But Boston was no longer her home.

Her pulse racing, she checked the time. If she left now, she would arrive in the middle of the night. That would be crazy. If she had any brains at all, she'd get a good night's sleep and wait till morning.

But who was she kidding? She couldn't sleep now. And the thought of staying in this big, empty apartment for one more night made her want to weep. She wanted to be home *right now*.

She set aside her laptop and popped to her feet, startling Graham. "Wanna go for a ride, boy? Huh? Wanna go home?" Graham's mouth curved into that familiar doggy smile.

CHAPTER 38

A TEXT AWAKENED Jonah from his fitful sleep. Judging from the faint light streaming into his cabin, the day was just dawning. He reached blindly for his phone.

The text was from Javi. *Morning. Thanks for lending an ear yesterday. Let's get together again soon.*

Jonah set the phone back on the nightstand. They'd gone snow-mobiling yesterday and had stopped at Birdie's Deli for a late dinner. Javi and his wife were doing much better now that the slow season was underway. Jonah was glad to hear it. When Javi had asked about him, Jonah tried to put on a good face. But Javi had seen right through him.

"I know you miss her, man. You don't have to pretend."

"I'm not trying to pretend. I just . . . There's nothing to be done, you know? It is what it is. I just have to . . ." *Forget her? Fall out of love with her? How did a person even go about that?* "Move on."

Javi leaned back in the booth. "Allison told me about Carson. Is that what's eating at you?"

Because, yes, Carson had gotten that residency in Boston he'd been hoping for. He'd soon be in Lauren's backyard for the foreseeable future. He'd probably already reached out and invited her to dinner or something. Jealousy twisted Jonah's gut. He should want the best for her. So why did the thought of her with another man make him crazy? "She deserves to be happy."

"She was happy with you. I saw it firsthand."

"Sadly, she doesn't remember that." He gave his head a shake. "She's made her choice. She doesn't want me anymore." Voicing the thought made his bruised heart ache.

Javi regarded him for a long moment. "I'm sorry. I really am. I'd hoped it would work out."

Jonah shoved the memory away and pushed out of bed. He just had to keep putting one foot in front of the other. These past seven weeks he'd powered through the days one hour at a time—and he'd go on doing so. What choice did he have?

He stretched out his back. Cedar didn't have the most comfortable mattress, but he'd refused to take Lauren's cabin. No way would he live and sleep in a place that still smelled like her.

But he couldn't get away from her. Everywhere he looked, there was Lauren. Not only in the cabin where she'd slept, but on the pier and in the lodge. The coffee shop, his favorite restaurants. Not to mention the barn. It turned out his parents had been right about that. Her fingerprints were on every square inch of the place. It was a monstrous monument to the woman he loved.

And there was no avoiding it because he had to maintain it and oversee its rental. A day didn't go by that the venue didn't absorb some of his time. Part of him wished he could just let the weeds claim it again, but that wasn't an option. The renovation had been costly. It would earn itself out, but that would take time. Maybe it had been a smart business decision, but it was eating away at his soul.

When he got down or felt lonely, he tried to imagine Lauren in Boston, living her best life. He pictured her thriving in her new job, happy and fulfilled. But there was no man in this imaginary utopia. He couldn't quite get there yet.

In reality he had no real idea what her life was like. She rarely posted on social media. But he had been stalking the Glitter website. A few weeks ago they'd added her professional headshot along with a bio. The brief paragraph told him nothing new. But he spent way too much time gazing at the beautiful photo, wondering if she was happy. If she missed him at all.

Enough wallowing.

Jonah went to turn on the shower. The best thing he could do was stay busy. So as he stepped under the spray of water he turned his mind to his job, mentally reviewing his chores and errands for the day. First on the list: restocking the dwindling woodpile.

A thud awakened Lauren. She stirred from the semiconscious state she'd been in since she'd flung herself into bed. She pulled the covers to her chin, hunkering against the morning chill as the memory of last night rose like fog in her brain.

She'd arrived at the resort around three and searched for a vacancy. Apparently Jonah had not taken her old cabin—the dusting of snow in front of the door was undisturbed. She made herself at home in her old bed and waited for morning.

She must've fallen asleep. She stretched, becoming more aware. Early dawn light seeped through the curtains. And the rhythmic thudding coming from outside jarred her wide awake. She smiled at the familiar sound. Jonah was chopping wood.

She flung off the covers and went to the window. Through the parted curtains, she spotted him down the way and her heart bucked.

Then slowly, trepidation leaked through her veins like poison. What if he'd given up on her? What if he didn't want her back? She'd left him in the dust for a *job*. How stupid she'd been. Why was hindsight so clear?

Graham nuzzled her hand and she petted him absently. Then she went to the bathroom for a quick refresh. The mirror revealed a disheveled, worried version of herself.

After swishing the complimentary mouthwash, she smoothed her hair and slapped some pink into her cheeks. "All right, girl. This is it. Be brave." She left the bathroom and put on her shoes and coat, then regarded Graham. "We're gonna do this, buddy. You ready?"

When she opened the door, he shot out like a torpedo. She followed in his path, watching as he approached Jonah. Watching as Jonah spotted him. He stopped midswing and turned abruptly, searching for her.

Then he found her.

Lauren froze as their gazes collided. She couldn't look away. The moment drew out, long and intense. Awareness crackled in the distance between them. Her heart stuttered, waiting for some sign from him.

Then his lips turned up.

And that was all she needed. She started walking, unable to keep from returning his smile. And the closer she got, the wider his smile stretched. The more his eyes sparkled.

He tossed the axe aside just in time to catch her in his arms.

She wrapped herself around him and held him tight. Breathed him in. *"Jonah."* It felt so good to have his strong arms around her. She never wanted him to let her go. She squeezed her eyes against the sting of tears. "I missed you so much. I'm sorry for everything I put you through."

He drew back, a look of relief in his eyes. "You got your memory back."

She chuckled. "No."

His smile wilted a bit and his brows knitted as he searched her face. "I don't understand."

She palmed his face. "Understand this, Jonah Landry. I love you. You made me fall in love with you—not once but twice. And I don't want to be apart anymore. I want to live here and work here and be with you forever and ever, if you'll have me."

He drank her in. "Wait. You love me?"

"I drove all the way here in the middle of the night, didn't I? I'm wrapped up with you like a burrito. I said the words out loud. Now are you gonna kiss me or what?"

He didn't waste a second. Just leaned in and brushed his lips gently across hers. There was so much in his kiss. Devotion, joy, want, hope. Her mind spun with all the sensations even as her heart healed with love's tender balm. There was something familiar in his searching kiss. In his reverent touch. In his exquisite taste.

Jonah tasted like home.

He withdrew, tears in his eyes. "You're really here. I thought I'd lost you forever."

She placed a hand on his bristly cheek and gazed at him, a promise in her eyes. "I'll never leave you again. So much has happened since I left. I can't wait to tell you everything. But later. Right now I just want to make up for lost time."

She kissed him again. And soon she was breathless and so warm that she was about to melt entire acres of snow.

Then he jolted away from her, bracing her with his hands on her arms. "Wait right here." He was already trotting toward the lodge, Graham on his heels.

"Jonah . . . ," she called with a chuckle.

"Be right back! Don't go anywhere."

She gave a huff of laughter as the door slapped shut behind him. "Where would I go?" She was already home. So she stood alone in the quiet pine forest, waiting, her thoughts spinning, her heart full. She was about to burst with the happiness welling up inside her. She wrapped her arms around her waist, reveling in how easily he'd welcomed her back into his arms, into his life.

Less than a minute later he exited the lodge and strode toward her. His expression was more serious now. His mouth set in a resolute line.

By the time he stopped in front of her, she was a bundle of nerves.

Then he dropped to one knee. And there was the ring, the diamond twinkling in the morning light.

She gasped.

He gazed up at her, love shining in his eyes. "Lauren Wentworth, you stole my heart. I was afraid to fall in love with you, but there was no stopping it. Those walls you put up guard such a soft, beautiful heart. Once I saw you, really saw you, there was no one else for me. You're it, honey. There's never gonna be anyone else." Tears gathered again in his eyes. "I want so much to spend the rest of my life showing you how much I love you. Will you be my wife?"

Overwhelmed, Lauren struggled to choke out words. She brushed away a fallen tear.

"That isn't the proposal I'd originally planned, but I wanted to ask before you changed your mind."

She framed his face. "I'm not changing my mind, you dope. And it was perfect in every way. My answer's yes, Jonah. Yes, yes, *yes*."

He flashed a grin as he stood and drew her into her arms. He kissed her again, that beautiful mouth of his demanding a response she was only too happy to give. Long moments later she was melting under his skilled lips. He was very good at this. She'd had many questions over the past few months, but right now there was only one: How in the world had she forgotten *this*?

When their breaths were ragged and their skin heated, he drew away, putting only a few inches between them. "I almost forgot how good this was."

"Well, I totally forgot, and now I'm kicking myself for all the time we lost. Jonah, you're everything to me. I've never been so happy in all my life. Thank you for being so patient with me."

"You're worth the wait, honey."

Her heart melted at the sweet words, at the tenderness on his face. Then a movement from her periphery caught her attention. "Um, Jonah, your parents are watching from the window."

"Well, I wouldn't let them come out."

She snorted.

"They begged."

Typical. She slid her hand up to his shoulder so she could admire the beautiful ring. The *familiar* ring. "Um, Jonah, I couldn't love the ring more. But full disclosure here . . . This isn't exactly the first time I've seen it."

He leaned back. "What?"

Just then Tammy rushed from the lodge, beaming at them. Tom lumbered behind her. They'd waited as long as they could.

"It seems we have company," Lauren said. "I'll fill you in later."

Then she was swept up into a hug. Tammy was gushing and blubbering. Well, all of them were blubbering a little. After an exchange of hellos and hugs and congratulations, their happy little party headed for the warmth of the lodge, Jonah's arm draped around her shoulders.

His parents entered ahead of them.

"Um, wait a minute." Lauren held Jonah back, then glanced back toward the barn. "I was just wondering . . . By any chance is my dream job still available?"

"Are you sure that's what you want? I can move to Boston, Lauren. I'd move there in a heartbeat to be with you."

Lauren shook her head. "This is what I want. This is my home."

He kissed her nose. "Then don't you worry, sweetheart. We've been holding that job just for you."

EPILOGUE

MAY WAS A perfect month for a New Hampshire wedding. Fresh green leaves clothed the trees, colorful tulips dotted the property, the town was not yet teeming with tourists, and business was slow.

Three months wasn't much time to plan a wedding. But when you knew what you wanted and your dream venue was at your disposal, the prospect wasn't too daunting. Lauren found her perfect gown on a trip to Portland with Sydney, Meg, and Tammy. The satin A-line dress featured off-the-shoulder sleeves with a fitted waistline. She felt like a princess in the elegant gown. It would be a smallish wedding anyway, with only seventy or so guests. Sydney and Meg would serve as her bridal party, and Javi and Tom would stand with Jonah.

Lauren swept her gaze over the barn's interior. Tomorrow this place would be filled with friends and family here to witness her union with Jonah. It was still afternoon, so she couldn't gauge the effects of the twinkle lights just yet. But sunlight would stream through the windows during the ceremony, making it perfect for photography. And by the time the reception was underway, the festive fairy lights would set a celebratory tone.

At the spot where they would exchange their vows, a beautiful archway stood, draped with blush tulle. Tomorrow peonies in blush, white, and ivory would be added. At the thought of exchanging vows with Jonah, Lauren smiled.

She'd only grown to love him more in the weeks since her return. He was everything she'd ever wanted in a man, in a husband, and she couldn't imagine her life without him.

After Jonah's proposal she'd given her two weeks' notice at Glitter, then spent her remaining time there helping her replacement acclimate—it was the same woman Olivia had originally been considering. After some initial frustration, her boss eventually came around—especially once Tammy called and told her how happy they were to be welcoming Lauren into their family.

Lauren had settled into her new role quickly and with a passion she'd never had for her so-called dream job in Boston. The Landrys had been clear from the beginning: the venue was hers to run as she pleased. And run it she had. The summer schedule was quickly filling up. Lauren had scouted out competent caterers, photographers, linen services, and three amazing florists. She'd scoured the area for talented DJs and bands. It seemed only right that the first wedding she'd planned start to finish was Jonah's and hers.

And then, in the middle of a snowy March, a memory from last summer surfaced from the recesses of her brain. It had been the day she over-booked a cabin and Jonah took her on a bike ride on the rail trail. It was a lovely memory, and after telling Jonah about its emergence, she held it close to her heart.

In the following weeks a few more memories, seemingly random, trickled in. Their time at Flume Gorge, Lauren tossing a pine cone at Jonah, a girls' night out with Meg and Tammy. They were precious pieces to a puzzle that might never be complete.

But those memories were a bonus, not a necessity. She loved Jonah fully even if her memory was incomplete. Speaking of Jonah . . .

He'd been very accommodating about the wedding plans. His only stipulations were a particular local band and the honeymoon locale. So

Lauren chose the color scheme, invitations, and virtually everything else—though he did assist her with all of it.

He and the Landrys had helped set up for tomorrow, and the space had turned out perfectly. White chairs were lined up with perfect precision on each side of the aisle. After the ceremony they would be swept away and replaced by tables while the wedding party posed for photos lakeside.

Arms slipped around her from behind as the familiar scent of Jonah's soap filled her lungs. "Just one more day until you're Lauren Landry."

"I can't wait." She folded her arms over his. "Do you like how the barn turned out?"

"It's beautiful. You're amazing at this—I knew you would be."

"Well, a girl envisions her wedding day. All I had to do was bring it to life."

"It's perfect. But truth be told, I'd marry you in a muddy pigpen as long as you promised to be mine forever."

She turned and slid her hands up his shoulders. "Well, let's do the beautiful barn wedding—and I'll still be yours forever."

"Deal." He gave her a quick peck. Then another, his lips lingering on hers for an extra beat. "It's been a busy week."

"Crazy busy."

Her mom had arrived this afternoon and was staying in Willow. They'd met up several times since their reunion in February and kept in touch via texting. Lauren didn't know if they'd ever share the kind of relationship Tammy had with her children—they'd been separated so long. But she was willing to build a relationship, and her mother seemed grateful for the opportunity.

Jonah nuzzled her neck. "I'm so looking forward to having you all to myself for seven sunny days in Bermuda."

"Ahhhh, I can't wait to lounge on the beach with an umbrella drink and soak up all that sunshine with my new husband."

"Are you in a bikini in this scenario?"

"I am. And it's red."

He groaned. "You're killing me. Tell me more."

She chuckled. "You'll see it soon enough, my love. Maybe we should go over a few details instead as we do have a wedding tomorrow. Did you pick up the tuxes?"

"For the record I'd rather think about the bikini. But yes, I picked them up this morning. And I took Graham to get groomed this afternoon. He smells like a spa."

"Perfect." Because, yes, Graham would be their ring bearer. Lauren had been working with him for weeks, and their sweet little mutt had his part down pat.

"Can I at least *see* the bikini?"

She snorted. "Let's see, what else? The rehearsal starts at five, followed by dinner at The Landing, but that's all set. The flowers will be delivered in the morning. Do you think we should start boxing up my things?" Jonah's parents had bought a little Craftsman near town, and Jonah and Lauren would be moving into their old place above the lodge when they returned from their honeymoon. It would be a new start for them all.

"I've already boxed up my stuff." His lease expired at the end of the month. "I think yours can wait till we're home."

Home. Such a nice word—and never more fitting. After years of searching she had finally found the place where she belonged. And the people with whom she belonged. Joy welled up inside her until she nearly burst with it.

"I have something for you." He reached down and lifted a manila envelope with a white bow from a chair.

"What's this?"

He handed it to her. "It's your wedding present."

"But I haven't even wrapped yours yet." She'd gotten him a watch he'd been eyeing online. She loved the idea—the gift of time.

"I can open yours later. I wanted you to have this a little early."

"It's a—a *document*?"

"Open it up."

She slid her finger under the flap. The envelope was about half an inch thick. "If this is a prenup, I should inform you that's not an appropriate wedding gift. Also, you have a very thorough lawyer."

"Funny. Stop stalling."

She reached inside and pulled out a sheaf of papers secured with a clip. There was only one line centered on the front page: *Before We Were Us*.

Her gaze darted to him.

"Remember that writers group we hosted back in October? I've been working with one of them—Donna—since you came back. She wrote our story."

Her eyes stung with tears. "Oh, Jonah. Thank you."

"It includes scenes from every date we went on and every interaction I could remember. I recorded it all—how we fell in love—and she wrote it all out in story form. I hope you like how it turned out."

She hugged the pages to her chest. "I haven't even read it and I already love it."

"Maybe you'll get all your memories back. But if you don't . . . I figured this was the next best thing."

"I can't wait to read it." She couldn't believe this man. Had never known there was someone so wonderful meant just for her. She was in awe of him.

"What's that look for?" Jonah smiled down at her, his expression full of love and affection.

How to describe the overwhelming, exquisite feelings flooding through her right now? "I'm just so happy. I can't wait to be your wife, Jonah Landry."

He leaned his forehead against hers. "I'm happy, too, honey. We've been through a lot already—and it's only made me love you more. Just imagine how much I'll love you fifty years from now."

Fifty years of Jonah. She grinned at the thought of their life together. "Imagine the story we'll be able to tell our children and grandchildren. Once upon a time, before we were us . . . we were just two lonely people in search of one another."

"I like the way our story begins."

She palmed his face. "I like the way it ends."

Jonah pressed a soft kiss to her lips, then smiled into her eyes. "And all the parts in between."

ACKNOWLEDGMENTS

Bringing a book to market takes a lot of effort from many different people. I'm so incredibly blessed to partner with the fabulous team at HarperCollins Christian Fiction led by publisher Amanda Bostic: Patrick Aprea, Savannah Breedlove, Kimberly Carlton, Caitlin Halstead, Margaret Kercher, Becky Monds, Kerri Potts, Nekasha Pratt, Taylor Ward, and Laura Wheeler.

Not to mention all the wonderful sales reps and amazing people in the rights department—special shout-out to Robert Downs!

Thanks especially to my editor, Kimberly Carlton. Your incredible insight and inspiration helped me take the story deeper, and for that I am so grateful! Thanks also to my line editor, Julee Schwarzburg, whose attention to detail makes me look like a better writer than I really am.

To accurately portray Pinehaven Resort, I located a similar resort and made a trip to the Lakes Region of New Hampshire. There the proprietors of Sunset Lodges, Rick and Lorraine Sager, were so kind as to sit down with me and answer all my questions. I fell in love with the beautiful shoreline property and cozy cabins, and I so enjoyed sharing a piece of it with you in this story. If you should find yourself in Wolfeboro, be sure and check it out (https://sunsetlodges.com/history-of-sunset-lodges/). They will make you feel right at home! Any errors related to the property that have made it into print are entirely my own.

Ronda Wells, MD, was kind enough to read my manuscript for medical accuracy. I'm so grateful for her help!

Author Colleen Coble is my first reader and sister of my heart. Thank you, friend! This writing journey has been ever so much more fun because of you.

I'm grateful to my agent, Karen Solem, who's able to somehow make sense of the legal garble of contracts and, even more amazing, help me understand it.

To my husband, Kevin, who has supported my dreams in every way possible—I'm so grateful! To all our kiddos: Chad and Taylor, Trevor and Babette, and Justin and Hannah, who have favored us with three beautiful grandchildren. Every stage of parenthood has been a grand adventure, and I look forward to all the wonderful memories we have yet to make!

A hearty thank you to all the booksellers who make room on their shelves for my books—I'm deeply indebted! And to all the book bloggers and reviewers, whose passion for fiction is contagious—thank you!

Lastly, thank you, friends, for letting me share this story with you! I wouldn't be doing this without you. Your notes, posts, and reviews keep me going on the days when writing doesn't flow so easily. I appreciate your support more than you know.

I enjoy connecting with friends on my Facebook page: www.facebook.com/authordenisehunter. Please pop over and say hello. Visit my website at www.DeniseHunterBooks.com, or just drop me a note at Deniseahunter@comcast.net. I'd love to hear from you!

DISCUSSION QUESTIONS

1. Who was your favorite character and why?

2. How did you feel about Lauren's decision to distance herself from Jonah after the accident? Did you feel she was justified?

3. If you were Jonah, when would you have told Lauren that she'd given up her dream job? Have you ever kept a secret from someone only to have them discover it on their own? How did that work out?

4. Jonah's parents seemed reluctant for him to take the helm at the resort. He misread the situation because he wasn't their "real son." Tell about a time when a miscommunication or misinterpretation has caused problems in your life.

5. Why do you think the job in Boston meant so much to Lauren given her background?

6. Discuss how the accident and memory loss instigated change in Lauren and Jonah. Talk about a time when a significant event in your life caused you to grow.

7. When Lauren's mother reentered her life, were you rooting for a reconciliation? Why or why not?

8. If a romance writer were to write your story, how might it go?

9. Because of her background, Lauren desperately needed a place to belong, and she found it in the resort and the Landrys. Where do you belong, and who are the people you call "home"?

10. Lauren fell in love with Jonah twice. Do you think couples are meant to be? What hand does destiny, fate, or God's will play in relationships?

LOOKING FOR MORE GREAT READS? LOOK NO FURTHER!

THOMAS NELSON
Since 1798

Visit us online to learn more:
tnzfiction.com

Or scan the below code and sign up to receive email updates
on new releases, giveaways, book deals, and more:

@tnzfiction

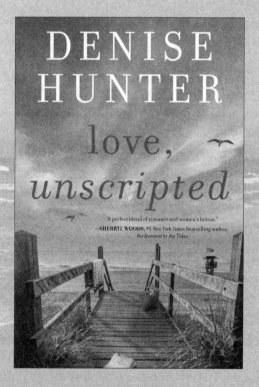

DENISE HUNTER

love, unscripted

"A perfect blend of romance and women's fiction."
—SHERRYL WOODS, #1 *New York Times* bestselling author,
for *Summer by the Tides*

Available in print, ebook, and audio

The Riverbend Romance Novels

Don't miss the Riverbend Gap romance
series from Denise Hunter!

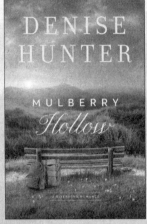

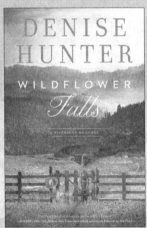

Available in print, e-book, and audio

ABOUT THE AUTHOR

Photo by Salve Ragonton

Denise Hunter is the internationally published, bestselling author of more than forty books, three of which have been adapted into original Hallmark Channel movies. She has won the Holt Medallion Award, the Reader's Choice Award, the Carol Award, the Foreword Book of the Year Award, and is a RITA finalist. When Denise isn't orchestrating love lives on the written page, she enjoys traveling with her family, drinking chai lattes, and playing drums. Denise makes her home in Indiana, where she and her husband raised three boys and are now enjoying an empty nest and three beautiful grandchildren.

DeniseHunterBooks.com
Facebook: @AuthorDeniseHunter
Twitter: @DeniseAHunter
Instagram: @deniseahunter